The Vault!

400 Boxes in 1st

LOOTED VAULT: Safecrackers left the vault of the Pioneer Safe Deposit Vaults, 701 First Av., a shambles after smashing open about 400 of 1,800 safe-deposit boxes in a carefully executed burglary over the weekend. The vault, built in 1884 for the Merchants National Bank, survived the Seattle fire of 1889, though the building housing it was destroyed. The burglary wasn't discovered until this morning. (See Page 5 for another picture.)

Av. Vault Looted

Jerome McDougal

THE VAULT!

ISBN 978-0-9835161-8-7

J. D. McDougal Publishing
4401 Aurora Avenue North
Seattle, WA 98103

Prepared for publication by Julia Ziobro, JAZyourWords.com.

Printed in USA by 48HrBooks (www.48HrBooks.com).

Table of Contents

Preface

The Vault! is a fictional novel based on a real happening. On Valentine's weekend, 1952, persons unknown to this day, broke a hole in the wall of the Pioneer Vault and spent three days inside opening four hundred fourteen boxes and collecting no one really knows how much money, jewelry, and government-issued gold certificates.

They even went out and got themselves sandwiches and coffee several times during the weekend and left the empty wrappers and paper cups on the floor (in my story). Most of the boxes belonged to officials of some stature from Seattle, Tacoma, Olympia, and who knows where else. Rumor has it one of them belonged to Jimmy Hoffa and the owners of the Fisher Flower Company had twenty-eight $100,000 gold certificates in one of the boxes. The rest was mostly all undeclared cash.

Reports said the persons only got away with about $5000. The reason they opened so many boxes was that they were searching for the Fisher Flower Company certificates; however, they left over $25,000 in ones and change on the floor.

I created a fictional storyline, charging some very unlikely people with the task of robbing the vault, while at the same time our two heroes find the loves of their lives. And through some humorous, very unlikely, and heart-warming experiences, succeed in pulling off the biggest unsolved to this day robbery in the history of the United States.

Through my own research I would guess the amount taken was somewhere in the neighborhood of $23,500,000, not counting the solid gold bars and jewelry. Some of it turned up in Las Vegas in 1980 in a pawn shop. Remember, back then, it was all silver and gold certificates worth much more today.

If a person looks carefully at the cover picture you can see they knew which ones they wanted to open... someone had a list, I think...

This book is very fun reading and exciting as five very unlikely persons travel to Seattle and meet through very possible circumstances and the plan comes together and the vault is robbed.

Exciting and intriguing. You just want to keep on reading until it is over and then you still want to know what happened after that...

The cover picture was in one of the Seattle newspapers in operation back then. I found it in an old garage and thought "what a nice story this will make".

One

He laid there half asleep, feeling and clinging onto the warmth of his own body, and the weight from the foot of snow that had piled up on the outside of the sleeping bag during the night. He half turned-over onto his back and felt the Winchester rifle under his left side. There were also assorted beer cans and loose things that had accumulated in the bed of his pickup truck during the past few weeks, including a very hard jack handle that was directly under and poking into his right shoulder blade. "Shit!" he muttered and moved, ending up on several other hard things he had moved to one side when he had laid down for the night. "Shit!" He moved back and a small amount of snow found its way through the head cover of the sleeping bag and down the front of his woolen shirt.

"Now I'm awake." He moaned in disgust and carefully threw the cover off his head, trying to throw as much of the snow away as he could. He succeeded about fifty percent; half of the powder went flying into the air and was blown away by the wind, the other half slid down into the sleeping bag. "Shit again!" he cried loud enough to be heard a hundred yards away, if anyone had been there to hear him. He was seven miles from the main highway, in the middle of the prairie, and several hundred yards from the dirt road he had driven down the night before looking for coyotes. He sat up, and tried to brush the snow off his chest and legs with one hand, as he tried to unzip the bag with his other, so that he could get out of it, only succeeding in letting a little more snow cover his lower half.

"Christ! How stupid can a guy get?" He cussed, then raised up on his knees, pushed the top half of the sleeping bag down, and finally managed to get free, except for the bucket or more of snow now settled around his lower legs. He stood up and looked down at the snow completely covering his feet, including the holes in both his socks.

"This has got to stop! You dumb fucking Indian," he said out loud to himself. "Jesus! I'm done with it!" He cussed and kicked the bag out of the way. He finally stood up. "I got to be smarter than this!" he moaned softly and reached for the few skins he had rolled out under the bag as a mattress of sorts. He used the four frozen skins to stand on as he tried to get into the cab of the truck.

It was Thursday, January sixteenth, 1963. It was eight-twenty in the morning, the temperature was eleven degrees and he was out in the middle of the state grazing land fifty miles west of Miles City, Montana. "And a hundred miles from nowhere," he muttered again as he tried to kick the snow off his pant legs.

Tommy Dollarhide stood in the back of his dented gray 1948 Ford pickup and tried to move the snow enough so that he could find a small dry space to stand upon on the cold metal bed of the truck without stepping on something. The four hides had already been covered with snow and he kicked the top one aside and stood on the second one underneath.

He flipped one of the pelts over and stood on the fur, and then he stood on one foot and leaned over the side until he could reach the door handle and managed to open the door. He then crawled over the side of the bed. He took the rifle and tossed it onto the seat and then managed to seat himself in on the seat next to it, behind the wheel. He pulled his socks down enough so his toes weren't sticking out, and pulled his worn-out boots on, being careful to place the strip of leather over the hole in the sole of his left boot.

He stomped his feet on the floor of the truck to loosen the stiff leather of his boots and then pulled the choke out, hoping his truck's battery was not dead. If it was, he had a long cold walk ahead of him.

He turned the key, hoping the old truck would start, while at the same time hoping he had enough gas to get back to Miles City, Montana, about fifty miles away (if he could get the truck out of the snow drift).

Tommy Dollarhide's wolf and coyote hunting days had come to a freezing and disappointing end. He pumped the gas pedal several times and pushed the starter button. The truck started and he sat back against the seat with his arms folded, trying to keep warm as he waited for the motor to get warm enough so he could turn on the heater and thaw out the windows enough to see out of them. With any luck, the tires would not be frozen to the ground.

"Christ!" he moaned. "How damn stupid does a guy have to get? I could die out here!" He took out one of the four cigarettes he had left in the pack, lit it with his stainless steel Zippo lighter, replaced the lighter in his pants pocket, and then looked at the 1912 gold Waltham railroad pocket watch hanging on the light switch, just right of the steering wheel. It read eight fifty-one.

His grandfather, Charlie Buck a' Skin, had left him the watch when he had died. He held it in his hand a few minutes and thought of selling it, then dismissed the thought. If he starved to death the watch would be in his pocket when he was found by whoever found him. Then they could sell it if they wanted to. He thought about when he had changed his name from Buck a' Skin to Dollarhide.

He was standing in line at the Marine Corps recruiting station when they had asked his name. He had, for some reason, answered Dollarhide, meaning Buck a' Skin. It was the name his grandfather had earned hunting deer for miners. He would sell the hides for one dollar each, or as they said back then, a buck, which meant one dollar.

A small area in the windshield was starting to thaw out, and he used his coat sleeve to wipe the melted ice away so he could see out. He sat and smoked another cigarette as he watched the ice slowly melt, making the small clear circle in front of his face larger and larger until it was large enough so he felt he could see well enough to drive. He put the truck in low gear and felt relieved when it moved forward. At least he wasn't frozen in the ice. He drove slowly at first, gaining speed, then shifted into second gear and plowed his way through nearly two feet of new snow, leaving a huge cloud of blowing snow and a seven foot wide trail behind him as he drove through the field until he reached the cattle trail, then down to the dirt road until he finally reached the paved road.

The watch read nine thirty-five. The truck was warm and moving easily along the good road. He put on his hat, leaned back, and relaxed a bit, but kept looking at the gas gauge which read less than one eighth of a tank. That told him he had about two gallons of gas and thirty-five miles to go. He might make it with a pint or less left. Maybe, but he knew his truck and he knew exactly how far it would go on a gallon of gas, and he knew if he drove at forty miles an hour, he could go thirty-eight miles or forty miles on what he had in the tank. "No problem," he said, and patted the truck on the dashboard.

Tommy Dollarhide was twenty-seven years-old and, was this day, completely broke, disgusted, fed up, hungry, but proud. He was a six foot three inch, two hundred thirty-four pound full blooded, bitter, Sioux Indian, driving his beat up old Ford pickup into a small, disgusting, no-hope, half-deserted, half-rundown town, to sell the four hides he had for sixty dollars at the Cattleman's Association.

He would sell his Winchester rifle to his brother-in-law, have a couple beers with Two Trees and Jack Jackson, say good-bye to his sister, pick up his saddle and gear, then go to Seattle and go to work for the Boeing Airplane Company, and buy a house with central heating, a big leather chair, a television, and a freezer full of food. He would buy lots of new socks without holes in the toes, and boots, and maybe a second freezer full of food, and everything else he didn't have, and more socks, wool ones, the kind that had the red stripe around the top.

He didn't know it, but he was also only ten months away from robbing the Pioneer Vault Company of a little more than twenty-two million, all in cash.

(The Pioneer Vault Company was, and still is, the largest unsolved robbery in the history of the Unites States, and to this date no one admits to it or even admits as to how much money was taken).

He had two things he kept to himself.

(Napoleon was short and he damn near captured the whole world).

He hated everyone over six feet tall, because he had to look at their belly as he walked by them.

John Tru-Day, seaman first class U. S. Navy, storekeeper and accountant aboard the USS Bonn Homme Richard CVA-31, which was about to tie-up in port, in the naval shipyard in Bremerton, Washington, at nine in the evening. At midnight his enlistment was up.

All one hundred thirty-four pounds and five foot one and three quarters inch of him stood in front of his locker, carefully and slowly packing his sea bag. He rolled each item and then stuffed it into the bag, removed another item from the small locker and stuffed it in the bag, until the locker was empty and the bag was packed. Finally, after three years, nine months, and sixteen days and nights, he was getting ready to start a new life in Seattle, where he had been offered a job as bookkeeper for the A. Charmichael Construction Company. The letter lay in front of him on his now stripped clean bunk.

His locker was empty. His bag packed. It was seven-eighteen pm January 16th, 1963. The temperature in Puget Sound was 49 degrees. It was raining and getting dark as the huge ship made its way through the choppy water, past the small islands. With the help of three tug boats it was finally pushed into dock at eight twenty-two.

His enlistment was up at midnight, but his obligation was over as soon as the ship had docked. His papers were signed, his bag packed and as the ship's crew threw lines over the side to secure the ship to the dock, John Tru-Day made his way up one flight of stairs and down a passageway, past the ship's barber shop, past the accounting office, past the administrative office, and came to the stores office.

He sat his bag down on the deck in the hall and went into the office. There, he sat at his desk one last time and

11

uncovered his typewriter, inserted a sheet of paper and typed:

I've been here three years, nine months and sixteen days.

I can't say I enjoyed it, because I didn't! So--

To whoever comes here to replace me.

   Enjoy!

And I leave you with these words of wisdom

   FUCK YOU AND

   FUCK YOU VERY MUCH!

   John Tru-Day

He replaced the cover on the typewriter, leaving the sheet of paper in it, and left the office, carried his bag up two more flights of stairs and stood on the hangar deck until the ship was secured. The gang plank set, and the officer of the day gave him permission to leave the ship at 19:32 hours.

"If I see a lot of smoke out there I'll know you're setting the world on fire." The officer laughed, after seeing his discharge papers.

"I left a message on my typewriter for you, 'Sir.'" Tru-Day replied with a smile.

John Tru-Day saluted and left the ship carrying his seventy-five pound sea bag on his right shoulder. "And fuck you too! You skinny fucker!" he said under his breath. He felt like he had just gotten out of jail as he walked the fifty feet down the gangplank onto the dock.

"Which way is the main gate to the ferries?" he asked a deck hand still tying the ropes to the pilings.

"Straight up the street, ten blocks," he answered.

"Any cabs around here?"

"Right outside the gate," the man answered.

"Thanks," John answered, then said under his breath, "I hope your fucking knot comes loose and the fucking ship floats away and sinks."

Then he began the two thousand foot walk to the gate, holding the heavy sea bag in place with both hands. He wanted to stop and rest several times, but his pride wouldn't let him. He wanted to just throw the bag away into a trash bin, but didn't dare too. He hated for people to think he was weak because of his size.

"Your problem is you got a Napoleonic complex, Tru-Day," his chief had told him.

"You damn right I do, look what he did," he answered, then added, "And I'm damn proud of it!"

The gate was now one thousand feet in front of him. He could see it and the yellow taxis waiting, seven hundred feet, his arms were aching. His legs were about to give out, he nearly sat the bag down, but saw people looking at him. He changed it to his left shoulder and kept walking. Five hundred feet, he began to count his steps, subtracting the footage as he walked 475, 473, 470, 397, 394, 391, 388 feet. A yellow taxi came through the gate and dropped off a rider a block in front of him.

"Hey! Hey!" he waved, and the cab came and stopped just in front of him.

"We can't pick up inside the gate. They have to check your papers," the cabbie told him.

Tru-Day threw his sea-bag into the backseat and said, "Fuck um. I'll meet you at the gate."

He walked the remaining block and a half to the gate and gave the guard the finger as he got into the cab. The Marine watched him stick his finger up at him, then yelled back at the short seaman. "Good luck! Out there! You little half-pint prick!" John Tru-Day laughed and thought about the letter in his pocket.

John,

Looking forward to seeing and working with you. I got you a room at the Madison Hotel. Check in and call me after the first of the month. There's some money at the front desk for you. Enjoy yourself for a few days.

Jack Charmichael.

"Where you going? Ferries?" the cab driver looked at the red-faced seaman in the back seat.

"Ya."

"You just missed it. The next one is in an hour," said the cabbie.

"So let's go get a beer and wait," John answered.

"Meter on? Or meter off?"

"On," John smiled then said, "I'm so fucking happy to be out of the Navy."

"Well, I'm happy you're out too," the cabbie answered, then asked, "Anywhere?"

"Anywhere," John returned, and then added, "You want to come in and have a beer?"

"Ya, I want to too, but can't, I'll wait for you."

The cab stopped in front of a small older tavern five blocks from the ferry terminal and the cabbie told him, "You got forty minutes. It's going to cost you about eight bucks if I wait for you."

"Wait." John answered and handed him a ten-dollar bill, then thought about it and said, "If I come back out and you're gone, I'll hunt you down like a fucking dog and break your fucking neck."

"OK," was all the driver answered, but he was smiling at the small man. He was at least twice as big as John Tru-Day.

John Tru-Day walked the few feet, pushed open the door, and stepped into the small tavern. There were two other people in the place, both of them sailors. Both of them looked down at him and smiled, not a friendly smile, but one of those "short ain't he," smiles that he hated. He walked to the bar, placed one hand on the bar, and his other one on the stool, then hopped up and sat on the stool.

"What can I get you, shorty?" the bartender asked, smiling.

"A pitcher of beer, you ugly son of a bitch! And don't call me 'Shorty'," Tru-Day answered.

"Hey! Watch your smart mouth," the bartender told him.

"Then get some fucking manners! I might be short, but I'm not a fucking prick!" Tru-Day answered, and then added, "So don't call me Shorty. My name's John."

"Feisty little bastard, ain't ya?" the bartender smiled again, but this time it was a friendly smile. He had been put in his place by the small man. "36 or 68 oz?"

"The big one," Tru-Day answered. Then as soon as he saw it, he knew he had made a big mistake.

"There's a lot of beer in there," the bartender told him, and sat the huge pitcher in front of him, then a glass, and asked for three dollars.

Tru-Day looked at the bartender, then at the two sailors watching him. He paid the money, and then he picked up the pitcher with both hands and began to drink. He stopped once, and then finished the pitcher. He got off the stool and walked back out of the tavern and got back into the taxi feeling the pressure building inside him. He knew he couldn't keep that much beer down for long. He could see the bartender looking at him through the window as he told the driver, "Drive around into the alley, hurry! I got to puke!"

"Don't puke in my car!" the driver cried, then floored the car and turned right, tipping John Tru-Day over on the seat, then right again, and tipped him over a second time, then slammed on the brakes, and slid him off the seat onto the floor as he stopped in the alley behind the tavern just in time.

John Tru-Day pushed open the door and leaned out, losing his hat as he fell forward, one second before 68 ounces of beer, part of his lunch, and two cups of coffee decided to exit his body with about the same force water exits a fire hydrant. It filled his hat and splattered over the ground. He nearly passed out from strain.

"God!" he moaned and sat back up.

"You anorexic or something?" the cabbie asked.

"Just stupid, I'm just fucking stupid!" he answered and wiped his face with a hankie. He looked up and saw the bartender looking out of the back door at him.

"I'm impressed," the bartender called to him smiling, then shut the door.

"Another bar? Or the ferry?" asked the cabbie.

"Ferry, I'll just wait for it," replied John.

The last ferry of the night left Bremerton at 11:03 and arrived in Seattle at 1:15. It was twelve o' six am, January 17th, when John Tru-Day again picked up his sea bag, and began the four block walk up the 11% grade of the Madison Street hill to the hotel. He made it three blocks before he had to stop and rest. He sat his sea bag down, and sat on it for several minutes watching steam come up out of a manhole a foot from the curb. It was raining hard now and he almost called for a cab, but he saw the sign on the hotel was too close, a block and a half away and across the

17

street. He picked up the bag and finished the walk, setting the bag down in front of the front desk in the lobby.

"I'm John Tru-Day, I have a room here," he told the tall reddish haired girl behind the desk. She looked down at him, put her glasses on and smiled, "Jack said you were coming, but he didn't say you were so cute."

He gave her a disgusted look and said, "I'm soaking wet, it's raining like hell out there."

"I know. I like the rain," she smiled and handed him a card to fill out. "So you're the new accountant? You'll like working for Jack," she said, then asked smiling, "So, how tall are you?"

"Tall enough to kick your ass. Give me my fucking key, and I'm supposed to have some money here too."

She handed him a key then took an envelope out of the drawer and handed it to him.

"You two should get along really good! You're both really rude!" she said.

He started to say "fuck you," but caught himself and answered, "I just walked up that hill out there carrying seventy five pounds of Navy shit! I'm wet, and I'm cold, and I'm hungry. I'm five foot one and three-quarters inches tall. I'm twenty-six years old and I weigh one hundred thirty-three pounds. Satisfied?"

"Two oh three, Room 2- 0- 3." she drew the numbers in the air with her finger as though he was a child and smiled. "The elevator is over there!" she pointed. "The restaurant is

18

open all night if you eat food," she pointed to a different door and turned away.

'You're pretty rude yourself," he answered.

"I try real hard!" she said looking back over her shoulder, and walked into a small room out of his sight.

"Ya!? Well I'd rather be dead, than red on the head," he answered.

She stuck her head around the door frame, looked at him like he was an idiot and smiled, "Are you retarded too?" she smiled and disappeared. John Tru-Day felt dumber than he had felt in three years.

He carried the bag to the elevator and rode up to the second floor. The room was better than the outside of the hotel showed. It was clean and neat. A full-size bed and television stood in the center, and there was a full bathroom with tub and shower.

He looked around and said, "Finally! A real room with a real bed!" He took of his wet clothes, showered, and put on his slacks and a white shirt. He still wore his black Navy shoes, but they were going away in the morning, as soon as the stores opened.

He opened the envelope and nearly did a number one in his pants. There were twenty-five one hundred dollar bills in it with a note:

Buy some clothes and rent a place on the southeast side,
somewhere around Rainier Ave. Be conservative, get laid a
couple times. There are lots of girls in the hotel.

Jack

He had spent thirty-eight months in the Navy living on eleven dollars a month, saving everything else he could save. He had saved twenty-three hundred dollars. Now he had more than that in his hand as a gift. "Jesus! What a fucking waste of time," he muttered, remembering all the times he had stayed on the ship so he could save a few dollars. He folded the money and put it in his pocket, thought about it, and put it in his right sock, keeping only thirty dollars in his pocket. He then went down to the restaurant to eat. At 2:16 am, January 17th, 1963, John Tru-Day was sitting in seventy-four degree warmth, in a soft booth, wearing gray slacks and a white short-sleeved shirt, eating a 12-ounce rib eye steak, feeling better than he had in four years.

Total Possessions:

$2,386 in his savings account.

$2,530 cash in his right sock, $30 in his pants pocket, plus what few dollars was in his sea bag, a job, a drink, and no one to salute.

He was happy and contented. He chewed his steak, sipped his drink, and leaned back against the leather of the booth. "How about another drink?" he asked.

Tommy Dollarhide was parked along the side of US 80 in nine degrees below zero cold, with his second of several flat tires. He was inside the cab of the truck, starting it every so often to keep warm, waiting for it to get light enough so he could change the tires and go on.

Twenty year old Patty McShane was hiding in a small storage shed full of empty oil drums, dusty boxes, and forty or fifty plastic bags full of aluminum cans, twelve hundred and sixty miles to the south of Tommy, in a small town named Alamo, Nevada, holding her five month old son in her arms and waiting for a car, any car, with out-of-state license plates to stop for gas at the Shell station sixty feet away so she could get a ride and get away from her husband, his friends, and his father.

Patty McShane was two hours and fifteen minutes away from taking the ride of her life.

Total Possessions:

One five month old boy.

One battered cardboard suitcase with a few baby clothes in it.

One pair of jeans and a few underthings.

One pair of tennis shoes.

One cotton dress.

Four hundred and fourteen dollars she had saved one dollar at a time over two years, given to her by the men she had been forced to have sex with.

Keith J. Shocko and Barbara Fieldsman were ninety-nine miles south of Patty McShane, on the outskirts of Las Vegas. Keith was sitting behind the wheel of the

1958 Buick station wagon waiting for Barbara to come out of the motel room where she had gone thirty minutes before with a man who had picked her up off the street. She came running out of the room and got into the car.

"Go! I got his money, he's in the shower." She closed the door and ducked down out of sight. Keith Shocko dropped the car into gear and headed out of town north on Highway 22, heading for Seattle, via Alamo, Nevada.

Total possessions:

A few clothes.

One 1958 Buick station wagon (not paid for).

Twenty-eight dollars Barbara had taken from the man's wallet when he went into the shower.

Tommy Dollarhide had driven straight to his brother-in-law's house and explained his intentions, then sold his rifle for seventy-five dollars, gathered his few clothes, his saddle, and gear. Not that he intended to ever use them again, but he might need to sell them before he got to Seattle.

At nine in the morning of January 16th, he sold the four wolf hides to the game department for sixty dollars and then filled his truck with gas. He bought three packs of cigarettes, four quarts of oil, and drove the three blocks to the Town Tavern, where he knew his friends would be.

He parked the truck across the street and walked over to where Two Trees and Joe Jackson were sitting on the bench in front of the tavern, as they did each and every day, unless they had something else to do, which didn't happen very often.

"Come on you bums, and I'll buy you a last beer. I'm heading to Seattle," Tommy said, and reached down to help Joe Jackson up to his feet. Joe had a stiff right leg from being thrown off a horse and stepped on when he was younger.

"You really going to Seattle today?" Two Trees asked.

"Just as soon as we have a couple beers and I say good-bye to H. C.," Tommy smiled.

"You gonna give it to him, Tommy?" Joe asked.

"Right in his fat gut," Tommy answered, and held the door open for his friends.

H. C. Morgan, the tavern owner, greeted the three men with his usual sarcasm. "Cash! Or no beer. Don't even bother to sit down!"

"I'm buying," Tommy answered.

"No hard stuff, just beer, and only three a piece!" Morgan told them, and then said, "Let's see some money."

Tommy paid for the three beers and carried them to the table.

"You really leaving? Going to Seattle, Tommy?" Two Trees asked again.

"As soon as I finish this beer, and something else I been wanting to do for a couple years." He looked over at H. C. and smiled.

"Just what you been wanting to do?" Morgan asked from behind the bar, and then said, "You'll last about one week in Seattle and you'll be walking home. You people don't know how to live in the city."

"Bring us three more!" Tommy called and placed six dollars on the table.

"Come and get them!" Morgan told him.

"Let's go over to the hotel and have one," Tommy told his two friends, knowing it would bring the fat man to his table.

"I'll bring them," Morgan answered, not wanting to lose the money he had seen Tommy take from his pocket. He knew the Indians would drink until all the money was gone. He carried the three beers to the table, and Tommy stood up holding the six dollars in his left hand, as though he was going to give it H. C. Morgan. Morgan sat the beers on the table and reached for the money. Tommy Dollarhide let him take it then with all the strength he could manage, punched the fat man in the pit of his belly knocking the wind out of him, then swung a good left hook and hit him on the side of the face, knocking him down to his knees.

"That's for being such a nice guy," Tommy said.

Morgan had a bad reputation for stealing from the Indians after getting them drunk, many were the times the men came and cashed their checks in the tavern and Morgan only gave them part of it and said he was short of cash and

24

told them to come back later to get the rest of their money because he didn't have enough on hand. The money was never repaid. Morgan stood for a second looking at the tall Indian, his eyes wide open with surprise, his mouth agape as he tried to catch his breath, and then he gasped for air and rolled over sideways, and lay on the floor gasping for air. He stayed there, holding himself up with his right elbow on the wood floor gasping for his breath with spit running out of his mouth and tears streaming down his fat cheeks, his eyes wide open, looking at Tommy Dollarhide with rage as Tommy drank half the bottle and dumped the rest on the man's head.

"I'll see you bums," he said, then patted H. C. on the top of his head and told him, "Be nice, it's easier," and left the tavern with H. C. Morgan trying to yell after him but not being able to speak.

He drove three miles out of town and stopped to say good-bye to his other sister, ignoring the bruise on the side of her face but wishing his other brother-in-law was home. He told his sister, "I'll send for you as soon as I can, sis," then drove out onto the highway heading for Seattle.

Total Possessions:

$113.23 cash.

One 1948 Ford pickup truck.

One American western roping saddle.

One bucking gear.

One bridle.

25

One 1912 gold Waltham railroad watch.

One stainless steel Zippo lighter.

Two pairs of jeans.

Three wool shirts stuffed behind the seat.

One half pack of cigarettes, because he had given one to Two Trees.

It was 12:20 pm January 16, 1963. He was not happy, but he wasn't mad, cold, hungry, or wet, and he felt good about punching the fat H. C. Morgan, even though he knew as soon as the man recovered enough, he would call the police and try to have him arrested. He kept a watch in his mirror for red and blue lights but no one ever showed, and after two hours, he stopped worrying. He was driving at forty-five miles an hour saving as much gas money as he could. Two hundred and six miles and five hours later he had his first flat tire. He changed it and bought a used tire for ten dollars in Billings, filled the truck with gas and had ninety-eight dollars and ninety cents left when he started for Butte. He already knew he wouldn't make it all the way to Seattle without working or selling the saddle, unless he was really lucky and had no more flat tires, but the ones on his truck were completely worn out and he still had over eight hundred miles to go. Sixty miles out of Billings at 8:15 pm, and in a snow storm, he had his second flat tire.

At 1:12 am January 17th, Keith Shocko and Barbara Fieldsman drove into the Shell station at Alamo, Nevada, and as Keith stood filling the car with gas, he and Barbara watched a small blonde-haired girl wearing a dirty white dress and carrying a child in one arm and a old suitcase in her other, come running out of the shed and then around to the back of their car, and without asking opened the back door and got in, then ducked down on the floor trying to hide.

"Please help me! I have to get away! Please help me!" the girl spoke in a broken Irish brogue.

"What's she doing in there?" Keith asked, looking through the window at the girl.

At the same time the owner of the station came walking out "Patty! What the hell do you think you're doing? Get out of there!"

"Please don't let him take me," the girl begged.

"Let's go, Keith!" Barbara cried, and Keith handed the man a ten dollar bill, dropped the still-running gas hose onto the ground, then shoved him back away from the car and got in.

"Does Glen know you're leaving?" The man yelled at her, trying to pick up the hose and look into the car at the same time as the car sprayed gravel leaving the station.

"Go Keith! Go!" Barbara screamed, looking back through the rear window at the man running back into the station.

"Get some place off the road. It looks like he's calling the cops."

"He's calling my husband. Please don't stop," Patty begged.

Keith drove at a break-neck speed for several miles and when they saw no one was following them, he pulled off onto a small dirt road and stopped the car.

Patty McShane was sixteen when she had been brought to the United States by her uncle with the promise of her going to a good school and living in a huge white farm house. Her uncle had sent pictures of it to her parents, telling them he owned a large cattle farm and she could live with him. In exchange for her helping in the house he would pay for her school and see to it she got a full education. She arrived only to find the huge farm house was a trailer house behind another trailer house in an old trailer park in a mostly deserted town. There was no farm, no horses, no cows, only her uncle and his son, and a dirty little old town in the middle of the Nevada desert. The second day she was there, her uncle had gotten drunk and tore off her dress, then raped her twice on the dirty worn-out couch, then passed out. Two hours later her cousin had done the same thing to her and so it had been for nearly four years. She had no idea who the baby's father was. Her uncle's, her cousin's, or any one of the several other men they had sold her to during the past three and a half years. Her cousin claimed the baby was his and had married her as soon as they found she was pregnant, not wanting anyone to know what they were doing with her. It had taken her nearly three years to save the four hundred fourteen dollars she had saved by keeping one dollar at a time from some of the men she had been forced to have sex with. She had waited over a year for her uncle and cousin to go to Las Vegas and stay a couple days. They had left at noon and she scrambled to get her money out of her hiding place and stuff a few baby things into the old suitcase and hide in the shed. She was in the shed at 1:15, standing in the corner looking out through a crack, holding her child, waiting for a car with a couple in it, or someone to stop that had out of state license plates. The green and white Buick with Washington plates was the first. She waited until she thought the man had just about finished filling the tank. Then, she scrambled as fast as she could, running, knowing that if Ray, the station owner, saw her before she got into the car, he would try to catch her and stop her from leaving. She felt a little scared, but safe, sitting in the back seat of the Buick holding her son as both the man and women turned and looked at her. "Big trouble?" Keith said, grinning.

"Shut up, Keith!" the woman said, and asked her, "Where are you going? Or does it matter? Just trying to get away? Husband? We're going to Seattle. You want to come with us?"

"I thought we were going to Chicago."

"Shut up, Keith!" Barbara told him, and pushed his head around so he wasn't looking at her.

"What's your fucking problem all of a sudden?" Keith returned in an angry voice.

"I ain't got no fucking problem, Keith! She's got a problem and I'm trying to find out what it is. All right?"

Keith turned around and started the car.

"Where are you going? Barbara asked.

"I'm just going," the girl answered.

"Shut the fucking car off, will ya? And wait til I'm done talking to her?"

Keith turned off the motor.

"I can get out here, if it's too much trouble," Patty told the woman.

"You're not getting out anywhere until we know you're all right. You got any money for a motel room? We're about busted flat."

"I have four hundred dollars. I'll pay if you drive me somewhere so I can go back to Ireland. I want to go to San Francisco and maybe get a job and buy a ticket."

"We're going to Seattle, Washington. You want to come with us? You buy the gas and we'll take you there, all right? You can get a ticket there. It'll probably cost less there than in San Francisco."

"All right," Patty smiled. "Oh, yes! It'd be very all right. Oh, thank you so much!" she reached into her bra and took out part of the money she had stuffed in it, all ones, and then handed it to the woman.

"This ain't four hundred dollars," Barbara told her.

"The rest is in the case there. Can we please go away? I'm afraid Ray may have sent someone to fetch me back."

"Who's Ray?"

"The man who owns the station. The man he pushed. Thank you," Patty smiled, looking at Keith.

Keith smiled proudly, then started the car and drove back to the highway and turned north. Barbara tried to talk to the girl but she was asleep in less than fifteen minutes.

"We need to get off this highway, Keith," Barbara told him, "Cut across and go up that old highway we came down on, the one that goes to Twin Falls. I think the turn is about fifty miles or so, we got enough gas?"

"Shit! We got almost a full tank." he answered laughing. "I gave that guy a tenner and got sixteen dollars' worth."

"What was that town we stopped in?"

"We stopped in a lot of towns. Which one?"

"Elroy or Leroy or something, the one with the motel we stayed at."

"I don't remember but it's on that old road a couple hundred miles from here."

"Go there, and we'll stop."

Barbara stayed awake until Keith turned onto the old highway, and after only a couple miles they passed a sign that read *Ely 198, Jackpot 378, Twin Falls 408*. Barbara leaned against the seat and went to sleep. One thing about Keith, he could drive for three days and never fall asleep.

Three hours after John Tru-Day had finished eating, and just about the time Tommy Dollarhide started the truck for the fifth time, Keith Shocko and Barbara drove into a motel in Ely, Nevada, with the sleeping Patty McShane in the back seat, holding her son. Barbara leaned over the seat and woke her up. "Hey! We're at a motel. You got some more money for the room?"

"It's in the case," Patty answered, and then opened the case and unrolled a wool sock. She took a hand full of the ones and handed them to Barbara.

"What the fuck? Were you selling joints or what?"

"What?" Patty answered, not understanding.

"All you got is ones?"

"I saved it one at a time, I was afraid to change it for bigger bills, someone would tell."

"What were you, a fucking slave or something?" Barbara asked, not expecting the answer she got back.

"Yes, I was. For three years, I never left the house except to have the baby. They kept me locked in a room for two of the three years."

Barbara did not believe her; she figured every woman was like her, completely self-centered and selfish. "Whatever," she answered, and got out of the car and rented a room. The room cost twenty-two dollars and she told Patty it was forty-six and handed her back two dollars.

They got twenty more dollars from Patty and brought food back to the room. Patty was asleep on one of the beds, her son next to her.

"Let's grab the money and go," Keith whispered.

"They got our fucking license number on the registration card, Keith. Use your head. Let's just take her with us."

"Fine with me," Keith answered, "She's got nice tits."

32

Barbara hit him with her fist on the arm. "Keep your eyes off of her, Keith. I'm not kidding!"

Patty McShane woke up at nine in the morning and took care of her baby, then waited until eleven for Keith and Barbara to get up and leave the motel. They took more money from her so they could eat breakfast, and then drove on north.

John Tru-Day woke up at seven-thirty, showered, and went down to the restaurant and ate breakfast, then went shopping for new clothes. He ordered two suits, and then bought three bags of new sweaters, slacks and shirts, plus an overcoat, and a casual coat, new shoes (brown ones), and a sixty-five dollar hat. "That's a start," he said when he finished, and headed back to the hotel. He got good and drunk in the bar.

Tommy Dollarhide was back on the road after fighting with wind and blowing snow. He finally changed the right front tire on his truck and managed to travel back thirty-five miles and buy another spare. He wanted to replace all the tires on the truck, but he didn't have enough money to pay for them. Now he was down to $77 plus some change, and less than one pack of cigarettes. He decided when they were gone he would quit smoking.

It was 11:00 am the 17th. Patty McShane was just going in to the restaurant to have breakfast and spend thirty-seven dollars, twenty-nine of it on Keith and Barbara.

Tommy bought a used tire and had it mounted on his truck, replacing his worst one. He then drove around trying to find another cheap tire, but he failed and headed back out onto the highway hoping for the best. He had no trouble for the rest of the day, and stopped in Billings in front of a used tire store, and slept waiting for it to open at eight in the morning. He bought himself a sandwich and a pack of smokes, and then he was down to $74 and change.

John Tru-Day woke up on the eighteenth and went shopping again. He picked up his new suits and wore the light gray one out of the store with a matching light gray shirt and soft brown colored tie. He bought new socks, and another pair of shoes, and another new hat.

"You look real nice, Mr. Tru-Day," the clerk told him.

"You look like a gangster! You and Jack should get along really good," the tall red head desk clerk told him, sort of laughing.

"Something wrong with the suit?" he asked.

She laughed and answered, "No, not really, I guess if you consider--"

"Consider what?"

"It's kind of short in the legs, ain't it?"

John leaned over as close to her as he could and whispered, "Fuck you, you stupid fucking broad."

"You even sound like him," she answered, and walked into her room out of sight. He put his clothes away and got drunk again. He was having the time of his life.

Tommy Dollarhide was cussing again, and changing the left rear tire on the truck. If he had another blow-out he was he was in trouble. It was almost a hundred miles to the next place he could stop. He pictured himself rolling a flat tire along the road and then rolling a repaired one back. He got lucky and made it to the base of the mountains just before dark on the eighteenth. He was about five hundred miles from Seattle and driving at forty-five miles an hour, chewing on a match stick, saving his last three cigarettes.

John Tru-Day was sitting in the bar drinking bourbon and water, and eating snacks from the bar. He noticed several girls coming in alone and having a Coke or a drink and then leaving. All of them looked at him and smiled or greeted him. None of them talked to him, and he spoke to none of them until the red headed desk clerk asked him, "You're not a homo, are you?"

"What?" he nearly screamed at her then said, "Give me my fucking key, you got a real problem, lady."

"You don't like women?"

"Of course I do, what business is it of yours?"

"I sent in seven girls and you never even said hello to them."

"What the hell you talking about?"

"Jack said I should send you some girls. He said you been on a boat for three years."

He thought about what she said for a few seconds and then remembered the note saying, "Get laid a couple times," and told her, "I can get my own women! I don't need you pimping for me."

"I'm not pimping for you, you moron, I'm pimping for the girls, they work here."

"What do you mean, they work here?" Then it came to him, the women were prostitutes. "Holy shit!" he muttered and went to his room, changed his clothes and went back down to the bar. He talked to several of the women but none of them turned his "want to" on, in fact most of them kinda made him want to tell them to get up and leave.

Keith J. Shocko and company were again stopped at a motel spending Patty McShane's money on a room, dinner, and drinks. Patty was starting to get worried that she had made a big mistake by getting into the first car that came along. She had already handed over nearly one hundred of the four hundred she had, but she figured she was still better off then she had been, no matter where she ended up.

The morning of the nineteenth, John Tru-Day bought a paper and started looking for a place to live.

Patty McShane started looking for an alternative and mentioned they should just let her off and she could take a bus from there to Seattle. Barbara took the rest of her money and told her not to worry. They would be in Seattle in one more day.

"But I'll have no money then," Patty answered.

"Don't you know about welfare?" Barbara asked.

"No," Patty answered.

"So don't worry, they'll take care of you, you got a kid," Barbara told her, and then told her to just go to bed in the motel room and not to worry. She went back to the bar where Keith was drinking.

Tommy Dollarhide went to a used tire place and bought his fourth tire for fifteen dollars, then filled his truck with gas and bought a hamburger. He was down to forty-two dollars. He figured if he had no more flats and no trouble he would get to Seattle with about one cigarette left and maybe two dollars. The motor in his truck was starting to miss from a bad spark plug wire or something else that had gone bad, and his mileage was down to about six or seven miles to the gallon. If he made it to Spokane by night fall he was going to be happy.

He made it to town within forty miles and had another blowout. He got lucky and bought not only a tire but a wheel too, at a junk yard for twenty-three dollars. It was ten-thirty in the morning on the eighteenth; he was forty miles from Spokane, and three hundred from Seattle.

Patty McShane was nine hours from getting the hell beat out of her by Barbara, and John Tru-Day was a few hours from finding out why God made people in all shapes and sizes.

It started about a hundred miles north of Twin Falls, Idaho, when Patty McShane took out her breast and began to feed the baby. Keith Shocko looked in the mirror and saw her, then adjusted the mirror so he could watch. Barbara saw him looking and slapped the mirror nearly off of the windshield, and screamed at him, "Keep your fucking eyes off of her teats, Keith," then she turned around in the seat and screamed at Patty, "You keep your fucking teats covered."

"It's only natural," Patty answered, but put the blanket over the baby's head. She was ready to get out of the car and find another ride.

Tommy Dollarhide was parked along the side of the road trying to figure out why the truck was running so rough. He found a spark plug wire had moved and lay against the exhaust pipe and burned through. He made a makeshift wire from a wire he had in the back and started the truck. It was better, but not good. He drove on through Post Falls and limped into Spokane at nine thirty at night, then had another flat right in front of a used tire store. He went to sleep in the truck wishing he had put his sleeping bag in the cab with him. It was in the back and wet. He was cold, his feet were wet, and he was hungry, with only eighteen dollars in his pocket and no cigarettes. He didn't want to waste his gas keeping warm so he gave up sleeping and walked across the street to a bar and had a beer, and bought a pack of smokes.

"Any work around here?" he asked the bartender.

"What do you do?"

"Anything right now," Tommy answered.

"Then there's work," the bartender told him. He sat in the bar sipping on a beer until one thirty in the morning when the bar closed and went back to his truck, started the motor and got it warm, then tried to sleep as best he could with his wet sleeping bag wrapped around him.

John Tru-Day sat in the bar and read the classifieds in the paper looking for a place to live. He remembered the note said try to find something by Rainier Ave. He found one ad that read:

Small one bedroom house close to Rainier Ave and bus, $250.00 a month.

Some rent in exchange for yard work. Perfect for one person or couple. No pets.

He called the number.

"Hello?" the voice said.

"I'm calling about the house. Is it rented?"

"Oh," the voice said, and then there was silence for several seconds.

"Hello?" John asked.

"I'm sorry, I just put the ad in last night. I didn't think anyone would call this soon."

"Should I call back later?" he asked.

"No, of course not. It's a small house behind my house. The rent is $250 but if you take care of the yard it's only $150."

I just got here and I'm staying at the Madison Hotel," he said.

"Oh! I'm sorry, do you have any children or pets?"

"No, I just got out of the Navy."

"Do you drink a lot?" she asked.

"No, not a lot, just a few beers."

"That's good. I drink a glass of wine every day," she answered and John thought, *"Like I give a shit what you drink lady, what about the house?"*

"Are you married?"

"No, I just got here two days ago. I've been in the Navy for three years."

"Oh, that's good." she said, then asked, "Where did you say you were staying?"

"At the Madison Hotel. Can I come and look at the place?"

"The rent is $250 but if you take care of the yard it's only $150."

"What do I have to do?"

"Just mow it, and things like that. I'm too small to push the lawn mower."

He thought, *"She's probably a shriveled-up old hag."*

"I'll have to find a way to get there. I don't know my way around here. I guess I could take a cab."

"Where are you staying?

"I'm at the Madison Hotel."

"Oh," the voice said again, sounding disappointed, and then silence, then, "I thought that was what you said."

"Is something wrong?" he asked.

"No, I was just thinking, I have to come to town tomorrow and I could pick you up if you like, then you could ride the bus back. A cab is so costly. It's really quite a ways from where you are. Are you married?"

"No," John told her again.

"No dogs or cats?"

"No."

"The Madison Hotel?"

"Yes."

"You'll have to meet me out front. I don't want to go in there."

"Alright."

"I'll be there at two-thirty. I have a 1959 green and white Ford Tudor."

"I'll be on the curb waiting for you."

"Fine. I'll pick you up. You sound like you're a nice man. You don't drink a lot, do you? I don't like drinking very much but I just had a glass of wine and that's why I sound so funny. I think it made me a little tipsy."

"No, I don't, just a beer now and then, and so do you, I mean, you sound like a nice woman too, are you, married?"

"I was," she answered flatly. "I'll see you at two-thirty. Bye." She hung up the phone.

John Tru-Day hung up the phone and thought, "that sounds good, $150 a month and a little exercise mowing the lawn. She can't be that bad, unless she's one of those old nosy ladies who are always asking questions."

What he didn't know, was how good it was going to be.

Patty McShane didn't know how hard a 119-pound woman could hit until they were forty-five miles from Boise, Idaho, and stopped to get something to drink. Barbara went into the store and bought snacks, keeping the change from the money she got from Patty. They drove north for a little over an hour when Barbara saw Keith looking in the mirror at Patty. She turned around and saw Patty feeding the baby again.

"Stop the fucking car, Keith!" she screamed.

"What's wrong?" he asked.

"Stop the fucking car," she replied.

Keith Shocko pulled the Buick off the road onto a turn out and shut off the motor. Barbara was already out of the car and opening the back door. Patty was nursing the baby, and Barbara reached in and grabbed her by her hair with both hands, and yanked her half way out of the car. The baby fell onto the floor and began to cry.

"What the hell?" Keith cried.

"I told you to keep your fucking tits covered!" Barbara screamed, and yanked Patty completely out onto the ground, and then stood there glaring down at her. Patty stood up and started to say something but didn't get the chance. Barbara swung her right fist and hit the girl in the left side of her mouth, knocking her to the ground backwards.

"Christ!" Keith screamed, "Are you crazy?" He was out of the car and running around to the passenger side. Barbara turned and headed for him, and he stopped dead in his tracks and stepped backwards out of her reach. The baby was screaming on the floor of the car. Keith stood frozen behind it as Patty McShane was just getting to her feet. Barbara hit her the second time. This time in the nose with her right hand, then on the side of her head with her left. Patty didn't go down this time, but grabbed the woman's hair with one hand and her shirt front with her other one, and tried to fight back. Both women ended up on the ground, Barbara on top with her knee in Patty's belly and hitting the girl with both fists. Patty turned over and tried to stand up with the woman on her back. Barbara leaned forward and bit into Patty McShane's right ear, biting a huge chunk of the lobe completely off. Patty came up off her knees screaming from the pain and bringing with her a rock the size of a soft ball in her right hand. She pushed the woman back and swung the rock at Barbara's head just as Barbara stepped forward and tried to hit the girl again. She stepped right into the rock as Patty swung it as hard as she could. It connected just above Barbara's left cheek bone and ended the fight. Barbara went down on her side unconscious for a few seconds, and rolled into the ditch. She hit her face twice, on rocks, as she rolled down the incline of the ditch. She lay there, not moving, with blood covering her face from a four-inch gash the rock had opened, and two smaller cuts on her face. Patty McShane stood there for a moment and felt the blood running down the side of her neck from her ear and her face. She ran her tongue over her bottom teeth and felt the three loose front bottom teeth nearly ready to fall out, then the gaping space on the left side where two had been knocked almost out and bent into her tongue. Her lip was cut open and so was her left eye. She looked into the car and saw the baby lying on the floor, screaming. She looked at Keith Shocko standing there, shaking. He was looking down at Barbara.

"Is she dead?" he asked.

Patty calmly reached in and picked up her baby, and stood in front of Keith Shocko. "Take me to a hospital, Keith."

Keith Shocko stood looking from one bleeding woman to the other for a few seconds, not moving until Patty screamed at him, "Take me to the hospital!"

"Alright," Keith answered, and got into the car with Patty McShane sitting in the front seat holding her child. He drove away leaving Barbara Fieldsman laying half-conscious in the ditch.

"You think you killed her?" he asked.

"Maybe," she answered, and didn't care if she had. She took the sock with the rest of her money out of Barbara's purse and put it in her pocket.

It was 9:16 pm January 19th, 1963. Tommy Dollarhide was walking across the road to the bar. John Tru-Day was getting drunk in the bar at the Madison Hotel.

Muriel Sue Boatwright was sipping a third small glass of wine and reading a book in her house.

Barbara Fieldsman was up on her knees looking at the tail lights of the Buick as it sped away. "You dirty rotten mother fucking son of a bitch cock sucker!!" she screamed at Keith Shocko, "I'll kill you, you mother fucker!!" she

44

screamed louder as the car went out of sight in the darkness. "I'll kill you, you fucking coward bastard!!"

She tried to stand up but fell over again. It took her three tries before she was able to stand on her feet. She also felt blood running down the side of her face and put her hand on it. It came away covered with blood. The rock had opened a huge gash on her cheek. "Mother fucker!" she muttered, and staggered over to the side of the highway. She stood there holding the skin together on the side of her face for several minutes until she saw a truck coming at her. She stepped out onto the pavement, opened her shirt, exposing her breasts, and waved at the truck.

Oscar Hines had been driving trucks for twenty-six years and had thought about a woman standing naked on the road a million times, and now, there she was.

"Holy H. Christ!" he cried under his breath, and jammed on both the tractor and trailer brakes at the same time, causing the truck to come to a screeching stop thirty feet past the woman, and leaving five pounds of tire rubber on the asphalt, plus moving his load a foot and a half forward from where it was supposed to be riding.

By the time he had completely stopped, the door opened and the woman was climbing into the cab. She stopped and looked around the cab, then at him.

"Where's the fucking seat?" she asked, seeing no passenger's seat in the cab.

"We're not allowed to have riders," he stammered.

"Ya, well you got one now."

"What happened to your face? Where's your car? Did you have a wreck?"

"It's up the road. I got hit with a fucking rock, and no. You got something? A bandage or something?"

"God! You're really bleeding a lot!" Oscar stammered.

"No shit, Sherlock!" she answered. "You got a fucking bandage in here?"

Oscar reached down into the pocket of his door and took out a first-aid kit, then turned on the overhead light as he handed the box to the woman.

"Can I help you?" he asked looking directly at her bare breasts.

She saw where he was looking and answered, "No, you just look and ... does this thing move?"

"You want me to go with you hurt like that?" he asked.

"You going to sit here until it heals in two months?" she returned, then said, "Take me somewhere so I can wash the dirt out of it, will ya?"

"Ya, sure of course I will," he answered, and started the truck moving. "There's a place a couple miles from here, you want to go to the hospital?"

"No. I want to go to Seattle," she answered, then muttered, "Be there, you mother fucker!" as she opened a sanitary pad and began to clean her face.

"What?" Oscar asked looking at her bare breasts again.

46

She saw where his eyes were looking and almost smiled.

"Nothing, just drive. What's your name anyway?"

"Oscar." he answered.

"Cute! A man named Oscar. I'm Patty," she told him, not wanting to tell him her real name.

"You don't seem to be very—hurt," he said, looking at her breasts again.

"What should I be doing? Bawling and crying?" she asked.

"Well, I don't know," he returned.

"I'm too fucking mad to bawl, Oscar," she said, then asked "You like my teats?"

He took his eyes off her breasts and looked back out onto the road.

"Look at them all you want to, that's what they're for, ain't it?" she said.

"Well, I--I don't know," he said.

"That's why they're there, Oscar, to look at and be played with, and for kids to suck on, other than that, they're a fucking bother!"

"If you say so," he answered meekly, and looked again. This time her nipples were sticking out.

"Good God, she's excited," he thought, and shifted the truck, missing the fifth gear and grinding the lever into place.

"Don't wreck the truck, Oscar." she said, then asked, "So where we going?"

"I'm going to Portland," he returned.

"We're going to Portland, Oscar," she told him, "After I wash my face and put it back together."

"I think you might need stitches."

"I'll tape it back, I've done it before," she answered.

He didn't answer, just drove the four miles to the stop and looked at her breasts about fifty times.

They stopped at a small truck stop café, and she went into the bathroom and cleaned her face. Then, using adhesive tape, she pinched the open skin back together and stuck the tape across the cut skin to hold it together. She was out of the restroom in ten minutes and back in the truck with a neat little bandage covering the side of her now-swollen face. Her left eye was black and getting blacker.

She climbed directly into the small sleeping compartment behind the driver's seat and took off her shirt and pants. Oscar watched her, turning his head several times as he slowly moved the truck back onto the road.

"You come back here when you get tired, Oscar," she said, and tossed her panties over his shoulder onto the dashboard of the truck.

Oscar Hines then became the most exhausted truck driver in the eleven western states. He parked the truck on a turn out and cut the engine, took off his shoes, and climbed in next to the naked woman.

"I don't care where you put it, Oscar, just don't hurt my face," she whispered, and turned her back to him, pressing her butt against his groin.

Keith Shocko drove Patty McShane into Boise, Idaho, and then followed the street signs to the first hospital he saw, he stopped outside the front door and asked her as she was getting out of the car, "Could I have some money for gas?"

"No," she answered, and carried the baby and the suitcase into the hospital. Two nurses took charge of her and rushed her into a room. One took the baby and told her he was going into the nursery. Patty didn't argue with them. She lay on a table and told them the story as the nurse filled out the papers. Patty explained where she was from and what had happened to her, leaving out the part of what she had been made to do for the past three years. A doctor stitched up her face and bandaged her ear, then put a plastic retainer on her lower teeth to hold them back straight until she could go to a dentist, telling her she would need plastic surgery to fix her ear right. They gave her a sedative and Patty McShane slept for twenty-nine hours straight.

She woke up at 6:16 the morning of the 21st of January. She asked for her baby and was told she could see it later after the doctor looked at her. He gave her another sedative and she slept until she was told it was too late to see the baby, he was asleep. The morning of the 22nd she was told he was with his father.

"But how?" she cried.

49

"He came and got him about two hours ago," the nurse told her.

"But how?" she cried.

"I don't know, you were asleep and he came with a sheriff and took the child. Here, he left you this." She handed Patty a card. "We had to call him, it's the law. I'm sorry."

Patty McShane read the card using her right eye, her left was swollen shut. "Don't ever come back," was all it said.

"Oh my lord!" she cried, "Oh my lord."

"I'm so sorry, there was nothing we could do about it; you were asleep. They wanted to take you too, but we wouldn't let them. I tried to make them wait, but they just took the baby and left." the nurse explained.

She laid there for most of the day trying not to cry, then sat up and looked for her dress. It was in a closet with her suitcase. She put on the dress and her shoes, and took the suitcase and walked out of the hospital completely unnoticed. She stopped outside the door and looked inside the suitcase for her sock with the remaining money in it. It was also gone. She dug through the clothes and found the other sock with some change she had stuffed into the back corner of the suitcase. She still had some money. She began walking, carrying the suitcase in front of her with both hands. She walked about six or seven blocks before she saw the sign "Greyhound," with a small arrow. She followed the signs to the bus station and bought a ticket to Seattle, Washington, for $19.43, paying with quarters and dimes and nickels as the man looked through the glass at her.

"You alright, Miss?" he asked.

"No," she smiled back, "No, I'm not, but thank you for asking."

Patty McShane sat on a bench in the bus depot all night and was asked several times if she was alright. Each time she said, "No, but thank you for asking." She left Boise, Idaho, on the bus at 10:50 pm the 23rd of January, sitting in the back seat with the suitcase on her lap and six dollars and twelve cents left in the sock.

Tommy Dollarhide was wide awake and waiting when the man arrived and opened the tire store. Tommy was sitting on his tailgate and the man looked at him.

"You look like you been shot at and missed, then shot at and hit, fella," he smiled.

"You should see me from the inside," Tommy answered.

"Looks like you need a tire. Hell, it looks like you need five of them. Where you headed?"

"Seattle."

"Good luck," the man said, then added, "I think I got a couple around here that will fit."

"I only got sixteen dollars," Tommy answered.

The man grinned and said, "You must be the guy I been waiting for."

Tommy smiled and answered, "I got a feeling about this," he laughed.

"Good or bad? The man asked.

"Um. You tell me."

"You had your coffee yet?"

"No."

"Well, come on in and have a donut and some coffee, and then we'll see what we can do for you."

"I need some work if you got it," Tommy said, and hopped down from the tailgate.

"Oh, we got work," the man grinned. "Lots and lots of work," then he paused and said, "If you want it."

"I want it."

"You don't know what it is yet."

"I don't care what it is."

"My kind of a guy!" the man smiled, then put his hand out, "Jake Smith."

"Tommy Dollarhide." They shook hands and Jake Smith held the door open for Tommy Dollarhide, and said over his shoulder as Tommy walked past him, "Come in, said the spider to the fly, I have a job for you."

"If it will get me a tire and a few bucks, I'm ready."

"It'll get you five tires and two hundred or more if you want to stick around and work for a few days."

"I'm here," was all Tommy answered. He was looking at the box of donuts on the table.

"Help yourself. The coffee is in the pot and the cups are over there in the sink. You'll have to wash one."

Tommy Dollarhide sat and ate four donuts and drank two cups of coffee with Jake Smith, then Jake asked, "You ready to ride, cowboy?"

Tommy smiled and got up. He followed the man out through the back door and around a neat stack of tires. There, in front of him, thirty feet away, was a pile of old tires fifteen feet high and twenty feet across.

"I figure there are about fifteen hundred of them there," Joe said, then smiled at him.

"At least," Tommy answered.

"Well, here's the plan ol' buddy Tommy," Jake smiled wider, then put his hand around Tommy's neck and on Tommy's shoulder and hugged him as though he might turn and run at the thought of so many tires.

"Walk with me, son." he said softly, like a priest might say, and made Tommy laugh again.

Jake Smith led him to the tire machine. As Tommy stood watching, Joe took one old tire from the pile and placed it on the tire machine.

"Here's how it works," he said, then asked "you ever use one of these things?"

"I worked at a tire shop for a while," Tommy answered.

"Wonderful!" Jake answered, then said as he put on a huge nut to hold it in place, stepped on a lever and an arm pressed the tire loose from the rim, then with a different lever he took the tire off of the rim and tossed it into a large trailer, removed the nut and took the wheel off, then tossed it into a different trailer, then handed the bar to Tommy, "I just made myself two bits," he smiled at Tommy and waited, half expecting him to do as so many others had done in the past, walk away.

"Piece of cake," Tommy told him, and took another tire and put it on the machine. He had done this before but only one tire at a time.

"Want some gloves?"

"No, I'm alright." Tommy broke the tire down and removed it, tossing the tire into the trailer, then the wheel into the other one.

"Put a chalk mark on the board there, so we know how many you do."

"How many are there?"

"I would guess fifteen hundred or better."

"That's how many I'll do."

"And I'll kiss your ass right in front of the shop!" Joe laughed and walked away, thinking he might do one hundred. The most anyone had ever done was fifty before giving up.

He had started a little after eight-thirty and averaged one tire every four minutes, but then he got into a rhythm and was doing one every three and a half minutes. By noon he had done fifty-six.

"You want some lunch?" Jake asked.

"Later, I'm just getting loosened up," Tommy answered.

"Don't get so loose you kill yourself," Jack answered, and went back inside the shop.

Tommy improved his method by tossing about ten tires over near the machine, then separating them and then tossing ten more. He worked until eight when Joe told him, "I got to close. If you want to keep working, you can sleep on the cot in the office but I'll have to lock you in."

"Lock me in," Tommy answered.

"Good man!" Joe laughed. "Do um all".

"I intend to," Tommy answered.

"There's about five hundred bucks there if you do. Take a week if you want to, they ain't going nowhere soon."

Joe left and locked Tommy's truck inside the gate.

He worked for another hour, then stopped and got the Waltham watch. He sat it on the chalkboard and timed himself, then broke down ten tires. It took him five seconds more than twenty minutes. He figured he could average three minutes a tire. Allowing for getting tired, he figured he could do the whole pile in 49 hours, non-stop. He worked all night, stopping every hour for five minutes to have a smoke and get a drink of water. He was still averaging one tire every three minutes, but he now had to walk further to get them.

Joe arrived at seven in the morning and looked out the back for Tommy.

"Holy shit! Man!" he cried. Both trailers were full, and Tommy had tires stacked around both of them. He had done a few more than five hundred in twelve hours.

"Christ! Take a break!" Jake told him.

"When I'm done," Tommy answered.

"Well, don't kill yourself, for God's sake," Jake returned.

"I'm just getting warmed up," Tommy answered, and Joe went back inside the store. He came back in a few minutes with some coffee and a handful of donuts.

"Take a break," he said.

Tommy stopped for fifteen minutes and ate the donuts and drank a cup of coffee, then started again.

Several times, Jake came out of the store with various other men, and stood watching him. The pile was getting smaller and smaller, while the other piles were getting bigger and bigger.

By the time Joe closed the shop, Tommy had finished over a thousand, and was still averaging about one tire every three and one half minutes, but he was starting to wear down, plus the fact he had to dig the last forty or so out of the ground where they had been pressed down so far by the weight of the ones on top of the pile. He finished some time after midnight. He sat and looked at the bare space on the ground where the pile had been, and felt good.

When Jake arrived in the morning, he found Tommy sleeping on the cot. He went out to look. The pile was done.

"That's one tough fucking Indian sleeping there," he told his first customer of the day, who was just about to sit down on the cot. "Don't bother him."

It was January 22nd, 1963, and Tommy Dollarhide was asleep on Jake's cot. Patty McShane was asleep on the back seat of the bus, sixteen hours from Spokane. Barbara Fieldsman was asleep in Oscar's truck, parked at a lumber yard in Portland, Oregon. Keith Shocko was awake in the Buick, parked near a tavern three blocks from Tommy Dollarhide's truck outside the tire shop, looking for something he could steal and sell for gas money to get to Seattle. He knew Barbara would be there sooner or later if she wasn't dead.

John Tru-Day was dressing and getting ready to eat breakfast. He would maybe shop for a few more things then come back to the hotel and meet a dark-haired, green-eyed, four foot eleven inch woman who in just over four hours from now was going to come and steal his heart.

Tommy Dollarhide woke up at nine in the morning from the noise in the shop and Jake told him, smiling, "Come on out front and drop your pants. I'll kiss your ass right in front of God and anyone who wants to watch. I said I would and I will. I never would have believed it. If I'd have known it was going to be that easy I'd have just done it myself and saved the money." He handed Tommy six one hundred dollar bills, the most money Tommy had ever held at one time in his life.

"I put some tires on your truck for you too," Joe grinned.

All Tommy could say was, "Thanks Jake, thanks a lot."

Jake shook his hand and asked, "You coming this way next year?"

Tommy laughed and answered, "I'm going to get me a job at Boeing, and stay there for thirty years, but first I got to get some food in me."

"I believe that!" Joe answered, and then added, "If you ever need a job. There's one here waiting for you."

Tommy walked out and stood looking at four nearly new tires on his truck, smiled, and waved goodbye at Jake, then drove five blocks down the street to a feed and seed store Joe had told him about and bought eight pairs of socks, one pair of Levi's, one new western shirt with designs on the pockets, three t-shirts, three pair of shorts, and a pair of new boots for sixty-nine dollars, then drove to a motel restaurant and stopped. He went in and ate, then rented a room. He took the first real hot shower he had in over four months and stood in it until the water turned cold, and then he went to sleep naked in an armchair, watching TV.

He woke up, put on his new clothes and went to eat again, and then walked three blocks back to the tavern and ordered a beer.

"You look a hell of a lot different," the bartender told him.

"I feel a hell of a lot different," he answered.

"You want a beer?"

"A couple of them," he answered.

"Jake said you did that whole pile of tires he had out back in two days."

"And I can feel it too," Tommy laughed.

"Well, we'll just put these on ol' Jake's tab," the bartender said, and walked away down the bar and told the guy sitting there, "Fella, you got to go."

He watched a thin man in his thirties get up from the stool and walked past him. He could smell the stale smoke inside the bar and the odor from the beer, and the smell of fear as Keith Shocko walked past him, hesitated, and then walked out of the tavern.

"He was trying to bum money from my customers. I don't go for shit like that."

"Don't blame you," Tommy answered, and finished the first of four beers before leaving. He walked out feeling almost real again. He lit a smoke, pulled his hat tight on his head, and walked back to the motel, and went back to bed on top of the covers on the queen size bed.

He woke up at eight-twenty in the morning. He went outside and found his saddle and bucking gear had been stolen out of the back of his truck during the night. He still had four-hundred sixty-three dollars in his pocket. He forgot about the saddle and gear. "I hope they needed it more than I do," he thought, and walked into the restaurant to eat. He ate and drove through town heading west to Seattle.

The bus stopped at every small town along the way and arrived in Spokane at three-forty in the morning. Patty McShane had to change buses and the second bus left for Seattle at 11:16 am, seven minutes behind Tommy Dollarhide.

Keith Shocko had sold Tommy's gear for fifty dollars at the same feed store Tommy had bought his clothes, filled the Buick with gas, and bought a half case of beer, and left Spokane a little after twelve.

John Tru-Day had gone shopping again, then went back to the hotel and waited on the sidewalk for the woman to come and meet him.

Exactly at two-thirty, a green and white Ford stopped in the street, and a woman got out and walked around the back of the car. "Mr. Tru-Day?" she asked.

The mighty John Tru-Day was dumbstruck. He looked at the small woman dressed in a light blue suit, with a white scarf around her neck, walking to him. He just stood there looking at the small beautiful twenty-four year-old woman in front of him. He saw her smile and say something, but he didn't hear a word she had said. He just stood there looking at her face, then her clothes and her white shoes, and then dark green belt around her small waist with the gold buckle, and the silver earrings dangling from her small ears, and her white teeth and red lips, and her black hair and eye brows, and her gray eyes, and as she came closer to him he was looking down at her face. Not up at her face. She was standing right in front of him and she was shorter then he was, by almost two inches, at least, and she had on high heels.

"Mr. Tru-Day? Are you John Tru-Day?" she asked.

He finally managed to say, "Oh for goodness sake. Yes, I am him. I'm here, I am here."

She laughed and asked, "Have you been drinking?"

"You're--you're--I'm sorry," he said.

"Short?" she finished.

"Beautiful!" he said.

"Why, thank you!" she said, then asked, "Are you alright? Would you like to go look at the house now?"

"Yes," he answered, "Yes, please."

He followed her to the car and opened her door, then returned to the other side and got in. He sat looking at her, her eyes, her hair, her nose and lips, the scarf around her neck, and the small outline of her small breasts under the small coat jacket she was wearing, the flowered pillow behind her back so her feet could reach the brake and gas pedals.

"Are you going to faint on me, Mr. Tru-Day?" she smiled.

"Maybe," he answered.

Muriel Sue Boatwright, unknown to John Tru-Day, was feeling just about the same as he was, she just controlled it better. They were halfway to the house when she stopped the car in a parking lot and turned to face him. He thought she was going to tell him to get out.

"Should we just go back to the hotel and get your things? We can rent the house to someone else. That is, if you want to."

"What!?" he stammered.

"I mean. You could just move into my house with me if you want to."

"What!" he stammered again.

"Maybe I should not have asked that," she said.

"Yes, you should have!" he answered.

"I mean, we're both the same size and--I'm sorry," she said, "I got carried away."

"No, you didn't," John answered.

"I'm very attracted to you," she said.

"Me too!" he returned.

"You're attracted to yourself?" she smiled.

"No! You! I'm attracted to you."

"Are you, John Tru-Day?"

"I need a drink of water," he said.

"Are you going to faint now?" she asked.

All he could think of to say was, "I will if you will."

She smiled and turned the car around and headed back to the hotel. She waited for him to get his things and load them into the trunk of the car and get back in, "You forget anything?"

"I hope not," he answered, then asked her, "Is this really happening?"

She reached over and pinched him on his leg just above his left knee. "It's really happening, John," she said, "Plus, I'm a good cook too."

It would take John Tru-Day over a week to wake up and walk straight.

It would take Barbara Fieldsman exactly three minutes to talk Oscar into renting her a motel room, another twenty to talk him out of a hundred-fifty dollars, and thirty seconds after he handed it to her to tell him it was time for him to go home.

"Thanks Oscar, you're sweet," she said and shut the door in his face.

It would take Tommy Dollarhide twenty-five minutes to drive through Spokane and onto highway 80, and it would take the driver of the Greyhound bus another sixteen minutes to catch and pass the 1948 gray Ford pickup with four good tires and a clean, warm, full bellied, happy Indian, with feet that felt wonderful inside the new socks and boots. Namely, Tommy Dollarhide, behind the wheel with a match stick in his mouth, a Pepsi in between his knees, and his hat pushed back on his head, and four-hundred fifty-three dollars in his right front pocket.

He saw the bus coming and he moved over to let it pass. As it went, by he looked at the rear window and saw something he had seen too many times back home in his life.

There, looking back at him out of the window, was a girl. A badly beaten-up girl with a bandage covering half her face and the other half black and blue. He smiled and waved at her. To his surprise, she smiled and waved back. Then the bus outran his truck and she was gone.

Keith Shocko passed the grey pickup two and a half hours later and he recognized it from stealing the saddle out of the back of it. He looked over at the driver and Tommy Dollarhide looked back at him. Keith Shocko was scared half to death. The guy would chase after him. He floored the Buick.

Tommy Dollarhide hadn't even really noticed him. He had been thinking about the girl on the bus and the times he had seen his mother and sisters looking like she looked, except they had never smiled after being beaten.

He drove on at forty-five miles an hour wiggling his toes inside the fresh new wool socks with the red stripes around the top, inside the new Justin boots, every once in a while, just cause it felt so good. The weather was almost sixty degrees and he had his window halfway down to let the smoke out. He had decided to quit smoking as soon as he got a job at Boeing, you can't smoke in an airplane plant anyway, he reasoned.

The bus stopped several towns and took a half hour rest in Ellensburg. Tommy passed it as it was parked in the bus stop. It passed him again seventy-five miles out of Seattle.

Again, he saw the girl in the back window. This time she seemed to recognize him and waved first, he waved back and smiled at her.

He drove on, up over the mountain and down the other side and into the rain and finally crossed the bridge across the lake and was in Seattle. He took the first exit and drove into the city looking for some sign that would tell him where Boeing was located. He drove until he found a gas station and asked where the Boeing plant was located.

"Four blocks straight ahead, then turn left onto Second Avenue and go south until you find it--about fifteen miles," the man said.

Tommy drove to Second Avenue, turned left and drove six or seven blocks, then stopped in the middle of the street and backed up. He parked the truck, then got out and walked back a half a block and stood looking down at a soaking wet, scared, battered, and broke, Patty McShane standing in the rain holding the suitcase in front of her with both hands.

"You need some help?" he asked.

"You won't hurt me, will you?" she answered, starting to cry.

"It looks to me like you been hurt enough, ain't ya," he answered.

"Yes. Thank you," she said, and let him take the suitcase out of her hands, then lead her to the truck. He opened the door, then helped her in, closed the door, and walked around and got in himself. He started the truck, and then turned on the heater as high as it would go. The girl was shivering something terrible.

"I saw you on the bus," he said and smiled at her.

"I saw you too," she answered, then said "Thank you," and started crying uncontrollably. For some reason she knew this time she was safe. Everything inside her came loose as she sat in the grey pick-up truck as Tommy Dollarhide drove south on Second Avenue looking for the Boeing Airplane company.

Tommy drove south until the street turned into highway 99 west. Three miles further, he found the Boeing plant and was told at the gate he had to go fill out an application at the office downtown. The guard gave him some papers. He drove back to the address and found it closed until Monday.

"Would you be too scared to stay in a motel room with me?" he asked the girl.

"No," she answered.

"You hungry?

"A little, I have a few dollars left," she started crying again.

He thought it best if he found a room so she could lie down and rest. He drove back south, past the plant, and found a motel near the airport with a restaurant in the front of it. He rented a room for a week at a cost of $88. He was thankful to Jake Smith as he paid the money over to the clerk and then parked the truck in front of room #11. He helped the girl inside and she lay on the bed. He went back out and got his few clothes and her battered suitcase.

"You hungry now?" he asked.

Patty McShane was asleep, curled up on the bed. He covered her with the blanket and left the room and walked across the parking lot to the restaurant. He ate two steaks, two baked potatoes, two salads, a second order of green beans, and three slices of buttered bread, then an apple pie, and drank four glasses of milk.

"You weren't hungry, were you?" the waitress asked, with the chef looking through his window at them both, when she picked up his second plate.

"I was, ain't now," he smiled back, and waved at the chef. "Thanks," he said, then asked for a take-out of chicken-fried-steak and soup for the girl.

Patty McShane was still sleeping, but he woke her up and told her to eat. She ate part of the meal and went back to sleep. He watched the TV for a while, then went to sleep on the floor next to the bed. He felt good.

John Tru-Day felt even better. He was as stiff as an oak plank lying on his back on the bed; with Muriel Sue sitting on him, leaning on his chest, and digging her nails into his flesh with both hands, as she rocked her hips back and forth against his pelvis moaning: "Oh God!! It's been a long time, John!"

She was happy. He was happy, except for the cramps in his feet, legs, and back, from having eight orgasms in nine hours. And the fact both his teats and his whole chest were sore from her digging her nails into it as she came, over and over. The weaker he got, the stronger Muriel seemed to get, until he finally pretended he was asleep. In a few seconds, he was.

Keith Shocko was sleeping in his car in an alley a few miles south of the motel Tommy Dollarhide and Patty McShane were staying in. He was completely broke and looking for something else to steal. He drove back north and turned into the motel and saw the grey pick-up truck. He drove out of the parking lot and went into town.

Barbara Fieldsman was sitting in a bar having a drink across the street from the motel in Portland, Oregon, with a man she was about to take back to the room. She turned five tricks, and earned two hundred-thirty dollars. She had three hundred sixty dollars when she went to sleep at three in the morning.

Two

Jack Charmichael and his wife arrived home from Hawaii at seven-thirty. They took a limousine car from the airport and arrived at their house in north Seattle at nine. The first thing Jack Charmichael saw when he got out of the car was a different car parked in his driveway, the windows were fogged over, and the car was moving.

"Son of a bitch!" he shouted, and then slammed the door of the limo open so hard he nearly tore it off its hinges.

"Hey! Watch my car!" the driver shouted.

"Fuck your car!" Charmichael screamed back as he got out of the limo, nearly slamming the door on his wife's feet as he slammed it closed.

"Jack!" she screamed, "Wait!"

He went to the car and yanked the back door open. There, on the back seat was his daughter and some boy on top of her. Both his sixteen year-old daughter and her boyfriend scrambled. He was trying to pull his pants up from around his feet, as she tried to push her skirt back down from around her waist.

"Daddy!" she screamed, "He made me do it!"

"No, I didn't," the boy cried.

"Yes he did! Daddy! He forced me!"

"Shut the fuck up, and get into the house!" he screamed at his daughter, then yanked her out of the back seat by her

69

arm, pulling her out so hard she landed on her knees on the driveway, her panties still down around her feet. He tried to kick her fat butt, but she scrambled away on her hands and knees until she reached the grass, then she got up and ran.

"What the fuck are you? A fucking animal?" he screamed at her as she was running across the lawn pulling her panties the rest of the way up around her waist, and trying to hold her shirt closed at the same time.

"We didn't do nothing!" the boy cried as he crawled over into the front seat, putting on his pants.

"Get the fuck out of here before I cave your fucking head in!" Charmichael screamed at him, and slammed the door, then kicked the side of the car several times caving in the door and fender.

"Yes, sir!" the boy cried, and started the car, then backed up straight into the front of the rented limo, smashing out both of the front headlights.

"I hope the fuck you got good insurance!" Charmichael yelled at him, and walked into his house, leaving the boy and the limo driver to settle the matter.

"She's up in her room, don't hit her please, Jack?" his wife said as she was pouring herself a drink. Jack Charmichael looked at first his wife, then at the gold framed picture of his daughter sitting on the nineteen thousand dollar piano he had bought so she could take three lessons on it then quit because it hurt her fingers to practice.

He laid the picture face down, then picked it up and threw it into the fireplace.

"Jack! For God's sake!" his wife cried.

"Shut the fuck up!" he screamed back, and walked out of the house into the garage, backed the car out of the garage, and then backed across his lawn to get past the limo and the kid's car. He drove to the Madison Hotel and proceeded to get drunk.

"Nice to see you back, Jack," the bartender started to say, and intended on telling him his new bookkeeper had arrived, but he only got the words "Glad to see you," out of his mouth when Jack Charmichael exploded.

"Shut the fuck up! And give me a drink! I just caught my fucking kid screwing some guy in the back seat of his car."

"They all start sometime," the bartender answered.

"Ya? Well maybe, but not in my fucking driveway with my fucking nosy neighbors watching, they don't!" he downed the glass of Cuttysark and said, "Don't that just frost your fucking balls for you?" I'm so God-damn mad I could fucking spit nails."

"It would me, Jack," the bartender answered, knowing when not to argue with Jack Charmichael. He moved to the other end of the bar and cleaned glasses.

"That bookkeeper guy get here?"

"Here and gone, Jack."

"Gone? What the fuck do you mean, gone? Gone where?"

"We don't know. He was here, then he checked out this afternoon and left with some really, really good looking little chick. She was cute, Jack. You'd have liked her."

"What the fuck are you talking about I would like her? Where did he go?"

"I guess he rented a house, or she took him home or-- hell, I don't know. Maybe she's his sister, for all I know. They looked to be the same size, Jack. Maybe he's getting laid. At least someone is having a good time."

"I'm sure the fuck not, here, fill this up," he pushed his glass across the bar. "Mary Forbes been in here this week?"

"Ain't seen her, Jack."

"No? Well I'll start out in the morning by kicking her fat ass."

"It's a big one alright, Jack."

"You make me sick! You fucking patronizing wimp," Charmichael laughed. "If I said shit was gold you'd agree, wouldn't you?"

"Yup! Every time!" he answered. "With you I would; I like my job here, Jack."

Jack Charmichael liked Bill Tacki more then he liked most men he had known, done business with, or knew now. He was sort of an antidepressant for Jack Charmichael. A couple drinks and a few minutes of conversation with the clean-cut fifty-five year old bartender always picked him up. He depended on him and trusted him with things he

72

didn't trust anyone else to know, and he loved the way the man gave advice.

"I ain't getting into that, Jack. Don't ask me, I'm only the bartender, and I can play maybe three tunes on the piano."

"I know, but what do you think about it?"

"I don't think about it, I'm only the bartender, want another drink?" And that was as far as it ever went, and probably why he had been behind the bar over ten years.

Charmichael thought at times, maybe he was gay, and had asked him if he was married several times, and had gotten the same answer: a good long blank stare and, "Need another drink?"

Then one day, on a Sunday, he saw him in a shopping mall with a woman and three children. They all looked like they had just come from church.

Bill Tacki had stopped for a second, put out his hand and shook Jack Charmichael's like he hadn't seen him in five years, but didn't introduce him to his wife or children. He merely said, "Hello, Mr. Charmichael, so nice to see you again. You're well, I hope," and he walked off with Jack Charmichael thinking, *"What the fuck kind of deal is this? I got something on my face, or something?"* He watched the family walk away.

Four nights later Jack Charmichael asked him: "What the fuck was the snub you gave me in the mall?" He got the same blank stare and the same answer.

"Can I get you another one, Jack?"

"Fuck you! You fucking stuck-up prick!" Jack Charmichael yelled at him, and left the bar. The subject of his life after work was never brought up again; that was eight years ago. He had never asked to borrow money, and was the only person who remembered his birthday every year and bought him a card. Charmichael had almost given him five thousand dollars last Christmas as a bonus, but couldn't make himself give that much money away for no good reason. He had started to hand the envelope to him across the bar, then stopped and took out three hundred dollar bills and handed them to him.

Bill Tacki had taken the bills, said "Thank you Jack," and dropped them into his tip jar, and went on about his work. It hurt Jack Charmichael's feelings a little bit, and he asked, "You see what I gave you?"

"Sure did! Thanks!"

"That's it?" Thanks?"

"Unless you want me to climb over the fucking bar and kiss you on the mouth, I guess so," Tacki answered, throwing Charmichael a two-sided curve. "But I will buy you a drink on the house, how's that?"

"With my own booze? Thanks a lot. You prick!" then he laughed.

Bill Tacki leaned over the bar and said softly, "You're such a good teacher, Jack."

"You are a fucking patronizing prick! You asshole!" Charmichael laughed harder, and sort of wished he had given him a little more, not much, but maybe another hundred or so.

That was a month ago. Now he sat and remembered the sight two hours ago, of his fat daughter's fat ass flopping across the front yard as she ran trying to pull her huge panties up over her fat butt, and hold her shirt closed with her other hand, and her bra straps hanging loose as she ran through the front door crying: "Momma! I got raped!"

Then he thought of his wife sitting on the sofa, drunk every time he came home, and then thought of Mary Forbes' fat butt. At least it wasn't floppy, fat, just big.

"So what did this girl, Trudur, or what the fuck is his name, leave with, look like?"

Bill Tacki leaned over the bar and rested on his elbows right in front of him.

"Jesus! I don't want a fucking movie script! Just tell me what she looked like. Cute?" Jack asked, leaning back away from the bartender's face, taking his drink with him, "I thought you were trying to kiss me," he said.

"She was a doll, Jack! I only got to see her through the front door, but man! She was even shorter than him, but her face--." Bill Tacki kissed the tips of his fingers "Perfect! Perfect! She was a living doll. I never seen a girl as attractive as her. Not attractive, that ain't the word. She was downright perfect, Jack, perfect!"

"Out of all the girls you've seen in here you never seen one as pretty as her?"

"She wasn't just pretty, Jack, but perfect. Dressed right, she stood right, and looked right. Green suit and white scarf, and small white shoes with gray buckles on them low heeled shoes."

"Jesus fucking Christ, Bill!" Charmichael exclaimed. "What? Did you do take a fucking picture of her?"

"She was just something. I thought so anyway. I doubt if I'll ever forget her."

"Christ! Tacki! I guess not. If she's so small maybe she's a fucking leprechaun, and cast a magic spell on you, you dumb fucking Irishman."

"But I ain't Irish, Jack. I'm English."

"Same thing. You both got your asses kicked by the Germans," Charmichael answered, and shoved his glass across under the man's chin.

"Fill that up, before your chin falls in it," he grinned, then said, "I hope she balling the hell out of him, at least someone is having a good night." He picked up his drink and carried it out into the lobby, then asked the girl behind the desk, "You see the woman that picked up the bookkeeper guy?"

"No."

"You talk to him? What's he like?"

She sneered and answered, "He's a shrimp! A smart-mouthed little shrimp. His name is 'Tru-Day'. He made a point of spelling his name for me like I was a child, it made me mad, Jack. I don't like him.

"A little jealous?" he grinned.

"Not a bit," she answered. "He dresses like a gangster in a bad movie."

"Can't be all bad then, can he?" Charmichael felt a tinge of pride and smiled at her, then went into the elevator and up to his apartment on the top floor, had two more drinks, and went to bed.

It was 12:16 am January 23, 1963.

Keith Shocko was looking out of the window of the Buick, into the bright flashlight of a police officer who had just tapped on his window and woke him up.

Keith rolled down the window and said, "Yes, sir?"

"You go find a rest area if you have to sleep in your car, don't do it around here or I'll have to take you to jail and have the car towed."

"Yes, sir," Keith answered and climbed over the seat and started the Buick. He drove out of the lot and headed for downtown, where he could steal something. He was again completely broke and about out of gas.

Patty McShane was sitting on the bed watching the TV and Tommy Dollarhide was sleeping on the floor next to it.

John Tru-Day and Muriel Sue were asleep in each other's arms.

Barbara Fieldsman was walking the street in front of the motel in Portland, Oregon, turning tricks. She had a little over five hundred in the right, knee high, ninety-six dollar pair of boots she had bought (a tool of the trade).

Jake Smith was still at his tire shop in Spokane, loading the wheels Tommy had removed the tires from, getting ready to bring them to Seattle and sell them for scrap.

Mary Forbes was in Vancouver, B. C., at her mother's house, visiting for the weekend. Both were sitting at the kitchen table talking about things that didn't matter to anyone in the world except themselves.

"We can't do that anymore until I get some birth control, John," Muriel Sue said as she served him breakfast.

"Okay by me," he answered, feeling his sore little ding-dong against his leg and his sore sheet-burned knees and his sore pelvis bone, from having so many climaxes in such a short time.

"You don't have to say it like that, John!" she looked at him with an astonished look on her face.

"Yes, dear. We shouldn't even think about children for at least a year or so," he answered, smiling at her.

"Don't go overboard, John," she answered, and picked up his still half-full plate.

"Don't you go overboard!" he laughed, and took the plate back.

They finished breakfast and Muriel told him. "I'm going shopping, John, you can mow the lawn if you want to, it's supposed to rain tomorrow."

"Rain makes the grass grow," he answered.

"That grass back there has grown too much, would you cut it please? The mower is in the garage."

"Be glad to," he answered, never having had a chance to look at the back yard.

78

He poured himself a cup of coffee and went out through the laundry room to the back door and stopped dead in his tracks. The yard was 140' by 80', completely grown over with foot-high grass.

"Miii'eee!! Lord!" he stammered, "That's a hay field!" He sat the coffee cup down and went to look for the mower in the garage; he found a push mower, an old rusty one. He went back into the house and waited for Muriel Sue to return. He met her at the car to help carry in the groceries.

"We've got to buy a mower with a motor," he said. "You got a hay field in your back yard."

"It's pretty bad, huh?" she agreed. "Maybe you can do it a little at a time."

"Not with that thing you got in the garage. It would grow faster than I could cut it. We'll go buy one with a motor."

"They cost a lot, John."

"I'll pay for it."

"They're over a hundred dollars, John."

"So? I can't do it with that push thing you got."

"Maybe we can get a used one," she said.

"Why?"

"To save money," she answered.

"I'm paying for it," he said. "If you want the lawn mowed, I'm buying a mower with a motor on it."

"Alright dear," she smiled, and then said, "You're the man of the house now. Just don't cut your toe off or something else," and she looked right at his crotch.

He laughed and they went down to Rainier Avenue and bought a mower at a mower shop. John bought the best one they had in the store; a self-driven wheel mower for $156.29. Muriel Sue nearly choked as she watched him pay out the money from a wad of hundreds he took out of his pocket. They carried the mower back into the trunk of her Ford and took it around the house. John put gas in it and pulled the cord, then pulled it again and again and again.

"I think you have to turn on or something, don't you? Maybe the gas or something?" Muriel said, trying to act dumb as she stood looking at the gas line with a valve in the middle of it turned off.

John looked and found the valve and turned it on, then pulled the cord three times and the mower started. He pushed it about two feet into the tall grass and was stuck. The grass was so tall and thick the mower couldn't pull itself through it. He pushed it a couple feet, and then tried to pull it back. He pushed again, three feet and he couldn't push it any further. He pulled it back and pushed it again, going about two more feet. He pulled it back and pushed it another foot and a half.

"Maybe we should pay someone to cut it this time, John. It won't be so hard after it's been cut."

"I can do it," he said, and pulled back, then pushed again. Muriel Sue stood and watched for almost fifteen minutes as he finally made it to the other side of the yard.

He turned the mower around and only used one third of the blade as he pushed it back to where she was standing.

"See, nothing to it," he smiled.

She looked at his red face, his puffed eyes, his panting chest, and the sweat running off his for head.

"Are you going to have a heart attack or something, John?" she asked, worried.

"I hope not," he answered, and turned the mower around and started back across the lawn. He had to stop four times before he made it to the other side of the yard. By the time he got back to Muriel Sue she had a glass of water and a towel waiting for him. He drank the glass of water as she wiped his head for him.

"Just do a little at a time, OK, John?" she asked.

"I'm fine," he answered, and started back across the yard. Already, his upper legs hurt and his calves were on fire. He hadn't worked like this in over three years.

He pushed and rested, strained and rested, drank water and rested, and pushed some more. It took him three and a half hours to finish mowing the whole back yard.

He sat on the back step and told her: "See, nothing to it."

"But you haven't raked it yet, John," she answered, kissed him on the cheek and went into the house. He stood up and got the rake and a basket from the garage, and raked the grass he had cut, put it in the basket, and carried it, basket, after basket, after basket, out to the alley behind the garage, it took him seven and a half hours to complete the whole yard, but it looked nice.

He sat in the big chair in front of the TV and Muriel Sue waited on him, bringing him first a beer, and then his supper on a TV tray.

"I'm so proud of you, John, I didn't think you would ever get it all done in one day."

"It wasn't that tough," he said. He was just glad she hadn't gotten the birth control pills yet. Every part of his body hurt, from his fingers to the bottom of his feet. He got out of the chair to go to bed and his legs failed him. He fell on the floor and couldn't get back up.

It was raining Sunday morning when they woke up. He got out of bed and fell down again. He couldn't walk; Muriel Sue had to help him into a tub of hot water.

"Rain makes the grass grow really fast! Did you know that John?" she kidded.

He rolled his eyes up at her and said, "Please don't tell me that."

It took three days of soaking and resting before his muscles had regained themselves enough for him to walk without limping, or having to bend at the waist, or hold himself up on the furniture as he moved around the house. Thank God she still hadn't gotten the pills.

Tommy Dollarhide took Patty McShane to eat three times on Sunday and had to make her eat. She ordered something small and he ordered something big each time. She kept saying she wasn't hungry but he told her, "Everyone gets hungry every day! Eat!"

"You eat a lot, don't you?" she said.

He stuffed a fork full of mashed potatoes into his mouth and pointed at the food in front of her with the empty fork, meaning for her to eat.

Monday morning he noticed her face had swollen and turned red around her neck. He looked closer at her and said: "We got to take you to a doctor. You're getting some kind of infection."

"I'm alright," she answered.

"No, you're not!" he told her, then looked in the phone book and found a doctor a few miles down the road, who would see her as soon as she got there, except as soon as the nurse looked at her face she knew someone had beat the girl up and she wanted to call the police, but the doctor told her to wait until he looked at her first.

Patty was sitting on a table in a small room when he came in and looked at her face.

"What happened?" he asked.

"I sort of got into a fight."

"Sort of?"

"I did," she answered.

"Who put these bandages on you?"

"The hospital in Boise."

"What were you doing there?"

"Coming here."

"That fellow out there do this to you?"

"Heavens no!" she exclaimed.

"He your husband?"

"No, he's in Nevada."

"Your husband's in Nevada?"

"Yes."

"Did he do this to you?"

"No."

"Can I ask how it happened?"

"I got into a fight with a woman named Barbara."

"And you lost," he said, taking off the bandage on her eye.

"I think I won," she answered.

He was half kidding when he asked: "Is she dead?" and Patty gave the wrong answer.

"Maybe."

The doctor sat and looked at her ear, then nodded to the nurse to call the police.

"I'll be right back, just sit there, OK?"

Tommy was sitting in the front room, and watched as two police cars parked in front of the office, and then a third. A male and a female officer came into the front room and the woman went into the back.

The man stepped right in front of Tommy and asked, "Having a little domestic problem?"

"I don't think so, why? Tommy answered.

"You got some ID on you?"

"Sure, something wrong?" Tommy handed him his driver's license and it was sort of worn so the officer asked:

"You got anything else with your picture on it?"

Tommy took out his reserve military ID and handed it to him, then asked: "This about H. C.?"

"Who's H. C.?" the officer asked.

"Some guy in Miles City I punched in the gut before I left."

"No," the officer answered and motioned for the third officer to come in and get the ID cards. He took them and went back out to his car as the first one stood there in front of Tommy.

"What's going on?" Tommy asked.

"Just hang on and we'll all find out," the officer said.

"Oh, they called you about Patty."

"Who's Patty?"

"The girl in there."

"What about her?"

"You better ask her," he returned.

"That's what we're doing," the officer smiled.

It took a few minutes, then the female came back out and said, "She says it was some woman who did it, and she hit her with a rock," then she walked out the door and talked to the other officer. Then both of them came back in and the female went back in to the back room again, then came back out and told the third one: "See if you can find anything on a couple named Barbara and Keith driving a Buick station wagon.

He left, then came back and said: "Nothing, but I got the word on this fella here. Then he handed Tommy back his ID and said: "You're quite the hero down there at Camp Pendleton, ain't you?"

"I don't think so," Tommy answered.

Then the officer said: "Well I hope you stick around here. Good guys are hard to find. You ever think of becoming a police officer?"

"I thought about it," Tommy answered, then said, "Not my kind of work."

"What's going on?" the second officer asked.

"I'll tell you outside."

"Sorry we bothered you," the female said, and they walked outside and stood by the cars for a few minutes.

"What's the story on him?"

"A Marine, the only one ever to get a Purple Heart and a Silver Star during peace time. I guess he took some guy off of a roof who was shooting at the parade field. He wounded five guys before that guy climbed up on the roof and knocked him off. He got shot twice in the process."

"So what about the girl?"

"She got a ride with the wrong people and they tried to rob her and I guess her and the woman got into a fight over in Idaho, and she hit her in the head with a rock, end of story. He's just helping her out, so she says."

"It's probably the truth," the male answered. Then they drove off.

The doctor told her she had an infection in her ear and her lower jaw. He gave her a shot, then changed her bandages and wrote out a prescription for her.

Tommy paid him $112 for the service and then paid another $22.69 for the pills.

The doctor told them both she would need plastic surgery to get the ear fixed right, and she needed to go to a dentist as soon as she could and get braces on her front, lower and upper teeth so they would not grow back crooked, then he told Tommy to bring her back Thursday.

"Please don't spend all your money on me," she begged him as he stopped at the drug store. "The shot will be enough," she argued, but he didn't answer, just went in and got the pills.

He left her back at the motel room and drove to the Boeing company office and filled out an application form. He was told they weren't hiring, but to come back every two weeks and check in, so his application would remain on the top of the pile and he would be one of the first to be called whenever they did start hiring again. He sat in his truck outside the room so she wouldn't see and counted his money. He had $206 plus some change left. He would have to find some kind of a job to hold them over until he got one at Boeing.

He figured after feeding himself and her, plus paying the rent for another week, he would be broke before the next week was up.

Tuesday he went looking for some kind of job. He went the state employment office, then to five different places and filled out applications. All of them told him the same thing. We'll call you, but check back in two weeks.

Wednesday he went through the wanted ads in the paper and filled out four applications with no result.

Thursday he took Patty McShane back to the doctor's office and on the way back saw a sign in the front of a night club six blocks from the motel that read:

"Wanted: Bouncer/Door Man

Apply inside, see Bartender

He left Patty McShane at the motel and went back to the bar. He parked his truck and went inside hoping they would not care about if he was Indian, or the fact he had on Levi's and a western-cut shirt. He thought he should have bought some new shirts, but didn't want to spend the money.

As soon as he walked in through the door, he stopped. There were half naked girls all over the place, some sitting, some standing, and one short skinny girl who looked to be about fifteen years old, sort of dancing on the small stage in the back corner of the large room. She was naked from the waist up and had almost no breasts, she had one leg wrapped around a stainless steel pole in the front of the stage and was swinging around on it. He thought she looked sick, or drunk, or on drugs. He saw only three men sitting at the tables. He was about to leave when he saw the lady behind the bar looking in his direction and smiling.

"I saw your sign out front. I was passing by and thought I'd ask," he said.

"You want the job? You look like you can handle it," she smiled wider at him.

"I need a job," he replied.

"It pays fifty-five a night, plus tips, all cash," she told him, then asked, "You interested?"

"I have to fill out an application or something?" he returned.

"No, just be here at six tonight and wear a white shirt and a pair of slacks. We don't allow Levi's or jeans."

"What do I have to do?"

"You don't know?"

He thought he had lost the job then and there, but she sort
of laughed and said: "You just sit by the door, check IDs,
and don't let anyone in here under twenty-one. You walk
the girls out to their cars so no perverts can grab them, and
if there's trouble you toss the guys causing it out on their
rear. You can read, can't you?"

"That's all there is to it?" he asked.

"We don't fire bouncers, they all quit, if you know what I
mean," she said.

"Oh, ya, I get it, rough sometimes is it?"

"Not too often, but sometimes when the military guys come
in. You want the job?"

"Ya, I do," he answered.

"Don't get me wrong, it ain't a piece of cake. It gets rough
sometimes, and some of the guys have been hurt. You got a
white shirt and some slacks to wear?"

"I'll get some," he told her.

"If I was you, I'd go down to Thrift City and buy some
cheap shirts, they sort of get torn up sometimes."

"What's Thrift City?"

"It's a second-hand store about five miles down the road,
past the airport. It's on the right side of the road, it's got a

big sign. I think some church or something owns it, they got really cheap stuff there but it's clean."

"So I got the job?" he asked.

"Ya! You got the job. What's your name?"

"Tommy Dollarhide."

"That's a neat name huh?" she smiled, then said, "You call me Jan, okay? And if you're a little late, don't worry about it, just get here as soon as you can. We got no one on the door."

"I'll be back as soon as I can," he answered, then said, "Thanks, thanks a lot."

As soon as he walked out, the bartender, Jan, asked a girl who had been sitting at the bar, "Wouldn't you like to crawl into bed with that?"

The girl smiled, and answered, "Maybe, if you were there too."

"I don't know how you girls can do that with each other," she said.

"You're not one of us," the girl answered, and smiled again.

"Well thank God, just the thought makes me sick," she answered, and the girl walked away.

He drove to the Thrift City store and bought three white shirts for $6, two pairs of slacks for $8, a bundle of new black socks for $2.50, three printed t-shirts for $1.50. He started to buy some jockey shorts, but decided he didn't want to wear used shorts.

He bought a pair of nice looking dress shoes for $3.50 that must have cost over fifty, new. He bought Patty McShane a bathrobe for 75 cents that was almost new, a pair of Levi's he thought might fit her, a dress and two shirts for another $7.25, a hairbrush for 25 cents, and some house slippers for another 50 cents.

He paid the woman $18.50, because some of the stuff was half price, and walked out carrying what he thought must be over a hundred dollars' worth of clothes. The Gentry/Leonard shoes new had cost $399 in London, England. Tommy Dollarhide only knew they looked nice and he needed them for his job.

He stopped at a store on the way back and bought toothbrushes and paste, some deodorant, shampoo, bath soap and powder, because he thought women liked powder, then some snack food for the girl, because he knew she wouldn't go eat unless he forced her.

He carried the things back into the room and put the sacks on the bed. He took out the shirts and told Patty McShane: "I got a job. It's not much of one, but at least we won't starve."

"I'm happy for you," she answered.

"Here, I got you a couple things. I don't know it they will fit you, but you can wear them around here."

He handed her the bathrobe.

"It's lovely!" she remarked looking at it, "Oh, thank you so much!" Then he handed her the pants and shirts and the house slippers, and told her:

"I have to go to work. I won't be back until real late so keep the door locked and I'll knock before I come in so you'll know it's me."

"Why are you being so nice to me?" she asked, looking at the robe.

"I like the way you talk," he smiled, and went into the bathroom to shower and change his clothes.

"You look very nice," she said, when he came out dressed in the brown slacks and the white shirt. He felt clean and his feet felt better than they had for the past two years, in the soft leather of the shoes. The boots felt good, but the shoes felt better for some reason. And new clean socks with no holes in them, loose fitting slacks, a nice clean white shirt. He folded his other clothes up and placed them on the dresser.

He took the two old pairs of Levi's he had brought with him and tossed them into the trash can.

"You're throwing them away?" Patty asked, thinking it was an awful waste of good clothes.

"I'm throwing my past three and a half years away," he answered.

She looked surprised at him and said, "I am too."

He smiled and told her, "I got to go. Keep the door locked. I'll be back about three in the morning and I'll knock."

"Bye," she said.

"See ya," he returned, and closed the door.

As soon as she saw him drive out of the parking lot she closed the blinds and got into the shower, she showered and washed her hair and cleaned her teeth as best she could without hurting the loose ones too much, and powdered her body, then put on the robe and slippers and brushed her hair. She sat on the bed with the robe tight around her and brushed her hair for an hour. Patty McShane had found a real live cowboy hero, or so she thought anyway. Tommy had found an almost gold mine, but didn't know it yet.

John Tru-Day had recovered from harvesting his hayfield, as he would later refer to it, and Muriel Sue had gotten her birth control pills, but had to wait 24 hours before doing anything. She sat on John Tru-Day's lap and whispered into his ear, "I know another way we can do it, if you want to, John."

Just as Tommy Dollarhide was walking into the Tropics Club, Muriel Sue was kneeling down in front of John Tru-Day undoing his belt.

Tommy Dollarhide arrived at the tropics at six ten, and was greeted by the bartender Jan who smiled and said, "Hi! I see you came back."

"Didn't you think I would?"

"Most of them don't," she smiled and handed him a sheet of paper. He looked at it and saw it had several pictures of state, federal, and military IDs printed on it.

"If their IDs don't match any of those they can't come in. Those army guys have got all kinds of fake IDs, some of them are only seventeen but they look older, so you got to look really close. Look at their eyes. If the color is off, the ID is a fake."

Then she said, "You look really nice. I love those Gentry shoes."

"What?" he asked.

"The shoes, they're Gentry/Leonard, from England."

"Oh, ya? Well, I got them down there where you told me to go, $3.50."

"Well, they're worth a hundred times that much if you bought them new."

"What?" he looked down at the shoes.

"Forget it, Tommy!" she kidded, and pushed him toward the front door.

He took his place at the door and sat on the stool. Not many men came in until after ten in the evening, but the girls kept him busy. One after the other came and asked him his name, and where he was from. Was he married? Did he have a girlfriend? Did he want one? And three came right out and asked him to have sex with them. One even said, "We can do it in the dressing room if you want to. No one cares. You make me really hot."

He checked IDs and stopped about ten men from coming in. He walked the girls out to their cars, and some of them several times. He figured they had a room close by and were going out to have sex with the men. Each time he walked one of them out she handed him some money and said, "Thank you, Tommy." Some of them kissed him on the cheek, some tried to feel his crotch, and others just handed him money and said nothing. Some of them tried to kiss him on the mouth but he turned his head. By the end of the night his right pocket was stuffed with bills and notes from the girls. He helped Jan pick up the chairs, then waited until she locked the money in the safe, then walked her out to her car. She handed him seventy-five dollars.

"I thought you said it paid fifty-five."

"Twenty is from the bar. It's the custom."

"Thanks," he answered, and put the money in his pocket.

"You did pretty good, huh?" she asked.

"I think I did really good," he answered.

"It's because you're so good looking and you're new. It won't last unless you play with them, you know, flirt and act like you like them. Make them jealous of each other and they'll all try to bribe you. Know what I mean?"

"Sort of, I guess," he answered, not liking the idea of playing with the girls like that, just to get money from them.

Then Jan said, "I'm not the jealous type. You want to go get something to eat?"

"No thanks," he answered, "I have to get back to where I'm staying."

"Girlfriend?" she asked.

"No. I have to go look for a real job. You know?"

"If you're smart, Tommy, you can make a lot of money here. Over a thousand a week, and all cash."

"How?" he asked.

"I'm telling you, just be nice to the girls and don't let them get to you. Just politely keep saying no, maybe tomorrow and they'll keep giving you their money. They just spend it on booze and drugs anyway."

"I'll keep that in mind, thanks," he told her, then said, "Goodnight."

"Don't I get a kiss?" She asked.

"Maybe tomorrow night," he smiled and patted her on her shoulder and said, "Thanks again Jan, thanks a lot."

"See you tomorrow," she answered, and drove away.

He went back to his truck and drove to the motel. He sat in front of the motel and counted the money. He had $364, plus seven notes. He put the notes in the glove box and went into the room, knocking on the door first. Patty opened it as soon as he knocked.

"I thought you would be asleep."

"I think I'm sleeping too much. Thank you for the clothes and hair brush."

He looked at her and saw she had brushed her hair down over the bandage on her ear. He thought she was a really pretty girl, except for the bruises on her face. She was wearing the Levi's and a plaid shirt. He told her, "You look a lot better, you're face ain't red no more."

"I know," she answered, then said "I guess you want to go eat?"

"You're right!" he grinned and took her across the parking lot into the restaurant and ate.

"I see you're feeling better," the waitress said to Patty McShane. She said nothing to Tommy Dollarhide except: "One or two steaks?"

He smiled, and answered, "One, a big one."

"One big one, Larry!" she called to the chef.

"You got it, big fella! The biggest one I got back here!" the chef called out through his window and waved at Tommy.

"You got it!" she answered, then asked Patty what she wanted.

"Can I have another strawberry milk shake?" she looked at Tommy.

"Anything you want," he answered. He was back to over $500 in his pocket. He felt like he was rich.

Friday morning he took Patty McShane to the Thrift City and he bought her sixty-five dollars worth of clothes, including two pairs of shoes, only because he kept saying,

"Here, this looks good! How about this? You need one of these don't you?"

"I never had so many clothes before in my whole life," she said, as she folded and put them away in the dresser drawer. "It's like Christmas. Thank you so much!"

Friday night was very busy and he understood why so many men quit the job on the first weekend. He had three small fights and tossed eight or nine men out of the club, broke up three fights between the girls, and fought off advances from most of the girls who were trying to see who could get to him first.

He came back to the motel on Saturday morning, down two white shirts that had been torn, but with a little over four hundred dollars in his pocket and eleven phone numbers from the girls, and one from some male customer.

Saturday night was different. He politely argued with three different girls and had three scraps with three different men. He threw two of them out. No hitting or shoving happened, he just smiled and said politely, "Don't make it rough, OK? This is a new shirt and if it gets torn, you're going to get torn," then he smiled and the men walked out.

The girls were different, two of them stood toe to toe with him and he finally had to laugh. He told one, "I ought to pick you up and kiss you. You're as horny as my sister is. I miss her, you got a sister?" She just looked disgusted at him, then walked away.

The other one he picked up by taking one arm around her waist and carried her back to his stool and held her on his lap with one arm wrapped around her as he checked IDs with his other one. After a few remarks from the men she started smiling and talking to him. She gave him a note and twenty when she went home.

He went back to the motel Sunday morning with $261, not as much as the first night or Friday but he thought it was a lot. He had $926 in his pocket.

Sunday night the club was closed because of a city law. He took Patty McShane to eat three times during the day and then they rode the bus sight-seeing around Seattle. He enjoyed it. Patty thought it was the greatest place she had ever seen, except for Ireland.

Monday he bought a second pair of boots at the Thrift City store, but they were like new. Twelve pairs of new shorts, twelve new t-shirts, and twenty-four pairs of assorted socks, all had been donated by some store going out of business.

"Why so many?" Patty asked.

"I ain't ever going to run out of socks again for the rest of my life," he answered.

He tried to buy Patty McShane clothes but she refused except for five pair of panties and three new bras. "It's more than I ever had in my whole life," she said, "I don't need any more."

Monday morning John Tru-Day called Jack Charmichael at 9:00 am, as he had been instructed to do, and as soon as he said who he was Jack Charmichael started, "So where the fuck did you go? I thought you were going to stay in the hotel. I hear you found yourself a friend and moved in with her?"

"You said to find a place near Rainier Avenue, so I did. I'm only three blocks from it."

"Good. The address is 4437 South Rainier Avenue. They're putting your office together as we speak, go down there and see if they're doing it right, and if you need something tell them about it. Don't be afraid to say something. Make it like you want it, so you feel at home. Fix it up the way you want. I'll call you there Friday morning," Charmichael hung up without saying goodbye. John Tru-Day looked at the receiver and said to it, "Rude Prick!" then he hung it up.

He left the house and walked the three blocks to Rainier, the street sign said 1600 South. It was too far to walk so he waited for a bus, but a cab came by and he waved it down. The driver told him, "There ain't no 4400 block on Rainier; it goes to 2700 then stops and starts again at the 8300 block south. It's got to be 14437 South, it's about eight miles from here."

"Let's go, then," Tru-Day told him.

They found the building, a low white block building that looked to be divided in half. It had a center entrance, but two doors, the one on the left read: *Charmichael Construction South Office*. It had a huge sign leaning against the north half of it and a truck was putting up another huge sign on the south side of the roof, both of them read the same:

Tru-Day Bookkeeping Services
14437 South Rainier Ave.

General Bookkeeping   *Expert Tax Service*
Phone 206 662 6666

He was surprised, to say the very least. He paid the cab and went through the two glass doors into the white block building. There were two doors, but only one hallway, a short hall with a brick planter at the end of it. It looked nice but the plants were fake. There was a door on each side. The one on the right read *Tru-Day Bookkeeping Services* on a large brass plate. The one on the left said *Charmichael Construction*, on a big brass plate.

He went into the one that had his name on it.

"You the bookkeeper guy?" a worker who was installing a door asked.

"I guess so, I didn't expect all this". "Call your boss, the phone is under the tarp on your desk. Sorry about the mess, we're a day behind. The doors just got here this morning."

He looked around for a few seconds, then found the phone and called Jack Charmichael.

"Found it all right, I take it," Charmichael said, then said, "I guess I gave you the wrong address. Anyway, look around and see if it's all right. I'll send a girl down there in the morning and you tell her what you need. You know, adding machines, books, pencils, pens. I don't know what the fuck a bookkeeper uses but get what you need, or whatever, I don't know. Whatever. She'll go get them for you. And if you don't stop her she'll suck your balls right out through the end of your dick. I'll call you in a few days." He hung up.

John Tru-Day stood there with the phone in his hand, wondering what he had gotten himself into, then muttered, "Don't you ever say good-bye?"

102

The worker took the covers off the furniture and carried them out through the door saying, "It's all yours, good luck."

He stood looking at the huge office. It had dark walnut paneling on all the walls, a soft green carpet covering the floor, a huge walnut desk in the center of the room a few feet from the back wall, with two matching leather chairs in front of it. Along another wall was a huge black leather couch with two matching chairs and glass top tables between them. A huge coffee table sat in front of the couch.

Along the wall closest to the street was what looked to him like a built-in bar with two louvered doors above and a counter with a sink below stocked with glasses and things from a bar.

He walked over and opened the doors and looked. It was completely stocked with about fifty different kinds of whiskey, gin, rum, vodka, and several other kinds of booze. He opened the bottom door and found an ice-making machine, a refrigerator, and other utensils for the bar, a blender, towels, and things. The other two doors were a coat closet and storage closet.

"Suit you alright?" a voice said behind him.

He turned and looked at a huge barrel-chested balding man with a huge scar on his face. It ran from his right eye to the bottom of his chin. He looked to be at least three hundred pounds. Standing in the door he filled the whole opening.

"I'm Jake Morrison. I'm next door. I run the construction company." He walked forward and put out his hand.

John Tru-Day put out his hand, but remained ready to pull it away if the man squeezed it too hard. He didn't. "Jack told me you were here. Everything all right? Look OK to you?"

"Looks fine, but it's a lot more than I expected. I thought I was just going to do bookkeeping in an office."

"You are, it just happens to be your own office," Jake said, smiling.

"It's kinda fancy, ain't it?" John asked, looking at the scar on the man's face.

"A piece of glass fell off a roof and got me," he explained, then said, "Jack does things right. He likes to impress people."

"I'm impressed," Tru-Day answered.

"Need something? I'm in the office there in the mornings until about nine, and then I go out into the field."

"So what am I supposed to do?"

"Beats the hell out of me." He laughed like it was a joke, "You're the bookkeeper," he said and walked out.

John Tru-Day walked around, sat at his desk, and walked around, sat in the chairs and on the couch, then walked around some more, and then a man came in and said, "You want to check out your sign, we got it up for you."

He walked out and looked up at the signs, "It's alright, I guess," he answered.

"It's OK, then?"

"It's fine, thank you."

"Far out! Have fun! I hope it gets you a lot of business."
The man got into the truck and left and John Tru-Day went
back into the office, sat on the couch, then in each chair
again, and finally behind his desk again. He slid the chair
around and turned it around, then opened the doors behind
him and below the counter. There was a built-in stereo
system with a remote control lying on top of it.

He started pushing buttons. The stereo came on, and then
turned off. He pushed another one and the doors above the
bar turned around and a huge TV screen swung around
taking their place. "Holy shit!" he exclaimed under his
breath, then pushed the TV ON button. The TV lit up and
he sat and watched it flipping through the channels, then
flicked it off and pushed the TV button again and the doors
came back around and the TV went into the wall.

"Holy shit!" he said again.

Jake came back and tossed him a set of keys. "I forget
these. You might need them. Oh Ya! The safe is under the
ice machine. It slides out, and then turns. Want me to show
you?"

Tru-Day watched him walk across the room, open the
doors, and then he pointed to a hidden button.

"It's here, right under the lip." He pushed the button and
the ice machine slid forward. He pushed it sideways and it
slid around to the side out of the way. There was a safe in
the wall.

"When you lock the front door it locks this cabinet, you have to unlock it every time you come in within forty-five seconds or the alarm will go off. See here?" He showed John a key and then where to turn off the alarm. It was located on the left side of the ice machine.

"Unlock this lock. Open the door and turn this one."

"OK," John answered flabbergasted by it all.

"I got to go clear the fuck across town," Jake told him and handed the keys to him, then walked out.

He heard Jake's truck leave and he sat back on the couch again wondering what he had gotten into. He knew he wasn't qualified to run an office like this one seemed to be.

The phone rang and he answered it:

"Hello?"

"Mr. Tru-Day?"

"Yes."

"This is Mary. I work for Jack."

"Yes."

"I'm coming down there in the morning. Should I bring you something?"

"What?"

"I don't know? Anything?"

"What am I supposed to do here?" he asked.

"Make yourself a drink and watch the TV. I'll see you in the morning. I hear you're really cute." she said goodbye and hung up. He thought about it for a few minutes, then made himself a whiskey and soda, then sat on the couch and drank it, made another one, and he walked around, going outside and around the building.

The back was fenced in and building material was stacked everywhere along with three old pickup trucks that looked like they were worn out. He went back inside and make a third drink, then decided he better stop. He went home at one in the afternoon after calling a cab.

Monday night Tommy Dollarhide went back to work at the Tropics club. Tuesday morning he left the Tropics club with $282 in his pocket, not as much as his first night but he had six more notes to add to his collection.

He got up and took Patty McShane to the doctor's again. This time he had to pay forty-eight dollars and was told he should take her to a dentist as soon as he could, because the teeth were starting to reset themselves crooked and she need to get the one replaced before the gums completely healed.

The nurse gave him the name of one a few blocks away and he took her there even though she didn't want to go. He sat and waited for three hours while Patty McShane got braces on both her upper and lower teeth, then a temporary tooth put into the vacant spot. She was told she had to wear them for five weeks at least.

Tommy paid the bill, $592.91, but it included the four weekly visits to have them cleaned and adjusted. Patty tried to say thank you but it came out a sort of "Aink uww."

"Now you really do talk funny," Tommy kidded.

Patty cried most of the way home, not because of any pain in her mouth but because someone really seemed to care about her for the first time in her life.

John Tru-Day had Muriel Sue drop him off at the bus stop on her way to work and he rode the bus (a twelve minute ride) to his new office that he had not mentioned anything about to Muriel Sue because he didn't know what to say or how to explain it to her.

He arrived a little after eight-thirty in the morning and sat doing nothing until after nine-thirty, and then he walked down the street a block and got a cup of coffee. When he returned there was a red Dodge convertible car parked in front off the door. He walked in and saw a pretty blonde-haired woman who looked to be about twenty-three, sitting on the couch, drinking a drink. The bar doors were open. He watched her sip from the glass, looking at him over it. The second thing he noticed was her huge breasts half way hanging out of a low-cut light blue sweater with no sleeves and a tan leather jacket lying beside her, then her short white skirt with a blue stripe, and then the black and white checkered scarf tied around her neck by a huge gold clip of some kind. It looked like a napkin-holder, but was carved and had small diamonds in it, and looked real expensive. She had rings on almost every finger and several bracelets on each wrist. Her finger-nails were bright red and long, she didn't type, and she didn't stand up, she just smiled and said "Gee! Lori was right! You are little."

He figured Lori must be the woman who worked at the hotel desk.

"You are?" he asked.

"I'm Mary Forbes." She said it like he was supposed to automatically know who she was. She scooted forward on the couch making her skirt slide up around her upper thighs, swung her legs in his direction, exposing something he didn't really want to see. He turned his head as she stood up and smiled down at him, then put out her hand for him to shake it. He didn't like her already and didn't want to take her hand, but he did, then he walked around his desk and sat in his chair, then looked at her.

"I'm supposed to run errands for you," she said, then added, "So what do you want?" Then she walked to the desk and handed him an envelope and said, "Here, you're supposed to buy a car with it. I'll take you somewhere if you want; and we're supposed to get some adding machines or something from the Office Supply, paper and whatever! I guess you need a lot of pencils too? That's what Jack said." She shrugged her shoulders, making her breasts bounce three times or more.

She turned and walked to the bar, bent over a little too far, and stayed that way a little too long, opened the lower door, got some more ice, and made herself another drink, then stood leaning back against the counter, looking as he opened the envelope and took out the money and a picture.

The picture was of her, naked, sitting sideways on the desk he had in his office with a drink in her hand.

"You like it?" she smiled.

"No," he answered, and laid the picture face down on the desk.

"What's wrong with it?"

"Nothing is wrong with it. I just don't like looking at pictures of naked girls."

"You queer? I thought you were in the Navy?"

"No! I'm not queer!" He was instantly mad at her. "I like looking at naked girls if they're not fat cows!" he answered.

"You are a little creep! Shrimp! Smart-mouthed bastard!" she said, and stomped out of the office and drove away. She was back in less than ten minutes. She walked in just as the phone rang, it was Charmichael.

"Hey! You tell that fucking fat ass to do what the fuck you tell her to do or I'm coming down there and--Is she back yet?"

"Yes, she just walked in."

"Give her the phone."

"He wants to talk to you, 'Fat Ass!'" John smiled as he handed the phone to Mary Forbes and saw she was scared half to death as she put it to her ear, then said, "I'm sorry Jack, I got mad at him. I'm sorry! He called me a cow! I'm sorry, I said I was sorry, Jack. I didn't try to do anything. I just showed him a picture of me, the one you took that time. Yes! Yes! I will, I will! I said I'm sorry, Jack." She held her hand over the mouth piece as she handed the phone back to him and said, "He's really pissed!" she grimaced her chin, and snuck away to the bar as he answered the phone.

"Yes Jack?"

"If she gives you any more shit just kick her fat ass."

"It might take a while, it's pretty big, "John Tru-Day answered.

"You got that right! If you need help doing it, call me." He hung up.

"He told you to hit me, didn't he?" she said, sipping her drink and looking over the glass.

"No! He told me to kick your ass."

To his surprise she turned around and lifted her skirt up over her bare butt and said: "Here it is."

"Christ!" He shouted "Put your-- Jesus! What the hell is going on here anyway?"

She dropped her skirt and turned around. "You don't have any idea what you're getting into, do you?"

"No, I don't. What?"

"Did you count the money?" She smiled, and sipped the drink smiling over the glass as she held it to her lips licking the rim.

He counted the money in the envelope; there was another $2500, all in hundreds.

She smiled, "That's nothing if you're smart," she said.

He stood looking at her licking the rim of the glass, and then finishing the drink, sucking an ice cube into her mouth, and then sucking on it.

"I love sucking things," she said, "I have since I was twelve years old," then swallowed the cube, straightened her face, set the glass on the counter and said, "Let's go, short stuff."

He was mad again, and answered, "Alright fat ass."

She stopped and said, "I don't think I like you very much."

"Haven't you noticed? I don't like you at all," he answered.

"Have you learned how to drive yet?" she asked as they locked the front door.

"Man, you're asking for it, ain't you?" he answered.

"You drive! There's a pillow in the backseat you can sit on." She tossed him the car keys.

He threw them back and said, "Just knock it off! Right now! Alright?"

She caught the keys and said, "Oh! I'm sorry, I forgot to bring the child's seat."

"One more and I will kick your fat ass! And I mean it!" He half yelled at her.

"Should I stop and buy you a foot stool to stand on?" she returned.

He started around the car to do something to her but she started the car and backed up a few feet, then stopped again and laughed. He walked back around the car to get in and she drove forward a few feet just as he reached for the handle. "Stop it, God damn it! You're not funny!" He cussed. She let him get in and said, "Want to go get your office things and then I'll help you buy a car. You do want a little one, don't you?"

"What the hell is your problem?" he asked.

"Don't call me a cow!" she answered.

"Don't call me a shrimp!" he returned.

"Then don't call me a fat ass."

"Don't call me shorty."

"Well! My name is Mary."

"Well! My name is John."

"Alright! John."

"Alright! Mary."

"Alright," she answered.

"Alright," he answered her back.

They drove to downtown Seattle and went into a store that sold office supplies and machines. Everything he said he needed she bought and had it put into the back seat of her car except the copy machine and the salesman who was not much taller than John Tru-Day himself said they would deliver it.

"So just deliver it all," she told them. The men took everything back out of her car and brought it all back into the store. John Tru-Day had already decided she was not the smartest girl he had ever met.

"So what kind of a car do you want?" she asked, "You know you have to drive a lot of miles every month so I'd get a big road car if I was you".

"Where am I driving to?' he asked her.

"You have to go to all the clubs and get the receipts and then bring them back to your office and do them."

"Oh!?" he answered.

"Get a Caddie or a Buick," she said.

"Just like that?"

"Ya!" She answered, "How much did he give you?"

"$2500."

"I got more," she said.

"How much more?" he asked.

"I don't know, a lot!" she answered "As much as we need."

She wanted him to buy a new gold-colored Cadillac for eleven thousand dollars but he refused.

They went to a Buick dealer and she bought a one year-old grey-colored Tudor hardtop Oldsmobile with only 12,000 miles on it for $3,700. She took his money and paid the difference from her purse.

"Jack is going to make you pay him back, you know," she said.

"I didn't expect him to buy me a car," he answered.

"He won't make you pay him back. You want my pillow?" she asked him when he got into the car and could barely see over the windshield.

He looked sheepishly at her and said, "It has electric seats," then he raised the seat as high as it would go and he was still too low to see safely.

"Ya! Give it to me."

She gave him the pillow by throwing it in through the driver's window and hitting him in the head with it, and he followed her back to the office in the Oldsmobile.

The truck arrived shortly after they did and Mary Forbes helped him put everything where he wanted it, in between making herself several strong drinks.

By the time they were done, she was drunk and could hardly walk around the office. He told her he was going home and she told him to go, she was going to lay on the couch for a while before she tried to drive back into town. He left her on the couch and went home driving the Olds.

Muriel Sue was very surprised, but he told her it was a company car. They were walking out of the house so she could look at it when she asked, "What company are you working for?"

"Well, it's kind of my own bookkeeping company, but Jack Charmichael is helping me get started.

"Oh! No! My God! John!" she cried, and stopped halfway out the door.

"He's a gangster! He has whorehouses, John! He has people killed!"

"He does?" John Tru-Day looked at her as surprised as she was.

"I wondered what the hell was going on with all this loose money," he answered.

"John! He has people killed!" she exclaimed again.

"He does?" he stammered, looking at her with his mouth half open.

"Yes! He does! You quit!" she cried, "You quit right now! Don't go back there!"

"He already gave me a lot of money, and an office, and equipment, and the car," he answered, "I can't quit yet! I have to--" she interrupted him.

"Oh God!" she cried, "You got to quit. Take the car back."

They went back into the house and he admitted now he was too scared to quit. He had to go ahead and see what happened. He told her, "I'll keep records and if he tries anything we'll go to the police."

116

"John!" she cried, "He pays the police, he pays everyone. I'm really scared, John."

"That makes two of us, Muriel Sue," he answered.

They didn't sleep well that night and in the morning it was a scared John Tru-Day who drove the Olds to his office. He saw no one all day. He sat around worrying and waited, but no one called and no one came in, at about two in the afternoon he made himself a drink, then another, and after four drinks in an hour he left at three and went home. He missed the driveway and drove over the curb; he decided he wouldn't drink so fast even if they were free.

Wednesday was the same. He sat at his desk, had a few drinks, worried, and went home. Thursday and Friday were the same.

Tommy Dollarhide on the other hand, liked his job just fine.

Monday night he earned $225.
Tuesday night he earned $266.
Wednesday night he earned $314.
Thursday night he earned $287.
Friday night he earned $344.
Saturday night he earned $366.

He had $1555, plus change, in a small toolbox under the seat of his truck, mostly all ones and fives from the girls' tips, and about fifty notes from the girls in the glove box. He had bought new boots and new Levi's, slacks for work, and shirts, a new overcoat and hat, a new belt, and several things for Patty McShane, all of which she said she didn't want, or need.

Sunday was his day off and he took Patty on two different ferry rides. She didn't like the water very much but she loved seeing the islands and the tall trees and nice houses along the shoreline.

Monday night two things happened. The first was a girl named Carol came up to him and asked, "How come you never answer any of my notes? Don't you like me, Tommy?"

"I haven't read any of them," he explained, saying, "I don't want to get involved with any of you girls because it might cause trouble." He smiled at her.

"It already has!" she snapped, and walked away. She left the club an hour later, giving him a dirty look as she passed, and didn't let him walk her out to her car.

A little while later, a thin, sort of balding, very clean looking man walked into the bar. He looked to be in his early thirties. Tommy admired his clothes. They were almost perfectly neat. A wide collared shirt, open at the neck with three gold chains showing. The creases in his trousers were so sharp you could fold a paper on them. His shoes looked very expensive, maybe the same kind as the ones Tommy had on. Both men looked at each others' shoes but said nothing. His face was almost shining, it was so clean shaven or he had oil on it, or something. He stopped directly in front of Tommy, stuck out his hand for Tommy to shake, then said without stopping, "Nice shoes, I been hearing a lot about you, big guy. A lot. I hear you're a really nice guy, that's what they need around here, and George says you're the best steak eater he's ever had in his restaurant. I'm Mike Cooper. I'm an actor. My friends call me Mikie, I hope you're going to be my friend too, Tommy. Sonia sure does like you a lot and that's good because she don't like too many guys who work here. I do TV commercials and things like that, a little theater too. Sonia Re'olo is my girl, that's her over there. She dances under the name of Mikie. I'm Mikie and she's Mikie. It's sort of a thing you know, I don't blame her for that though, girls like to be silly most of the time, it don't hurt nothing. Do you think it does? No, of course not. I don't like her working here, but she likes to dance and the money is too good to let go if you get my drift. Someone sure did a number on your truck, didn't they? It was probably one of the girls here, they get jealous for no reason. You got to be a real politician to get along with all of them and not make any of them mad at you. Sharon, that's her over there by my girlfriend. She called me and told me when she came in and saw your tires had been cut, so I came down to see if you needed some help getting them replaced. I know everyone on the south end. We have an association of sorts. I got a friend with a tire shop, he'll come and change them for you. If you want me to, I'll give him a call. Oh, she's done. I'll be back, Big Guy."

And Mikie 'the actor' Copper was halfway across the room before it soaked into Tommy's brain what he had said about his truck tires being slashed. He walked out and looked. All four of his nearly-new tires were flat; someone had punched holes in the side of them with an ice pick or something sharp.

"Son of a bitch!" he muttered, and went back inside.

"Want me to call my friend, Tommy?" Mikie the actor asked.

"Would you?" Tommy answered, wondering how much four tires would cost him.

119

Three hours later a man walked in and handed him a paper. It was a bill marked PAID for $88.00. "I gave them to you for wholesale. You didn't need tires, just a patch over the hole and some new tubes. Mikie took care of it, here's your receipt."

"Why would he pay for them?" Tommy asked.

"We don't really pay for things amongst ourselves. We just sort of--trade," the man said, then shook Tommy's hand and left.

He looked for Mikie the actor but he had left the club with Sonia Re'olo. Later, one of the girls came up to him and said, "It was Carol," then walked away. He then looked for the girl Carol but she had not come back.

He went home with only $126, a little disappointed, but only five girls had shown up for work, and only about twenty men came in.

Tuesday it was better. He went home with $210 in his pocket. Wednesday, the girl, Carol, came back in, stayed only a minute, and before he could ask her about his tires, she left, then, few minutes later, came back in and smiled at him, then walked away into the back room. He was going to wait until she came back out to confront her but ten minutes later some man came in and told him, "Someone poured red paint all over an old pickup truck out there."

He knew it was his truck as soon as the man said it. "Damn it," he muttered, then walked out the door and looked. It was his truck. She had poured the paint all over the hood, front fender, and the driver's door. He came back in, and then went straight to the back room.

The girl, Carol, was standing completely naked in front of her locker. She smiled at him and started to say something but never got the chance. He said nothing, just grabbed her by her arm and pulled her away from the locker and over to a bench the girls used. He sat down on the dressing bench and pulled her down across his lap. He held her down and put his leg over hers so she couldn't kick, then began spanking her bare butt as hard as he could hit her. At first, she cried out, screamed, "Let me go!" kicked and screamed, as she tried to fight her way loose from his grasp, but he had his right leg over top of hers and held her down with his left hand on the back of her neck as his right hand slammed down across her bare butt sixteen or seventeen times. After about eight or nine good whacks on her butt, and as most of the girls came running back into the back room because of her screaming, looked and left again as fast as they had come in, her screams sort of turned into moans and little cries of something he didn't understand.

Then, as he spanked several more times, telling her she was going to pay for having his truck re-painted, the cries sort of turned to moans and she put her hand down under his left leg and in between her own legs and started rubbing herself and crying: "Oh! Oh! Oh God! Spank me harder! Spank me, Tommy! Oh spank me, Tommy! Hit my ass! God! Hit my ass with your hand! Harder! Hit me harder!"

He stopped with his hand in mid-air and stood up letting the girl fall onto the floor. He looked down at her thrashing body as she laid there on her side with her knees bent and her hand in between her thighs crying and moaning, making herself climax. Then she straightened her legs out and cried, "Oh God! I did it!! Oh God I did it!!!" He nearly ran out of the back room pushing four astonished girls out of his way.

He sat on his stool dumbfounded as Jan the bartender stared at him with her mouth half open, holding an empty glass in her hand for several moments, then went into the back room still carrying the glass with her, then came back out laughing and looking at him, then laughing some more. She came up to him and stood there laughing.

"Boy! Did you turn her on? Or what?!" She laughed. "You spanked her? She must have liked it a lot!" She laughed and went back behind the bar.

"It's not funny, she poured paint on my truck."

"She'll probably buy you a new one now. You really turned her on," she laughed again.

Several other girls stood looking at him and laughing, hitting and shoving each other like it was the best thing they had seen in their whole lives.

"It's not funny!" he shouted, but they kept laughing until the girl, Carol, finally came out of the back room, fully dressed and walked out of the club. She stopped and handed Tommy a folded piece of paper.

It said, "I'm so sorry. I'll clean it off, Tommy." And had a bunch of X's on the bottom of the sheet.

"What the hell do X's mean?" he showed the note to Jan.

She started laughing and showed the note to the other girls, they all started laughing and she handed it back to Tommy.

"So what does it mean?"

"It means you turned her on, big boy! Those are kisses, you probably made her have the first orgasms she ever had, she's in love, Tommy. With you!" Then they all laughed again.

"It's not funny!" he said.

"Oh yes it is!" Jan laughed.

It was the talk of the club all night long. He nearly left several times but didn't want to give up the money. He went home with $380, plus several notes he was afraid to even look at. He tossed them away without reading any of them.

All night long the girls had kept turning their butts to him and patting themselves like they were getting a spanking and laughing. Several of them came over and tried to lay across his lap until he smacked one named Julie real hard.

"Owwwuch!" she cried, "I was teasing you."

"Well, stop," he said.

He was mad as hell about the paint on his truck. Thursday morning he went to a paint store and bought five gallons of paint thinner and rags, then spent most of the day cleaning the red paint off his truck at a car wash. Then the owner of the car wash came and cussed him out for dumping paint down his drain and in the tank that recycled the water.

"I ought to make you pay for having it pumped out, you stupid fucking moron," the man yelled.

"I'm sorry. I'll pay for it," Tommy answered, not realizing what he had done.

"Just get the hell out of here and don't come back," the man yelled at him.

Monday, John Tru-Day did nothing. Tuesday nothing. Wednesday, Mary Forbes came to the office, had two drinks, insulted him several times, and gave him an envelope with a thousand dollars in it.

When she left, she took her pillow from his car, and he had a hard time driving home. He got a pillow off Muriel Sue's couch to drive back to work in the morning.

At three in the afternoon, Thursday, Jack Charmichael called and said, "I'm sending a guy down there, his taxes are all fucked up, don't touch them, just tell him you'll fix them for him."

"You don't want me to do them for him?"

"You can't, you're not a CPA, but he don't know that. Just take whatever he brings you and Mary will pick them up Friday. We'll do them in the other office and give them back to you. Charge him about fifteen hundred. He's an asshole anyway. He's a roofing contractor and he screws me every time I let him work for me." He hung up. An hour later, a fat, badly dressed man, carried, into his office, three cardboard boxes of papers.

"I sure hope you can help me, Jack said you were the best in town. I'm really in trouble. The IRS is about to lock me up and take everything I got. I ain't filed for over eight years."

"Oh ya? Well you probably got a lot of tax credits coming then." Tru-Day told him, smiling.

124

"Think you can fix them for me?"

"If I can't, I'll bring you cigarettes," John kidded, but the man didn't laugh. He just looked scared, thanked him, and left the boxes.

Friday morning, at nine-thirty Mary Forbes came and got the boxes. She asked him, "Well, ain't you going to carry them out for me?"

"I can't lift them. I'm too small," he grinned.

"Creep!" she said, and carried the boxes out herself, then left.

He went home at three in the afternoon, stopping to buy his own pillow.

Saturday, he mowed the lawn, and then raked it. It took him only two and a half hours and five beers to complete the job.

Sunday, he did nothing except watch TV and play with Muriel Sue.

Thursday, Tommy went home with a little over three hundred. Friday, $284.

Saturday night, he went in and Jan handed him a package wrapped in gold paper with a silver bow and a card. The card said:

I hope this will make up for me being such a bitch.

It had five X's below the name. It was signed by Carol. He opened it and found a solid gold chain bracelet with two small diamonds and his name engraved on it. It was spelled "Tommie."

"I bet she paid plenty for that," Jan said, and then told him, "Maybe you better give her another good spanking, huh?"

"You're not being funny! Or a spelling lesson," he said. He put the bracelet in his pocket and took his place at the door.

The girl, Carol came in around nine and stopped in front of him, touched his knee, and said, "I was going to have your truck painted for you."

"Forget it," he said.

"I'm really sorry, Tommy, I was such a bitch. I really like you a lot and I just felt rejected."

"It's over and done with. Forget it," he answered.

"Did you get my present?"

"I got it."

"How come you're not wearing it?"

"I will, just not here," he nodded his head at the other girls. "They might get jealous and really paint my truck," he said knowing he would never wear it.

She stood in front of him several seconds trying to think of something else to say and finally said, "I'm going to dance just for you, OK, Tommy?"

"If you want to," he answered, and wished she would go away. She did, but came back about fifteen times during the night, touching his legs and trying to be friendly.

"Man O' man! Has she got the hot pants for you!" Jan said, sort of singing it and waving her head back and forth as they were closing. "You know who her dad is? Carl Glen Miller. He owns a bunch of sporting good stores, and a couple jewelry stores. She's rich and spoiled and lonely. And I guess, kinda kinky?"

She turned her eye brows up and smiled.

"Ya? Well she can take her hot pants somewhere else," he answered.

He went home with $302, fifty of it from the girl, Carol.

Sunday, February 14th was Valentine's Day. He bought Patty McShane a card and a small bunch of flowers. She carried them with her all day as he and she went to a park and then to the Seattle Center, and watched the workers building the Space Needle. Patty told him when they returned to the room, "I wish you wouldn't sleep on the floor."

He could almost understand every word she was saying now, as she learned to talk through the braces on her teeth.

They went to bed and he slept on his back with Patty McShane lying next to him, her head on his shoulder. It was all he could do to keep his hands to himself.

Patty McShane was wishing he would do something but was too shy to make the first move.

Barbara Fieldsman was still in Portland, Oregon, moving from one motel to another, turning tricks, saving money, and buying clothes. She was thinking about going to Seattle. She stayed two more days, and then bought a train ticket and moved to Seattle, and to the south end where she used to live in a different motel. The owner knew her and told her: "Any trouble and you're out of here. No hooking."

"I don't do that anymore. I'm a bartender now," she answered.

Keith Shocko was still sleeping in the Buick, eating at the mission downtown, and stealing whatever he could steal, then selling it and buying more beer with the money.

Jack Charmichael was in the Madison Hotel talking with Bill Tacki about nothing, getting drunk, and thinking about taking the girl Lori from behind the front desk and up to his apartment. He made up his mind at eleven and walked out to the front lobby and told her: "When you close, come up to my place," then he said, "Just close the front door now, and come up. I got something to give you."

She had heard about his gifts to girls, black eyes and broken teeth, and decided to not go up, but then got scared. She had heard he put girls into his houses and kept them locked there turning tricks for months at a time without ever letting them go. She was scared, but still locked the front door, then took the elevator to his apartment. He was standing by the window, looking out.

"Raining like hell out there," he said.

"I know," she answered, still standing by the front door.

128

He turned and told her, "Don't be so shy, come here, make yourself a drink."

"No, thanks," she said.

"Suit yourself," he said, and motioned for her to come to him.

"Don't beat me up! Please? Will you not, Jack?" she said.

"What the fuck kind of talk is that?" he asked.

"I'm scared," she said.

"Scared of what?" he asked, moving closer to her, "You a fucking virgin or something?"

"Please, Jack," she started backing up as he came forward, thinking he was going to hit her, until she was against the back of a chair.

Charmichael leaned forward, put one hand on her right breast and squeezed it, and whispered in her ear, "Turn around, bend over, and take your panties down."

She was too scared not to. She did as she was told, then held herself up with her hands on the chair as he raped her, pulling out then saying, "So was that so bad? Did it hurt you?"

She was crying from being so scared, and tried to tell him she was going to call the cops if he hit her.

"I'm going to tell if you--"

He slapped her on the side of her face, knocking her down and told her, "You say one fucking word and I'll stick you in a house and let you rot there! Keep your mouth shut and do what I tell you to do. You got it?"

"Yes," she cried, scared half to death. She scooted away, sliding backwards on her butt, thinking he was going to kick her.

"Go sit on the couch!" he told her.

She got up, then went and sat on the couch and waited for an hour, thinking he was going to come over and beat her up, but he stood drinking and looking out of the window, then he told her, "There's a hundred on the table, take it. Go on, get out of here! And keep your mouth shut! I mean it! You run away, and I'll have someone come get you. You talk, and I'll have someone kill you. Got it?" Then he said, "I'd like to know who's the cocksucker who starts all these fucking rumors about me."

"Yes," she cried. She left.

She found another envelope with three hundred dollars in it in her drawer the next day, with a note saying:

I was drunk, I'm not that bad of a guy. I just don't like to be threatened.

    Jack.

She wanted to run away, because she knew it was only a matter of time until he put her in a house somewhere. It never happened; he just treated her like any other employee from then on. He told Bill Tacki she was a lousy piece of ass, not worth bothering with.

130

Bill Tacki didn't answer, just walked to the other end of the bar and waited on a different man sitting there, drinking Kessler's whiskey on the rocks.

Barbara Fieldsman was back in Seattle, in a motel five blocks north of where Tommy and Patty were staying. She was getting ready to go to the Tropics and ask for her old job as a bartender back.

Monday morning John Tru-Day went to work and was just starting to wonder what he was going to do all day long, when Jack Charmichael and Mary Forbes arrived. Jack Charmichael was carrying a small black case and Mary was carrying an arm-load of several canvas money bags with locks on them. Charmichael sat the black case on his desk and Mary dumped the bags on the couch, then went to the bar and started to open the doors.

"Sit your fat ass on the couch and stay there! Don't be drinking this early. For Christ sake! You're getting to be a fucking lush." Charmichael yelled at her. Mary Forbes sat on the couch and folded her legs, then folded her arms under her breasts. Jack Charmichael looked at her, then said: "Where are the maps?"

"I'm sorry," she answered, then got up and went out, then came back with a large brown envelope. She handed it to Jack Charmichael and sat back down on the couch, refolded her arms and crossed her legs, then sort of looked at the ceiling, trying not to be noticed.

"Alright!" Charmichael started, "Here's where you start earning your money, a lot of money if you're smart."

Tru-Day didn't answer, he was too scared. He looked at Mary Forbes and she smiled a forced, knowing smile back at him, as if to say, "Now you're in trouble."

"It's simple if you pay attention," Charmichael told him, then opened the black case. "You know what this thing is?"

"Ya, it's a money counter/bundler. I used them all the time in the service every payday."

"Well that's half the battle right there then." Charmichael took out of the envelope a map and several papers. The papers had addresses on them, numbered from one to fifty-eight.

"These are clubs I own or manage. Your job is to go to each one of them each month and collect the money, and account for it. You go here first, and then follow the list. You open the safe and take out the money and count it. Sixty percent of it you put into one of those bags with a signed form, one of these." He showed John a small book of forms. It listed the bills: ones, fives, tens, twenties, fifties, and hundreds. "Count them, bundle them, and write the total, then the complete total, and the amount you put into the bag. What happens to the rest, I don't give a shit. That part is theirs. You just make sure they sign the receipt every time. Don't leave until they do, and if they argue about it, call me, I'll straighten it out. And you steal from me, I'll kill you. Take all you want from them, but I wouldn't if I was you," he smiled. "They'll kill you worse than I will," he smiled like it was a joke but when John looked over at Mary she wasn't smiling, she was nodding her head, "Yes he will."

"Here's the map showing you where each club is located. You leave here on the twentieth of each month and be done by the first. It's as simple as that. Bring the money back and put it in your safe."

He handed John a credit card. "Use this for gas and food and a motel room if you need it. If you leave real early you can get to Portland and back in one day easy. It makes a twelve hour day out of it, but you can do it. And you go alone. Don't take no one with you. Got it?"

"I think so," John answered.

"Don't think so, know so. If you got questions, ask me. If I ain't around, don't ask no one else, and don't be calling me telling me you're lost or something."

"I guess it's simple enough," John said, looking at the map, "After the first trip I'll know where they all are, so I should be all right."

"The better job you do, the more you get paid, fair enough? And I'll tell you this, there ain't nothing illegal about what you're doing, your license says you got the right to carry money for other people and count and deposit it. Everyone thinks I'm a fucking crook but I ain't. I'm just a little smarter than most and I don't give a shit how I make my money, but I'm telling you right now. I'm completely legal. If the cops hassle you, tell them to go fuck themselves and call me."

He looked at Mary Forbes, "Where's the license and his car papers?"

Mary Forbes dug into her purse and handed the papers to Jack Charmichael. He handed them to John Tru-Day, "Hang em on your wall."

There was the title to the Olds, insurance papers, and two licenses, one business license, and another courier license.

"Carry this one with you, if you get stopped by the cops they can't open the bags without a court order, and they can't remove them from your car without a court order and my attorney being there, but you won't ever get stopped unless you're speeding or something like that, and even then, it ain't got nothing to do with your job. So don't worry that you're running money gained illegally or something. Every club is licensed and legal, and all the licenses are up to date and it's just a job to you, nothing more. It's just so God damn fucking hard to find someone who don't steal. The cock suckers don't ever learn. Greedy bastards. You got any questions?"

"How do I open the safes?"

"Damn near forgot that part," Charmichael said, and laughed, "And I'm supposed to be perfect! Right, Mary?"

"Right Jack," she answered looking at John Tru-Day.

He handed John a funny looking key, "Make sure you lock them back, or the bastards will rob me blind. Any questions now?"

"No," Tru-Day answered.

"Good, now, Mary, get up off your fat ass and make us a drink."

He turned to John Tru-Day and said: "She's dumb, but she never lets me down. Do you Mary?"

"No, Jack," she smiled.

"You like your job don't you, Mary?"

"Yes I do, Jack," she answered.

"Show John here your tits."

She turned and raised her sweater, and then her bra.

Charmichael smiled, and Mary lowered her sweater, and then finished making the drinks.

"He don't like me," she said, and handed Jack his drink.

"Where's his?"

"Let him get his own," she answered, and then realized she had made a mistake. Before she could back up far enough, Jack Charmichael slapped her on the side of her face, nearly knocking her down.

She went and got John Tru-Day's drink and brought it to him, then went and sat back on the couch. Charmichael finished his drink and told Mary Forbes, "Sit on the floor, Mary."

Mary Forbes got off the couch and sat on the floor.

Tru-Day didn't think it was funny.

"It's Monday the fifteenth. So you leave here on Saturday morning. OK?"

"OK," John answered.

"OK," Charmichael said again, and sat his drink on the desk and walked out, leaving Mary Forbes sitting on the floor.

"You going with him?" John asked.

"I'm supposed to stay here and help you."

"Do what?"

"I don't know!" she yelled.

"Well, get up off the floor, will you?" he said.

"As soon as he leaves I will, he might come back in and see if I'm still here."

"Get off the damn floor!" he yelled at her.

She got up off the floor and went to the bar, then made herself a drink, turned and said, "I wish I was smart enough to get him, he makes me so mad sometimes."

She drank the whole drink and poured another one, straight Scotch, then another one, and sat back on the couch looking at him.

"So you're just going to sit there looking at me and getting drunk all day?"

"I might!" she answered.

"You might not, too!" he answered.

"I bet your dick ain't even two inches long is it? Creep!" she laughed.

"Get out!" he screamed at her.

"I'm telling Jack you told me to leave."

"Fine! Tell him anything you want to," he yelled at her, and she got up, setting the glass on the carpet, and left him standing behind his desk half mad and half scared.

He studied the maps and the addresses for three hours, made himself a drink, and went home, then drank three beers and was half way potted when Muriel Sue got home at five-thirty. He explained the whole thing to her and showed her the license, and she felt a little better that he wasn't working directly for Jack Charmichael.

Tuesday, he got a real customer from off the street wanting him to do their income taxes. He worked three hours on their taxes, finished them, and spent three hours studying the maps, and went home. Wednesday, he got two more customers off the street, and one Jake Morrison had sent to him, all income tax problems. He wondered if he was supposed to give this money to Jack Charmichael too, or keep it. He called and asked him.

Charmichael laughed and asked him, "Are you really that fucking honest!? Keep it! Build yourself a business." He hung up, then called back and asked him, "You want me to find you a secretary to be there while you're gone?"

"If it ain't that Mary girl," John told him.

"I'll find you one. You want a young one or a good one?"

"A good one," he answered.

"You're smart," Charmichael returned and hung up.

"Don't he ever say good-bye?" John asked himself, and replaced the phone.

John Tru-Day had two drinks and went home, then had three beers before Muriel Sue got home.

Thursday, he got two more customers from the sign above his office, and Friday, he got four, all income tax. Saturday morning he left at five am and was in Portland at eight. He did the five clubs there and headed back to Seattle with no problems.

His money bundler had counted and bundled 75,200 ones, 28,962 fives, 11,793 tens, 24,658 twenties, 13,303 fifties, and 11,203 hundreds. He had the bags in the trunk of his car and was scared half to death all the way back to his office. He locked the bags in his safe and went home. Sunday, he went to Tacoma and did eight clubs there, and was home at nine in the evening. He carried with him a total of $173,859.

Monday, he went to Vancouver and brought back $91,245. Tuesday, he went north and counted $166,580, and brought a little over ninety-five thousand back with him. Wednesday, he went to three small towns and brought back a little over $55,000. The rest of the week he stayed in Seattle doing the remaining clubs. His bundler had counted and wrapped over two million three-hundred thousand dollars. He was done and back in his office Friday the 26th at four in the afternoon and had $1,668,593 in his safe.

He called Jack Charmichael and told him he was done.

"I know," Charmichael answered, "You did good! Wait there and an armored car will come get the money."

The truck was there in fifteen minutes and John Tru-Day had three drinks of straight whiskey. He needed them all.

Barbara Fieldsman had found a sugar daddy on Tuesday and moved into his apartment for four days. The man was over sixty and in two days she got eight hundred dollars in cash and another thousand from him in a blank check he gave her to buy clothes with, plus a lot of spare cash she talked him out of. She left him in a bar and went to his apartment, got her things, several pieces of his dead wife's jewelry and left, then got on the train heading back to Seattle.

Tuesday night, Tommy Dollarhide was still getting ribbed about spanking the girl, Carol. She took every opportunity she could find to stand next to him and touch him and try to talk to him. Wednesday, when he came in, there was another present for him, a ring. Jan watched him open the package, and then as soon as he opened the box she grabbed it and said, "Holy shit! Tommy! Those are real diamonds! Her old man is going to shit when he gets the bill for this thing. I bet you she just took it from one of his stores. You better sell it fast."

"This has got to stop right now!" he said, and put the ring in his shirt pocket.

Carol never came in, but every girl in the place came and asked to look at the huge diamond ring.

Wednesday night she didn't come in, but she did Thursday, and he stopped her at the door and tried to give the ring back to her.

"I didn't buy it, it was given to me by some guy when I was in France," she answered, then said, "Just keep it, please,

139

Tommy, I want you have it. Save it for a rainy day." She walked away.

"She's so full of it!" Jan said, "She buys things for guys all the time, keep it, sell it, Tommy! She probably paid three thousand for it, or her dad did, or she just took them. He came in here once looking for some things she took. Have you seen her car? Not the one she drives here, the other one?"

He shook his head *no*.

"It's some kind of English sports car. Mikie says it's worth over two hundred thousand dollars."

"Oh Ya!" Tommy said, and decided to keep the ring.

He thought it might pay for the surgery on Patty McShane's ear.

Friday, he went home and again had a little over two thousand dollars saved in the tool box, plus the ring and the bracelet.

Saturday, he took home $260, fifty from Carol, but he was getting tired of her and was a little worried about how far she might go, and if she was maybe a little dangerous.

His intuition was right. She was at the restaurant when he and Patty McShane went to eat Sunday morning. She walked in carrying two packages. She came to the table and handed one to him and one to Patty McShane.

"These are for you guys, Tommy," she said and walked back out.

"Who was that?" Patty asked, looking surprised.

"A nut cake," he said, and got up from the table and tried to catch the girl, but she was already in her car and driving out of the parking lot.

He went back in and Patty had opened the present. It was a very expensive set of necklaces and earrings.

"Give me those," he said, and took both packages out to his truck and put them behind the seat.

He told Patty McShane they maybe should start looking for a different place to live if she wanted to stay with him.

They went to a park, a movie, and then to dinner. Patty McShane asked about the girl about fifty times until Tommy explained what had happened. Patty McShane didn't think it was so funny and asked Tommy if he wanted another girl. She cried and Tommy got madder and madder at the girl, Carol, and finally told Patty to just stop talking about her.

"That's what the whole thing was about! She was trying to make you upset. She's a nut cake," he almost yelled at Patty but caught himself and explained it in a nice soft voice that Patty didn't believe.

It was all Patty McShane could do to contain herself and she gave into her feelings that night as soon as they were in bed.

She rolled over against him then reached down and slid her left hand inside his shorts and said, "I think it's time, don't you?"

She felt him growing and pushed her panties down with her other hand as she pushed his shorts down with her left one.

Tommy rolled over on top of her and they became a couple.

She had never told him what had happened to her and he had never asked. In the morning he saw her stretch marks and she saw him looking at them. She realized he knew she had given birth to a baby. She started crying.

They talked almost all day Monday and she told him the story about how she had gotten so beat up, and about her cousin/husband and Tommy listened, and then said, "Well, let's go eat and look for a house."

They looked in the paper for a house so he could buy a freezer and a TV and a leather chair.

Monday night, all hell broke loose in the club. Jack Charmichael came in and started yelling right off. "Where the fuck is Doug?" he said after he came out of the office.

"He don't stay here at night," Jan explained.

"Like fuck he don't." Charmichael yelled, then told her, "You call that bastard and tell him he better get his ass down here."

Jan tried to call Doug Hicks and couldn't get a hold of him. Jack Charmichael sat at the bar and drank three drinks and ate three packages of cashew nuts. He looked at the girls and then stomped out not saying a word to Tommy Dollarhide. He came back around nine and the manager, Doug Hicks, was following one step behind him.

Tommy could hear them clear across the club. Rather, he could hear Jack Charmichael cussing the man out and knocking things around. Everything sort of stopped and the girls all seemed to disappear somewhere.

"Maybe he'll fire him," Jan said. "I hope he does, he does too much coke."

Jack Charmichael came out of the office and turned around, "I'll be back here in one hour and you better have that shit straightened out, you got it?"

Doug Hicks stood at the door and said, "Yes, sir, Jack, I will."

Jack Charmichael walked by Tommy Dollarhide and stopped, then patted him on the shoulder twice and said, "Jan says you're doing a hell of a good job here, thanks." Then he pointed with his thumb back over his shoulder at Doug Hicks and said, "He's a fucking moron," and then he left.

Tommy Dollarhide waited for him to come back but he never did.

Doug Hicks stayed for three hours in the office then left without speaking to anyone.

The mood was bad the rest of the night and Tommy went home with only $112, his worst night ever.

Tuesday night Doug Hicks was there sitting at the bar half drunk, he didn't speak to him and Hicks left at eight. Tommy did better, he left with $165.

John Tru-Day had eleven new customers he was working for, and was pretty contented until his first secretary showed up Wednesday morning.

Barbara Fieldsman was back in Seattle, in a motel five blocks north of where Tommy and Patty were staying. She was getting ready to go to the Tropics and ask for her old job back. Keith Shocko was in the Buick in a parking lot in north Seattle. Jack Charmichael was in his office downtown, waiting for Mary Forbes to come in. She arrived ten minutes late and was told about it. Jack Charmichael handed her a bag and a list, she left to make the monthly payoffs. Jack Charmichael left and drove to the Tropics club. He arrived at three in the afternoon. He talked with Doug Hicks, cussed at Doug Hicks, then called a small dark-haired girl into the office.

She walked into the office and said, "Hi, I'm Mindy."

Jack Charmichael closed the door, then took her by her arm and pulled her over to a sofa, then pushed her forward until her head was down on the cushions. He pulled down her small skirt and shoved himself into her, finished, and then Doug Hicks took his turn as Charmichael sat at the desk, watched, and had a drink. Charmichael left and walked out of the club. Doug Hicks sat in his chair and watched the girl sitting on the floor crying.

"Get the fuck out of here!" he told her.

"I'm calling the police," she cried, "You're both going to jail!" She tried to stand up, but Doug Hicks was still mad at Jack Charmichael and he just snapped. He came out of his chair and before he thought about it, he hit the girl in the face, knocking her backwards across the office. He watched her head snap as her neck hit the bottom rung of a heavy wooden armchair, and she lay on the floor limp. Her head turned half way around from her shoulders, and before he even touched her he knew she was dead.

He stood there trembling and then locked the office door. He stayed in the office sitting at his desk for eleven hours, looking at the small dead girl on the floor, all during the time the club was open.

When Jan and Tommy came to put the money in the safe he called through the door, "We're busy in here. Leave it on the floor and lock the front door."

He left the club at four in the morning with the girl wrapped up in a small rug from the storage room. He drove to a dirt road several miles away and dumped her body down a bank into the brush. He stood on the bank trembling with fear, watching the body roll down into the brush. A thousand thoughts ran through his mind as the body of the girl un-wrapped itself from the rug and tumbled down into the brush, leaving the rug hung on a branch. He stood there remembering his childhood, and his mother, and what she had done to him, the beatings, and the men she had brought home. Doug Hicks stood on the road, on the bank of the gully, in the rain, and plunged into insanity, partly from what he had done, partly from the booze and cocaine he had used all day long every day for the past eight months, but mostly from past memories and fear. He stood looking down into the brush seeing only the girl's naked legs sticking out of the leaves. Then, he imagined her standing up and then climbing her way back up the steep bank, hanging onto brush as she climbed up through the foliage until she reached the road. She stood in front of him, her knees covered in mud and her hands dirty from clawing her way up the bank, and he stood there believing what he was seeing. He stared down at her red toenails then at the black hair around her crotch, and then at the small white top she still had on around her waist, then up into her dead sightless eyes.

"You're not a very nice person, Doug Hicks," she said softly, "look what you did to me. I was going to get married."

He stood there imagining he was seeing the girl in front of him.

"You're going to be sorry you killed me," she said softly, "Now you're going to get put in jail and they're going to kill you."

He watched her turn and walk away down the dirt road, then she stopped and turned and called back at him, "You're going to be sorry Doug! And so is that other guy," then she faded away.

Doug Hicks maybe screamed, maybe he cried. He didn't know what it was, but some sound was coming out from inside of him. He turned and ran back to the car, then ran back and climbed down the bank and got the rug, then he drove to his house. He sat in a chair in the dark and looked at nothing for several hours, then went back to the club. He came in and sat at the bar in front of the day bartender.

"You want a drink? You look like shit," the bartender said.

"I'm fucking crazy!" he answered, "I hear voices in my head. I been seeing dead girls." Then he got up and went into the office and opened the safe, filled his pockets with money and left the club, dropping money from his pockets as he walked out. He got into his car and drove south, not knowing where he was going.

The bartender called Jack Charmichael several times during the day and finally reached him at five in the evening, and told him, "Your manager took too much coke, Jack. He flipped out. He was talking about seeing dead girls and left. He took a lot of your money too. He had his pockets stuffed full of it. He was dropping it all over the floor and the parking lot as he left."

"Did you pick it up?" Charmichael sort of screamed.

"Most of it, but the wind blew a lot of it away across the street and I couldn't leave the bar to go chase it."

"So why didn't you have one of the girls go get it?"

"I did, but she never came back. She probably just took it and took off with it."

"Which one was she?"

"Hell, I don't know. I was just trying to get the money off the floor before the girls all grabbed it."

"Christ! How much did he take?"

"I don't know, maybe twenty thousand, maybe more. I don't know how much was in the safe. He had all his pockets full."

"Son of a bitch! The fucking moron!" Charmichael screamed, and hung up. He called Mary Forbes and told her to meet him at the club in an hour.

As soon as Tommy arrived at work, Jan told him to go stand by the office and "don't let no one in," and if Doug Hicks came in to keep him here until Jack got there.

Before Tommy could walk to the office, Jack Charmichael and Mary Forbes came in and went passed him straight to the office.

Jack Charmichael sat in a chair while Mary tried to figure out about how much money had been taken.

"Maybe seven or eight thousand, Jack," she told him.

Charmichael sat and watched Mary Forbes go through the desk drawers and look at all the records and notes. She found a book with several girls' names in it; also, Doug Hick's company checkbook that was kept to buy supplies.

"How much has he got in the bank?" Charmichael asked.

Mary Forbes called the bank, turned and looked at Jack. She smiled at him.

"He's been stealing from you. He has nineteen thousand in his personal checking account," then she showed him a check Doug Hicks had signed for some unknown reason. She smiled.

"Stupid fucker!" Charmichael remarked, and then hesitated, "Well! That was easy."

Charmichael smiled and stood up. "Fill it out," he said.

Mary Forbes filled out the check in the amount of $18,841.12, the exact amount left in the account, then showed it to Jack Charmichael.

"Fucking moron," he muttered in disgust, "There ain't no good help left," then told her, "Go get yourself a drink."

Charmichael had looked across the room and saw the smear of blood on the arm of the chair and some on the floor. He figured Doug Hicks had done something stupid, like beaten the girl up. As soon as Mary Forbes had left the room he took the wooden chair out the back door and tossed it over the fence into the alley. Then he and Mary Forbes sat at the bar and had several drinks. They left about one hour later and Charmichael told Jan, "You're the new manager until I can find someone. Don't go fucking nuts on me either."

Mary Forbes got into her car and put the check into her glove compartment so she wouldn't lose it, and two minutes later she had forgotten it was there.

All the girls kept asking Tommy what had happened to the girl Mindy, but no one knew.

Tommy had another slow night, only $96. The worst. Thursday he took Patty to the dentist and had her braces adjusted, then back to the doctor. She had her bandages changed. On the way back he bought a paper and they sat in the restaurant and looked for a house to rent. She found an ad in the paper that sounded good.

Small one bedroom house near Rainier Ave.
Large yard and garage $250 a month
$50.00 off for yard work.

(The fifty was John's idea but he had already done the hard part).

Tommy called the number but got no answer.

Thursday night, things were somewhat back to normal. He went home with $226.

149

"I called about the house," Patty told him, "We can go there Saturday. Tommy, it has five trees in the yard."

"And five million leaves," he kidded, thinking about the yard work part of the ad.

Muriel Sue told John Tru-Day about the girl calling and wasn't surprised when he answered, "I hope her husband is a big guy who likes to mow grass."

"Don't get too excited, she talks really kind of strange," Muriel said.

Friday night, the talk was Doug Hicks had run off with Mindy and stolen ten thousand dollars from Jack Charmichael. At around seven-thirty a girl came in with a bad scar on the left side of her face, and went right up to the bar and said hello to Jan. Jan called her Barbara and told Tommy she was starting to work there, then said, "Watch her! And I mean watch her! She's a bad one, she steals everything she can get her hands on and she fights with the girls. If she gives you any shit, just throw her out."

He watched the girl and she only stayed an hour, then left with a man and didn't come back, she didn't want him to walk out with her. He went home with $245 and another gift from Carol that he didn't open.

Barbara Fieldsman went back to the man's hotel room, which just happened to be two doors down from hers. He went into the bathroom and she grabbed his wallet and started for her own room but didn't quite move fast enough. She got as far as the front door of the room then she opened the wallet and saw a badge, *Seattle Police Dept.* then she saw the man standing in the open doorway of the bathroom smiling at her. Barbara went to jail and paid $300 to a bondsman to get her back out Saturday morning. If she had gone all the way out through the door she would have been charged with robbery.

Tommy Dollarhide and Patty McShane went to look at the house. He parked the truck in front and walked up to the front door, knocked, and no one answered. They walked around the house and just as they came to the backyard they were met by a short man tucking his shirt into his pants.

"Hi! We sort of sleep in on Saturday," the man said, "You want to look at the house?"

"I like it already," Patty said, "It's nice. Look at the trees, Tommy."

He looked at the evergreen trees and answered her, "Ya! No leaves either."

"You like doing lawn work?" John asked.

"I don't mind it," Tommy answered.

"The mower is in the garage. I'll show you where it is," John Tru-Day told him, and had every intention of having him mow the yard, but Muriel Sue came out of the house and stopped him.

"Really, John!" She sort of laughed, but wasn't happy about it. "Don't you think we should at least let them look inside before you put him to work?" Then she turned to Tommy and asked him, "You do have a job don't you?" She was looking at Patty McShane's face as she finished.

"I'm going to start at the Boeing Company in a few weeks," he answered, not wanting to tell her he was a bouncer at a topless bar.

"Oh!" she answered, and then asked, "But you do have money for the rent, don't you?"

He grinned and said, "I have a temporary job until they call me."

"Ok!" John said to Muriel, "You show her the house and I'll show him the lawn mower. We might as well get it done," then he turned and asked, "You drink beer?"

"John! Stop it!" she smiled, and said, "I'm Muriel Sue, and this," she pointed at John, "is John. I guess you might have guessed he don't like mowing the grass."

"Tommy, Tommy Dollarhide, and this is Patty."

Patty looked at Muriel Sue and told her, "He didn't do it. I go into a fight with a nutty woman when I was coming here."

They all shook hands and Muriel took the keys to the house out of her pocket and opened the door, letting them in. Patty McShane loved the small house and Tommy thought it would be a good starter house. He intended on buying one as soon as he could.

Muriel Sue told them the rent and the deposit was five hundred dollars, and then said, "Mowing the grass is John's job, really."

"No, it ain't," John chirped, "It's his. He's twice as big as I am."

"I'll mow the grass," Tommy said, laughing.

"Can we have it, Tommy? Can we live here?" Patty asked, looking at Tommy's smiling face.

"Do you have furniture?" Muriel Sue asked.

"You can get furniture," John interrupted, "There's a used furniture place just down the street."

"John!" Muriel Sue gave him a look.

"Well?" he said, and Tommy laughed again, and then kidded, "He *don't* like mowing grass does he?"

"The first time he mowed it--he--"

"Muriel Sue!" John interrupted her, this time not wanting her to tell about his three days in the tub recuperating.

They went into Muriel Sue's house and signed the papers. Tommy went out to his truck and took five hundred dollars out of the toolbox and paid for the house, explaining it would be a week or so before he could get enough furniture to move in with.

Muriel Sue told him, "We'll start the rent once you're moved in."

"So everything is settled?" John said, standing up.

Tommy laughed, and said, "Okay, let's go mow the grass. I'll mow, you rake."

"I'll go get some beer," John said, "right after you get started." Then he took Tommy out to the garage and got out the lawn mower. He watched Tommy guide the heavy mower across the yard and back with ease, then drove to the store and brought back beer and snacks. It took Tommy forty-five minutes to mow the whole yard, another twenty-five to rake it, and he was finished. "You should have been here when I mowed it. The grass was up to my ass," John said.

"Maybe up to just past his ankles," Muriel Sue corrected.

All four of them sat in the backyard and drank the beer John Tru-Day had bought. Tommy and Patty left at two in the afternoon and went to eat. He went to work and came home Sunday morning with $246 from the girls and his wages.

Two detectives had come in around seven and asked him about the girl Mindy. Did he know her real name? Where was she from? Had he seen her boyfriend?

He told them he had only talked to her one time for a few minutes. He didn't think she was doing cocaine or turning tricks, she didn't leave during her shift like some of the other girls, and then they asked him and several girls about Jack Charmichael and Doug Hicks. The detectives left after talking to several of the girls and Jan the bartender.

Three hours later a tow truck came with two police officers and took her car from the parking lot.

Sunday the 7th of March, Tommy Dollarhide and Patty McShane went shopping at the used furniture store and bought a bedroom set for $225. They carried it back to their new house in his truck and put it in the bedroom. Then they sat and talked with John Tru-Day and Muriel Sue for a while before leaving.

Monday morning the 8th of March, the sun was shining and it was warm outside. Tommy took Patty back to the doctor and she had the stitches removed from her lip, ear, and above her right eye. The doctor told him he had a friend who was a plastic surgeon and he would contact him.

The two detectives went to see Jack Charmichael. He went out the back door of his office when he heard they were in the reception room. He left for Mexico after calling his attorney.

John Tru-Day went back to work at nine in the morning and three more customers from off the street came in with their taxes, also a woman who said she was his new secretary and had been hired by an agency the past Friday. She was about forty years old, tall and not very good looking, she stood in front of his desk and told him, "I don't work over-time, and I don't like smoking anywhere near me. I don't like drinking, or cussing, I expect to be treated like a Christian woman, and I won't work for anyone who is even slightly dishonest. I expect a morning and an afternoon break, and a full hour off for lunch. I like to read the good words of our Lord."

John Tru-Day listened politely, then got up from his desk, opened the top drawer and took out a cigar, then walked to the bar, made himself a drink, turned round and looked at the woman, lit the cigar, lifted his left foot off the floor, grunted, then farted, took a sip of his drink and smiled, then blew a cloud of smoke into air, and said, "I bet I could have lit that one on fire, huh?"

She turned red, put her fingers over her nose, then turned around and walked back out of his office. He went back to his desk and worked on the taxes.

Tuesday, Mary Forbes came down and handed him a envelope then said, "Here! Creep!" she tossed it on his desk, smiled, and then said. "John, really, tell me how big it is."

"It's bigger than your fucking brain!" he said, but she was already leaving. He opened the envelope and counted $1000 in hundreds. He put the money in the safe and reclosed it.

Wednesday, the 10th of March, Tommy Dollarhide came home with a little over three hundred, and then he and Patty went shopping again and bought a sofa and a leather chair for the living room.

Tommy and one of the salesmen loaded them into his truck and Patty helped him carry them into the house. He went to work at six and the police came back into the club a little after seven looking for Doug Hicks and asking the girls about Jack Charmichael, and how long had both of them been in the office with the girl Mindy.

The mood was again ruined and he took only $158 home with him.

Thursday the 11th, John Tru-Day interviewed his second lady for the job; it lasted less time than the first one.

Barbara Fieldsman went to court and said she had been tricked. The guy had told her to leave and go to her place because his girlfriend might come by to see him. He had given her the wallet to buy some beer with, and nothing about having sex for money was ever mentioned. The cop had to agree because he hadn't gotten that far. He said if he hadn't had to pee so bad he was going to but he went into the bathroom and she left. The judge looked at her, then at the cop and dismissed the case against her, telling the cop to have a backup witness next time he arrested someone like that.

Keith J. Shocko was driving through town looking for a pickup truck with tools in the back he could steal at exactly the same time Barbara walked out of the county courthouse. He didn't see Barbara Fieldsman walking down the sidewalk, but she saw the Buick, and then him driving, and stood looking at the Buick going down the street and said to herself, *"Find me! Motherfucker! Find me real soon, you bastard!"*

Barbara Fieldsman went into a sporting goods store four blocks from the courthouse and bought a nine inch hunting knife with a bone handle. She told the man, "I'm going to give it to a boyfriend of mine."

"Does he like to hunt?" the man asked.

She thought for a second, and then answered, "I don't know, maybe." She went to work at the Tropics and went out with a man two hours later and earned a hundred-fifty dollars.

Keith Shocko slept in the Buick three miles from where she was staying.

Doug Hicks was sitting in a motel room in Roseburg, Oregon, doing cocaine and drinking Jim Beam whiskey from the bottle. He fell asleep and dreamed he was home at his parents' house in Denver. He dreamed he was with the girl Mindy and she was dead lying in bed with him. His mother was standing by the bed watching.

The girl's body was stiff and cold and swollen out of shape. Her eyes were pushed out of their sockets and her tongue was halfway out of her mouth.

"Don't you want to kiss me, Doug?" she said, and opened her mouth.

He looked at her dry black tongue and woke up sweating, then stood up and ran across the dark room thinking he was in his bedroom at his mother's house and ran straight into the partly open bathroom door, knocking himself down and opening a cut on his forehead. He lay on the floor and cried until he passed out again.

Friday morning, Tommy Dollarhide went home with another present from the girl, Carol, and $280. He took Patty McShane to the Thrift City and they bought three big boxes of dishes, pots and pans, two lamps, a toaster, a small radio, two end tables, and various towels and things, then stopped at a department store and bought sheets and blankets and pillows for their bed.

Patty wanted to stay in the house but neither the heat nor the electricity were turned on.

John Tru-Day interviewed his third potential secretary. She was the best one so far, but she was just too dumb for him. She reminded him of Mary Forbes. She even sort of looked like her in the face, and had just as big a butt as Mary had. He said he'd think about it and sent her on her way

March 13th was Saturday. Tommy came home with $326, a good night. They went to the house and he asked Muriel where he had to go to have the lights and heat turned on. She walked out to the back porch, opened a box, and flipped a switch.

She smiled up at him and said, "Nowhere."

"I knew that," John Tru-Day added.

"Oh you did not!" Muriel Sue laughed, and then said, "God, John! I swear!"

Patty McShane and Muriel Sue went to a store and bought household things and groceries. Muriel Sue nearly had a fit when she watched Patty McShane buy eight huge steaks at $1.96 per pound for Tommy. They then spent the day fixing the house while Tommy mowed the lawn and John Tru-Day watched, drank a few beers, and commented about places Tommy had missed.

Tommy left to go change clothes and go to work while Patty McShane stayed in the house cleaning and arranging things. She was completely happy. She turned on the radio and put the groceries away, then cleaned every crack and corner of the small house.

John Tru-Day had a couple drinks, ate supper, and Muriel Sue took him into the bedroom, and there they stayed the rest of the night.

Tommy changed his clothes and told the manager of the motel they had found a house and were leaving.

He went to work and found another present from the girl Carol waiting for him. He gave the bracelet and the other presents still unopened to Jan and told her to give them back to Carol or sell them, then changed his mind when Jan showed him what they were: a gold Rolex watch, a gold belt buckle with silver inlays in it forming a picture of a rider on a bucking horse, a solid gold necklace that

159

weighed about a pound, and a stainless steel engraved 357 Magnum Colt handgun in a walnut wood case.

"She's got to be nuts!" he said.

"She is, she's so lonely she hasn't got a clue about how to get a man," Jan told him, then said, "She's rich and spoiled. Tommy, keep them! She just comes here to get men. You give them back to her and she'll wreck your truck real good, or worse, then just give them to some other guy who will dump on her."

He decided to keep the handgun and the belt buckle, and sell the ring, the watch, and necklace. At nine the same evening, the girl, Carol, came in and he stopped her, then took her into the back room and sat her down. He sat next to her and told her, "You're a really nice girl, Carol, and you're really pretty too, but trying to buy a guy is the wrong thing to do. I really like all the things you got me but I don't want you to give me anything else. I want you to just be your sweet pretty self and let some good guy find you that you like. I don't want you to do anything else to my truck again and I don't want you to cause me or Patty trouble. I want you to promise me you'll just be my special friend and be happy, okay?"

"I'm kinky, huh?" she said.

"I don't know. I knew a girl in school who liked to play with dogs. Now she's married and has five kids, maybe she still does it. I don't know, but she don't go around dumping paint on trucks or poking holes in tires."

"I understand," she said.

Tommy Dollarhide put his finger under her chin, turned her face up and kissed her lightly on her mouth.

"You really helped me a lot by giving me those things, Carol. I won't ever forget it."

He watched her eyes light up and she said, "Really?"

"Ya! Really" he answered then said, "I got to go back to work."

"Alright," she answered.

He left her sitting on the bench and went back to the door. She walked out a few minutes later carrying her costumes without saying anything to him. She just smiled and left, he never saw her again.

"She's gone?" Jan ask him, "What did you tell her?"

"Thanks for the presents and she was a nice girl, too nice to go around pouring paint on trucks," he answered.

"You're Mr. Magic!" she remarked, and went back to the bar.

Tommy went home Sunday morning to his new home with $244 plus the belt buckle, and the gun, and the ring he intended on selling to pay for the surgery on Patty McShane's face and ear, and the remaining things from the motel room.

Sunday he spent doing some shopping with Patty, buying a TV set with a built in record player, several 33-1/3 albums of songs he liked, all country, some bathroom things, two new black iron skillets, and a huge black iron stew pot Patty said she needed.

He spent a little time in the garage straightening things out and sweeping the floor clean, even though there was nothing in it except the new mower and one old one sitting in the corner, then he sat in his leather chair and listened to the music, then watched his TV as Patty cooked his dinner and he rubbed his feet together inside the new cotton socks he had on. He felt better than he could ever remember. He had been gone two days less than two months and his life had changed so much. He thought he must be dreaming. He rubbed his feet together inside the new socks.

He had been wearing a new pair every day for two weeks. He got up out of the chair and patted his belly with both hands like it was a fat drum. It sounded full, but he went into the kitchen and sat down to eat a steak, and some mashed potatoes and brown gravy Patty made from a package, and some green beans, and bread and butter, and drink a couple glasses of ice cold milk, and look at the pretty face across the table from him smiling back at him.

He and Patty McShane went to bed and did what John Tru-Day and Muriel Sue had already done twice, and were doing a third time. It was ten-thirty, Sunday night, March 14th, 1963. The Tropics was closed.

Jack Charmichael had gone to Mexico until the thing about the girl, Mindy, was over with. Barbara Fieldsman was sitting in a different bar crossing and uncrossing her legs picking up a different man. This time she asked him outright if he was a cop. Keith Shocko was asleep in the back seat of the Buick with his knees doubled up and his hands between them, only three blocks from her, parked in the driveway of an abandoned house.

Jack Charmichael's daughter was in a car with her boyfriend, running away from home with $1600 of her dad's money she had taken from a dresser drawer. Her mother was sitting on the sofa drinking gin over ice by the glass-full, watching the television, and not really seeing it or paying attention to it. She just sat there sipping from the glass, too drunk to go refill it. She had heard her daughter say she was leaving forever and had answered, "Alright dear, you go ahead." She sat and remembered how it used to be a long time ago, when she was young and thin and pretty. It all seemed to end when she had the baby. Jack didn't like the stretch marks, or her sagging breasts. He looked for sex in his bars and she decided to drink about thirty five hundred fifths of gin during the next fifteen years. Her liver was bad, and she knew it, and her eyes had large bags under them, but she didn't care much about her looks anymore. She used to have her hair done once a week, now it was gray and thin so she just brushed it and put a bandana over it to hide the gray. She liked wearing bandanas, and she liked thinking about how it used to be a long time ago, so she just remembered and drank and remembered again. She thought about the man in Mexico, five years ago, she had slept with, and then felt guilty and told Jack about it.

He laughed and told her. "That was a birthday present for you! I paid the guy a hundred dollars." She had stood on the veranda for a long time watching him down on the patio sitting and drinking with some women and thought about jumping the five stories into the pool, or maybe missing the pool and landing on his table, but decided to just drink instead.

She turned sideways, putting her feet up and laid back, then closed her eyes and fell asleep letting the half-full glass slip from her hand and spill onto the carpet, blending in with the hundred or so she had let spill there before, over the past dozen years.

Doug Hicks was in a different motel room in Sacramento, California, dreaming. He dreamed he was back home again, in his house in Denver, and he was twelve, maybe younger, maybe a year or two older. The dream was foggy. He was in his bed and he dreamed his mother was standing over him, cussing because he had wet his bed again. Then he was in the garage with the girl Mindy and she was naked, but a young girl and they were running around the garage. He tried to catch her but she ran away and stood looking at him, then she got older and looked dead. Her eyes were dried out and her lips black. "I'm still here, Doug, and you're going to be sorry for what you did to me." He dreamed he ran back into the house and his mother screamed at him.

"You pissed your bed again, damn it! Go take a shower, then change your sheets!" Doug Hicks, still asleep, got up and walked into the bathroom and turned on the hot water in the shower. He stood there several moments, dreamed he was taking off his shorts, and then stepped into the 138 degree water fully dressed and stood there until it soaked through his clothes and the heat woke him up. He screamed and dove from the shower onto the bathroom floor, lightly scalded over most of the front of his body. He turned on the cold water and got back into the shower and stood there until his body started to cool down, crying and thinking about killing himself and trying to cool his body off. He left the motel room at six in the morning because he was too scalded to sleep. He just drove, not knowing where he was or even that he was in Sacramento.

He was out of money and out of rent time in the motel room. He drove around through the streets slowly looking at the houses and yards and people until almost noon, then realized his car was about out of gas. He parked on a side street under a large oak tree and sat there sipping the last of the last bottle of whisky and looking at a garden hose rolled up in the front yard of the house he was parked in front of, wondering if there was enough gas left in the car and if he put the hose in the tail pipe and into the window would the car run long enough to kill him. He searched the car looking for lost bills under the seat and found a twenty and a few others he had dropped. He drove to a store, bought another fifth and returned to under the tree and sat drinking until he finally passed out and slept until daylight. He woke up, drove five blocks and ran out of gas. He sat and finished the fifth and slept again.

During the next week nothing really happened except John Tru-Day rejected three more girls who applied for the job. Too tall, too fat, too dumb, too everything he didn't like. He had to find someone before Saturday, because he had to start his round of the clubs early on Monday morning. He had gotten eight more customers from the sign above his office.

Wednesday, Mary Forbes came in and tossed an envelope on his desk, then told him, "Here's your money! Creep!" She walked back out without saying another word. There was another thousand dollars in the envelope. He put it in the safe and locked it.

Thursday a girl came in and said she was a bookkeeper herself and seemed really nice. She was about thirty, well dressed and polite. He explained the job and she said she could handle it without problems. He explained it was only ten days a month and she said that was also fine with her. He told her to start the next day, Friday, and he would show her what to do. She agreed and left the office.

John Tru-Day left an hour later for home and saw her standing at a bus stop three blocks from the office, he almost stopped, but saw her drinking from a brown paper sack and drove right past her.

"Ain't that a pisser?" he muttered.

She came in a little after eleven on Friday and he could tell she was half drunk. He told her to leave. He placed a sign on the door saying he would be back in ten days, or to call him at home during the evening hours. He left for Portland, Oregon, at four thirty am Monday the 20th. He came back with nearly $200,000 in the trunk of his car.

Tommy Dollarhide took Patty back to the dentist on Monday and had her braces adjusted again. Tuesday he took her to the doctor for a talk about the plastic surgery. The doctor told him he had talked to his friend who worked for a free clinic but did work outside, he said he would try and get Tommy a good deal. Tommy asked Patty to wait outside the room, and then he took the ring out of his pocket and handed it to the doctor to look at.

He looked at it and handed it back to Tommy. "What do you want me to do with it?"

"You think it will pay for her surgery?"

"I don't know anything about rings, what's it worth?"

"I don't know, a lot I think," Tommy answered.

"Sell it," the doctor answered, and then said, "I would guess around three thousand dollars."

"You think it's worth that much?"

"I don't know what it's worth, the surgery will probably cost around three thousand dollars."

"How much is a gold Rolex watch worth?" Tommy asked.

"A lot more than that ring! I'm sure of that," The doctors eyes lit up, "Why? You got one of those too?"

"This girl gave me the ring and watch," he answered.

"Why? Was she rich and crazy?"

"A little, maybe, I think mostly rich and lonely," Tommy answered.

"Let me see the watch. I think I could talk him into a trade, maybe give you a little cash back too."

"I'll bring it in tomorrow," Tommy told him.

John Tru-Day came back from Tacoma with $116,612. He put it in the safe with what he brought back the day before.

"Alright, and I'll see what I can do," the doctor told Tommy. "Have Patty come back in here and we'll take pictures so I have something to show him."

Patty McShane came back into the back room and the nurse took pictures of her face and her ear. They left and went home. Tommy changed, ate and left for work. He asked Jan for the watch and she got it from the safe in the office, then gave it to him. He told her to sell the ring, bracelet, the earrings, necklace and belt buckle.

"You know that thing is worth about seventy-five hundred bucks don't you?" she said as she handed the watch to him.

"I do now," he grinned.

Wednesday John Tru-Day brought back with him $116,244, almost the exact same amount from the day before. He thought maybe Jack was sort of testing him and the money had already been counted by someone else. He counted it twice to make sure it was exactly right.

Wednesday Tommy Dollarhide took the watch to the doctor on his way to work and left it with the nurse. Thursday, he called, and the doctor said he was sure the watch would pay for the surgery, plus change.

"You keep the change," Tommy answered, "I just want her face fixed."

"You call me next Monday, Tommy, and I'll let you know."

Thursday John came back with the biggest haul of the week, almost $220,000.

Doctor Ronald R. Ricketts called his friend, Doctor Richard R. Richardson, and set up a meeting for that evening. They had drinks and agreed to play golf the following day. Dr. Ricketts told Dr. Richardson he knew this little Irish girl who was about maybe seventeen, and had gotten beat up by persons unknown to him, and she needed his skilled hands laid on her pretty, but sadly scarred face. Then he showed him the pictures. Dr. Richardson looked at the six photos and said, "I can't do it, as much as I would like to. I'm booked solid for over four months at the clinic. I can't get her in because there just isn't a room opening."

"How about using my office or I'll pay for the hospital. I'll use my earned free time."

"That might work, but there are still the material costs," Richardson answered.

"So how about we split them?" said Dr. Ricketts, then said, "You have to see this poor kid, she is so pretty, and half her ear is gone."

"I got the pictures right here. So how about you giving me those Arnold Palmer clubs I've been wanting, and you assist me, and we use your free time, and your nurse?" answered Dr. Richardson.

"I'll give you the clubs if you trade me for the oak file cases I've been wanting in your garage, and I'll pay all the costs."

Dr. Richardson looked at the pictures again, then laid them face up on the table in a row, studied them for a few moments and answered, "You pay for the recovery drugs and x-rays and all outside costs and ten rounds of golf,"

169

then he said, "I can't believe I'm doing this for a set of golf clubs and losing my file cabinets in the deal."

"Man, you're so cheap! How about six rounds of golf?" Dr. Ricketts said.

"The clubs, the bag, seven rounds of golf, and you buy all the drinks, including lunch, and we have a deal," Richardson smiled.

"I'm getting cleaned, but OK. Wait until you see her."

"I can see the pictures," he answered, "she's pretty."

They left the clubhouse and finished the golf game, Dr. Ricketts paid Dr. Richardson $22.00 for the 11 strokes he lost by, bought three more drinks in the clubhouse, and drove home with the $9,900 Rolex watch on his left arm.

A profit of about $7600, plus a set of oak file cabinets worth another five hundred, all for a set of golf clubs he had bought at a yard sale for twenty dollars three years before, and used only the one time when he happened to get lucky and beat Dr. Richardson with them.

He called Tommy Dollarhide at the club and told him Dr. Richardson would do the operation for the watch. "And I have to be honest with you," he told Tommy, "I made him give me a set of file cabinets to boot."

"Good for you," Tommy answered.

Dr. Ricketts hung up and said, "Good for me is right!" He looked at the gold watch and decided it was time to go home.

Tommy Dollarhide was pleased.

John Tru-Day brought back $83,881, and he had three more clubs to do on Friday and he was done for the month. He had collected almost $1,800,000.

Tommy worked on Friday night. Saturday night he worked. He was off Sunday, Sunday night, and Monday throughout the day. He watched television, worked on his truck, mowed the yard, trimmed the bushes, ate steaks, baked potatoes, and cans of green beans, snacked, drank beer, went shopping for things he never had before but had wanted, bought things for Patty, and ate some more steaks and apple pie, and drank more beer.

He was contented, happy, and thirteen pounds heavier than he was the day he left Miles City, Montana, plus he had over fifty pair of new socks he had never worn yet, folded neatly in a dresser drawer, along with twenty-four pair of shorts, twenty-four new t-shirts, seven pairs of slacks, eight white shirts, seven western shirts he found at the Thrift City store for four dollars each, six colored ones, two new pairs of boots, five pairs of new Levi's, two new belts, and a new pair of tennis shoes, and still had a little over fourteen hundred dollars in his tool box under the seat of the truck. He was very happy. He sat there thinking about his sister back in Miles City.

John Tru-Day was starting to become a little worried. He hadn't noticed it on the way down, but once he stopped at the first club in Portland, he saw a white Chevrolet park a few spaces away from him. The car had two young men in it. He watched them a few seconds and saw they weren't getting out. They were gone when he came out of the first club and he sort of forgot about them. His bundler had counted and wrapped 10,613 ones, 11,193 fives, 9,287 tens, 5,314 twenties, 3,961 fifties, and 2,278 hundreds.

He had carried the bag out, and as he put it in his car he saw the white car was still there, but had moved down the street three spaces and across the street in front of his Olds. He watched them in his rear view mirror and as he passed them, they pulled out and followed him. They were at the second club and the third, then they were gone. He didn't see them again until he was almost back to Seattle, then he saw them following him a few cars back. He saw it again as he left his office.

He tried to call Jack Charmichael and ask if he was being followed by some of his men but he got no answer on any of the three numbers he had. Sunday, he went to Tacoma and didn't see the car but he saw a different one and it looked like the same two men were in it. He counted and bundled a little over $232,000 of which $146.000 plus change belonged to Charmichael. He bagged it and carried it back to his office. The men were parked across the street and down one block. He left the office and drove north. They drove away south down Rainier Ave. Monday he went south to Vancouver and saw them again in still a different car, a red Corvette. He knew he was being followed by someone. What he didn't know was, who, and why. He was getting scared. He tried calling Jack Charmichael and was again told he was gone for a while.

"How long is a while?" he asked the woman.

"I don't know, just for a while," she answered.

Tuesday he went north and didn't see them. Wednesday he didn't see them. Thursday they were right behind him, then in front of him, waiting for him, and even drove alongside of him and looked straight at him. Almost all day long they followed him, from club to club, around Seattle, then back to his office.

He spent the rest of the week looking in his rear view mirror, up and down each street and around corners, but didn't see them. Every time he took the bags out of his trunk and carried them into his office he expected to be shot or at the least robbed. He finished at six in the evening on the 29th a few pounds lighter and scared half to death. He didn't know if they wanted to rob him or just protect him or-- he had no idea who the hell they were. He called Charmichael's office and told the woman, "I'm being followed."

"That doesn't surprise me," she answered, then said "Ya, that sounds like Jack."

"Where's the truck?" he asked.

"What truck?"

"The truck that comes to pick up--" then he thought that maybe she didn't know about the money. He decided he wouldn't say anything.

"Never mind," he told her.

"You want me to call Jack and have him call you?"

"Why didn't you tell me that eight days ago?" he asked.

"Tell you what?"

"That you could call him."

"You didn't say you wanted me to," she snapped back at him, then said, "I'll have him call you right back."

Three minutes later Charmichael called and said, "Getting a little nervous down there?"

John Tru-Day was relieved but still scared. He told him he was done and he was being followed.

"Ya, that's George, don't worry about it," Charmichael told him, then said "I'll call the truck, wait there."

Twenty minutes later, the truck arrived and took the money, and he felt a lot better. He had two more drinks and went home.

Jack Charmichael called a police officer who was on his payroll and told him, "Someone is following my bookkeeper. Nab the fuckers, will you? Hang around the office down there on Rainier and see what you can find out."

John Tru-Day had found out one little thing during the week. None of the club managers had the slightest idea how much money they took in because no records were kept in case they got raided by the law. He spent Thursday and Friday in his office doing taxes and thinking about all the money he could have miscounted if he had wanted to. He gave up the thought and went home, then he and Muriel Sue went to the coast and stayed in a motel for the weekend.

Wheels were turning inside the head of the mighty John Tru-Day. Every club, all fifty eight of them, took in a total of about two million, three-hundred thousand each month, all in cash.

Where did it go? Who got it? No one could really know exactly how much money was taken in, except the guy who counted it. (John Tru-Day). All the money was cash and dropped into the top of the locked safes through a slot and left loose in the bottom. Maybe the managers kept a record in a book or something, but he doubted if they were very accurate. He figured all of them were stealing a little each day, and then, on top of that, Charmichael had to be paying off a lot of people. Somewhere there was a hell of a lot of un-declared money. Millions of it.

Now the questions were: how much is it? Where is it? How? Should I? Should I even be thinking about it?

He sat on the beach and watched Muriel Sue fish, sipped a few beers and thought about all that un-declared money hidden somewhere in Seattle.

Sunday the first of April, several things happened.

At ten in the morning three people hiking in the woods saw the body of a young woman lying in the brush. They called the State Police.

Doug Hicks woke up in his car in Sacramento, California. He was drunk on whiskey and high on cocaine, completely out of money and gas, sick and dirty. He walked several blocks down the street to a shelter and told them he was hungry. They wouldn't let him in until that night, but they gave him a sack lunch, and then pointed him to an outside shower. He never took the shower. He ate and then couldn't remember where he had left his car. He began walking around town looking for it. He was arrested for being drunk in public. The jailer gladly gave him a shower with a hose.

He was in jail for three days and about to be released when he started talking in his sleep about seeing dead girls and saying he was sorry he killed the girl, Mindy.

The jailer told the sheriff and the sheriff did a check, and then went and asked him, "Did you kill a girl in Seattle?"

"I didn't mean to, I'm sorry," Doug Hicks answered, and the sheriff sent the message to Washington State Police, and Doug Hicks stayed in jail but was moved to a private cell.

Barbara Fieldsman let Keith Shocko find her. She wanted to give him the present she had bought for him, plus, she wanted the Buick. She saw him drive by in the Buick as she was walking to the motel office to pay her room rent. She knew he was driving up and down the road, and probably looking in clubs around Seattle looking for her. So she walked out and stood on the side of the road until he drove back by. She let him see her then went back to her room.

He parked across the street, afraid to face her. She let him sit across the street in the car until Tuesday evening. She left her room several times and went to the bar and back to her room. Each time he just sat in the Buick watching her.

"You chicken shit son of a bitch!" she muttered under her breath, and fondled the bone handle of the knife she had bought, and was keeping in the bottom of her purse.

Jack Charmichael returned home from Mexico at eight-thirty in the morning. At six in the evening he was sitting at

176

the bar in the Carlton Hotel having a drink and checking papers. The six o'clock news on TV told of finding the dead girl, Mindy. Charmichael recognized her picture from the bar, he finished his drink, went up to his apartment, then home and repacked his suitcase. He left again for his house in Mexico at eight the same evening.

At seven that evening, Tommy Dollarhide took Patty McShane to the hospital and checked her into a room. She was to have her face fixed at nine-thirty, Monday morning. He was told to go wait somewhere and come back in two hours. Then he could spend some time with her until nine-thirty, and then he had to go home and come back in the morning.

At ten that evening Jack Charmichael's daughter's boyfriend got sick of her and dumped her out on the street in Hollywood, California. She sat on the sidewalk crying for an hour, then dug through her purse and found enough change. She called her mother for money to come home.

The girl, Carol, was sitting in a small bar in north Seattle and after her making several rude remarks the bartender told her, "What you need lady is a good hard spanking on your bare ass."

Carol smiled at him, and then as he watched, she wrote her phone number down on a twenty dollar bill and handed it to him. "You're right! I do," she answered, and said, "Call me when you get off work."

John Tru-Day and Muriel Sue were back home getting ready for work on Monday morning.

Tommy Dollarhide was across the street from the hospital having a beer, waiting until he could return back up to Patty

McShane's room and spend time with her. He was on his second beer when Mikie, the actor, came into the bar, walked up to him, leaned against the bar, and said without stopping, "Hey! Hey! Big guy! Heard you were bringing Patty to the hospital. I was close so I thought I would stop and see if you needed anything, Dr. Ricketts's nurse is a good friend of ours and she told me what was going on, or rather she told Sonia yesterday, some guy traded a Rolex watch to have his girlfriend's face repaired, and I just put two and two together and figured it must be you and Patty. So I asked her when you were having it done, and she told me. So I came to see if I could do something to help out. Billy! Give us a couple more beers here! This guy is one of us. His girl is too. She's having an operation in the morning. Dr. Robertson is doing it. You play pool, Tommy? I do. I'm good at it too. It might take your mind off Patty. You can go back and see her in about an hour, so we might as well spend a little time together if you want to. If you don't I'll understand. I talk a lot, but I make sense. A lot of people who talk a lot don't. So at least I got that in my corner. Right? Ya, sure it is. They found that girl, Mindy. Hicks killed her. I know he did. He's hiding out somewhere, and Charmichael was there too. Sonia told me he was there just before she disappeared. It's not the first time. There's been girls missing before, and one of these times he'll get caught. I hate the bastard! The way he treats people, someday someone is going to nail his ass to the wall and I'm going to be right there holding the hammer for them and handing them nails. So how about a game of pool? Hey Billy! Two more beers if you got time." He stopped talking and thought for a second then went on, "We got you and Patty a present for your house, but haven't brought it over to you all yet. We'll wait until she's out of the hospital and then bring it over. That John guy is a kick, ain't he? Funny too! He's doing some work for my friend, the one who gave us the tires for your truck. You

178

remember him don't you? That Charmichael has his fingers in too much stuff! You know the last guy who worked for him got bumped off. They found him stuffed in a fifty-five gallon drum, floating in the sound out there about five months ago.

"Stop!" Tommy said, and held his hand up in front of Mikie's face.

"What the hell you talking about?"

"Your friend John. The short guy you rent your house from, or, his girlfriend, is who you really rent the house from, but he's Charmichael's bookkeeper. Didn't you know that? Or, not really a bookkeeper. Ya, he's a bookkeeper, but that's not his real job. He's the guy who goes and collects the money from the clubs. It's not a good job if you get what I'm saying. Oh, it pays a lot, but he better be watching himself at all times or, well you know what I'm saying don't you?"

"No, I don't!" Tommy answered.

"You know the guy, John, who lives with the woman you rent your house from? He works for Jack Charmichael. He goes and collects the money from all of Charmichael's whorehouses and dance clubs."

"You're kidding me!" Tommy exclaimed.

"I don't kid," Mikie answered.

"John Tru-Day works for Charmichael?"

"Whatever his last name is, ya! He works for Charmichael. He collects his money and the guy who used to do it ended up in a drum in the water out there. Charmichael probably caught him stealing. So he better be watching his ones and fives and make sure none of them end up in his dresser drawer."

"I thought he had his own bookkeeping business."

"He probably does on the side, but you can bet Charmichael is backing him and bookkeepers don't last too long around Charmichael. They get to know too much! How about that game of pool? You feel like it?"

"Ya, sure," Tommy answered, but his mind was going in a different direction. He was thinking maybe his job at the Tropics wasn't such a good job after all, and maybe he better get back to Boeing and make sure his application was on the top of the pile like the woman had told him to do.

"Man! That gives me the willies," Tommy said.

"Funny you should say that. That's the guy's name they found in the drum. William Gordon. Everyone called him Willy," Mikie smiled.

"I think I need a new job," Tommy answered.

"You and your friend both!" Mikie returned.

"Mikie, you got a phone call here," Billy called and held the phone across the bar to him.

Mikie said a few words then told Tommy, "I guess the pool game is off. I got to go. See ya, big guy. I'll stop by the club tomorrow. You're still going to work there for a while ain't you?"

"Until I find something better," Tommy answered, and Mikie turned and walked out.

Tommy finished his beer then went back up to the room where Patty McShane was laying in bed watching the TV. He stayed there talking to her for an hour, but his mind was at the house in front of his, and on his friend John Tru-Day, and Jack Charmichael. He thought John and Muriel were asleep when he got back to his house, so he sat and listened to music and thought about what he was going to do. In the morning he was going to Boeing and reinstate his application.

John Tru-Day was not asleep, but laying in bed next to a naked Muriel Sue, thinking about a lot of undeclared money lying hidden somewhere in Seattle.

Barbara Fieldsman took a shower, then got dressed and walked out of her room and across the highway and up the driver's side of the Buick. She knocked on the window, then moved back because of the stench coming from inside. She kicked the door and woke the sleeping Keith J. Shocko up.

He sat halfway up, then started shaking from fear as soon as he saw she was next to him. "Bring the car over and park it in the lot, then come up to the room. It's 113," she said, and walked back across the road. Keith moved the Buick and then went up to the room. He almost didn't open the door from being so scared but looked in and saw Barbara sitting on the bed.

"You want me to come in?" he asked.

"Come in and close the fucking door!" she answered, then as soon as he was inside, she told him, "Go take a shower. You stink like rotten feet."

He took a shower, then put on his dirty pants and came out.

"Throw those fucking pants out! I can smell them! Throw all your clothes out! I'll get you some clean ones in the morning."

Keith took his smelly clothes and set them outside the door, and stood naked looking at Barbara.

"Get a fucking towel!" she said, and climbed in under the covers, then told him, "You can sleep on the other bed, but stay away from me until I tell you not to."

"Thank you, Barbara," he answered. "I been having a really hard time. I'm sorry I left you, but I was so scared and I thought she had killed you."

"Ya? Well, she didn't!" Barbara answered, then turned off the TV and turned her back away from him. She laid there smiling, thinking, "You'd be a lot better off if she had killed me, bastard!"

Keith Shocko went to sleep in a bed for the first time in several weeks, feeling halfway safe again. He was back with Barbara and after she got over being mad at him she would take care of him like she always did.

Barbara Fieldsman got up in the morning and took a cab. She bought Keith a set of clothes and brought them back, took him to breakfast and told him, "I want you to spend the whole day cleaning the car. It stinks! Clean it really good inside and out. As soon as I have enough money, we're going to Chicago and you're going to get a real job and I'm quitting."

Keith J. Shocko was ecstatic. He spent the whole day washing and cleaning the foot smell out of the Buick, washing the windows and changing the oil.

"It looks really good, Keith," Barbara told him, then handed him some money and told him, "Get yourself some beer if you want, I'm going to work."

She left driving the Buick, and Keith sat and drank beer all night while he waited for her to come back.

Tommy Dollarhide spent the second day of April at the hospital waiting until after one in the afternoon to see Patty McShane. She had bandages covering most of her face, and had to talk through a small hole in the bandages where her mouth was, "You look like a mummy," he told her, and then asked, "Does it hurt?"

She shook her head no.

"Did they fix everything?" he asked.

She shrugged her shoulders.

He stayed with her until after five, and then went to work. He wanted to talk to John Tru-Day but didn't have time.

Barbara Fieldsman was sitting only a few feet away, when Mikie, the actor, came into the club, stopped in front of Tommy, and said without stopping, "Hey! Big Guy! How's Patty? What's her last name? McShane? Isn't it? She's an

Irish girl, huh? Where did you say she came from? Nevada somewhere? Oh, it don't matter. Just don't you worry big guy, ole Doc. Richardson is the best. She'll look like new when she comes out of there Ricketts's nurse told Sonia he did it for a set of golf clubs. I don't know how you swung that deal but I'm glad you're on our side. We need smart guys like you on our side. They got Hicks down in California. I guess he confessed to killing little Mindy. They're bringing him back sometime this week. I got to see Sonia about something personal. I'll see you in a few." Mikie was gone across the room.

Barbara Fieldsman sat looking at the man sitting on the stool and realized the woman she had beat up and the one they were talking about were the same person. She decided not to wait, knowing that if Mikie found out it was her who beat up the girl she would be in real trouble. She got up and as she left the club she handed Tommy Dollarhide a fifty and told him, "Give this to your girlfriend."

Tommy took the money and said, "Thanks."

"Ya, sure," Barbara answered and left the club. She drove across town and got a job at a different club, then returned and told Keith they were moving to the north end until she had enough money to leave with. They rented a different room in north Seattle and Keith sat there and drank beer as Barbara turned tricks in the room next door for two weeks.

Tommy went home with a little over three hundred dollars, mostly gifts from the girls because someone had told about his girlfriend in the hospital. He knew it was Sonia Re'olo Mikie's girlfriend.

At ten-thirty in the morning of the third of April, they took the bandages off of Patty McShane's face. There, sitting in front of Tommy Dollarhide was the smiling, perfect face of a soon to be twenty-two year-old Irish girl. No scars, no missing parts, her ear looked like it had never been damaged.

"I told you I was good," Dr. Richards said.

"Are they gone? The scars?" Patty asked.

"I even fixed your nose a little," Dr. Robertson told her laughing, then handed her a mirror.

"Thank you all so much," she started crying.

"Remember," Dr. Robertson told her, "don't wash your hair or your face for three days." He gave her some wet towels in paper wrappings, she was supposed to use, then told Tommy, "Don't kiss her for at least fifteen days or her lips might fall off."

Patty looked at Tommy, then at the doctor.

"I'm kidding," he said, and walked out.

On the fourth of April, John Tru-Day hired a secretary to work the last ten days of each month, a nice fifty-two year-old woman with little experience, but she was nice and lived only a few blocks away. She spent three days helping him and learning what he wanted, then the phone rang and Jack Charmichael said, "This is Jack Charmichael! Where's Tru-Day?"

"Does he work for you?" she asked.

"That ain't none of your fucking business, lady," Charmichael returned.

She sat the phone on the desk and said, "It's for you," then she walked out, never to return.

"You just scared my new secretary off," Tru-Day told him, "she quit and walked out."

"Fuck her!" Charmichael answered. I'm sending another guy down there with a shit box full of tax stuff. Mary will come pick it up." He hung up.

On the ninth of April the guy came in with two huge boxes of folders and sat them on the floor. "I hope you can do something for me. That other guy really fucked them up!" he handed Tru-Day his card and left.

At ten in the morning on the eleventh, Mary Forbes came in. She said, "Hi, Creep!" and handed him his envelope, then dug through her purse and tossed three pieces of wadded up paper into his trash can, took the boxes and left. He sat there and opened the envelope. There were twelve one-hundred dollar bills in it. He laid the money on the desk and reached down and took the wadded up papers out of his trash can and spread them out to look at them.

What he saw was two and a half pages of three rows of:

BK-137-11.00   *NNR-66-350*   *BB-093-1222*

RCH-41-700.- -   *PR- 212- 600*   *LKM-576-3200*

CC-66-0275   *TG-111- 1100* *JML-11-1400*

RMD-365,100   *HO-123-2200 DD-254-1600*

RBC-450 1K250

And the list went on for two and a half pages. It took John Tru-Day exactly fifteen seconds to figure out the sheets were the pay-off sheets and the money went to a safe deposit box somewhere.

The first two or three letters were the person's name. The second numbers were the box numbers. And the third was the amount they got each month. He sat at his desk and added the numbers.

Jack Charmichael had paid off two-hundred and three people that month. The smallest amount was three-hundred fifty dollars and the largest was six thousand, for a total of $973,860. He had carried back to the office $2,213,877, leaving Jack Charmichael a balance of $1,340,017.

He sat looking at the figures, and then made his mind up. He was going to rob Jack Charmichael, if for no other reason than he was such a prick and never said goodbye when he hung up the phone. His sharp little brain sat inside of his head, on top of his small frame, that sat in the big chair behind his big walnut desk in his nice fancy office for two days thinking and counting inside his head.

He came to the conclusion that somewhere in the Seattle area was a safe deposit vault with at least three hundred seventy-five boxes in it. Inside those boxes was a lot of money no one would ever admit they had, if it turned up missing.

Most of the money would just lay there for months at a time until whoever owned the box went somewhere to spend it so it couldn't be traced back to them.

Now, all he had to do was find out where the vault was, how to get into it and get away without getting caught. He made himself a drink, sat on the couch and said out loud, "It has to be easier than hiring a fucking secretary."

He went home at four ten in the afternoon of April 14th, 1964.

Ten wheels were turning, four on the Olds and six inside his head as he drove up Rainier Ave.

The fourth, fifth, sixth, and seventh of April, Patty McShane stayed inside the house letting her face heal. It was a little bit sore, but not so bad. She looked in the mirror a hundred times, trying to see what Dr. Robertson had done to her nose. Tommy finally told her he was joking and had done nothing.

Saturday morning, the seventh, Tommy took her to get her braces off her teeth. They returned home and Tommy started mowing the grass. John Tru-Day and Muriel Sue came out and stood looking at Patty.

"You're all new again," John said.

"You look wonderful, Patty," Muriel Sue told her.

Patty McShane spent the day going shopping with Muriel Sue, and John Tru-Day spent the day with Tommy, watching him do the yard work.

Tommy put the mower away and finished the raking, then sat in a lawn chair beside John Tru-Day, opened a beer and said, "So you work for Jack Charmichael too?"

"What do you mean, too?" John returned.

"I sort of work for him. I'm the bouncer at the Tropics."

"Really?" John smiled, then said, "Don't tell Muriel Sue."

"Patty don't even know where I work. She never asked, and I never told her."

"You're smart," John answered, then said, "I guess you know what I do then, don't you?"

"Sort of, but not really, and I don't want to know either. As soon as I get called to work at Boeing I'm out of there."

They spent the afternoon drinking beer and talking about nothing, while the two women cooked and did girl things. Tommy went to work at five and Patty McShane tried to bake a cake. It didn't come out very good, so she fed it to the birds.

On the ninth of April, Jack Charmichael made the first step to his own downfall. Jake Morrison called him and told him he was having problems with an inspector on the apartment house job.

Charmichael told him, "I'll stop over to your house tonight and we'll talk about it." "Talking" meant Charmichael would give Jake Morrison an envelope full of money and Jake would give it to the inspector. Charmichael stopped at

Jake Morrison's house on his way to one of the clubs in north Seattle and Jake led him into his den. Charmichael tossed him the envelope, and then sat across from Jake's desk, and as Jake talked, Charmichael looked out through the door at Jake Morrison's seventeen year-old daughter Linn, who was standing at the bottom of the stairs looking in at him, smiling.

She was seventeen, blonde haired, and her good looks were only surpassed by her greed. She looked knowingly in at Jack Charmichael, and then slowly walked up the stairs, taking off her sweater. Just before she was out of eyesight she lifted the sweater off up over her head and turned halfway around making sure Jack Charmichael saw her large breasts, then ran up the stairs out of sight.

Jake Morrison leaned over and looked out through the door trying to see what Charmichael had been looking at.

Jack Charmichael felt Jake Morrison looking at him and asked, "Where did you get that carpet?"

"From the carpet store," Jake answered.

"Get me some. I need to replace the one in my office." Jack Charmichael got up and walked out of the house.

Linn Morrison was standing at her window as he walked to his car. He glanced up and she smiled at him, her bare breasts in plain sight through the upper bedroom window.

He drove to the club in north Seattle and sat at the bar, having a drink and eating cashew nuts from small packs, looking from one girl to another, watching them dance on the small stage until he saw one that resembled Linn Morrison. He then took her into the office and pushed her down on her knees in front of him. He un-zipped and crammed himself into her mouth, making her gag for a few seconds until she caught up to his excitement from thinking about the girl Linn. He finished and he dropped twenty dollars on the floor, zipped up his pants and walked out of the office, leaving the girl there still on her knees trying not to throw up. He left the club and went to the Madison Hotel.

"You got a call from some chick named Linn," Bill Tacki told him, then handed him a slip of paper.

"When did she call?"

"About an hour ago."

"She leave a message?"

"No, just said to tell you she called."

Charmichael thought about his own daughter running across the grass pulling her panties up over her fat butt, and then remembered Linn Morrison's small round butt in the tight jeans as she was standing halfway up the stairs showing him her breasts. He compared her to the girl in the club and decided there was no way the girl in the club could ever compare to Linn Morrison. He then looked at Bill Tacki.

"Something on your mind?" Tacki asked.

"Ya! Something that shouldn't be there!" Charmichael answered, and then asked for another drink.

Tommy Dollarhide went to work and was introduced to the new club manager, a man named Paul. He seemed like a nice person. He was well dressed, in a suit, but Jan said he had just gotten out of prison and had worked for Jack Charmichael before. "Watch him," she said. "He beats people up."

"That's all I need," Tommy answered, and took his place at the door. An hour later Paul asked him to come into his office, and then told him, "I get a cut of your tips, twenty percent."

Tommy grinned at him and answered, "You're trying to fuck the wrong dog here, Paul."

"You saying no, Tommy?" Paul asked.

"I'm saying no, Paul," Tommy smiled again.

"You like your job here? Or would you rather be in a hospital bed, Tommy?" Paul asked.

"You like lying in a hospital bed, Paul? You're welcome to try me if you feel like getting hurt," Tommy answered.

The manager looked at him for several seconds, stood up, and answered, "Alright, not you, but the girls all pay up or they're out of here."

"Tommy looked at him then said, "No way, fella."

Paul stepped closer and tried to fake a punch to Tommy's belly, then swung his fist forward. Tommy moved his head sideways and hit him. One punch just below the left temple, knocking him unconscious, then half carried him and half dragged him out through the front door and tossed him into the parking lot on his face in the rain.

Jan was on the phone when he came back in. She looked over at him about fifty times as he sat on the stool waiting for something to happen, wishing he had carried the gun Carol had given him to work.

One hour later Paul was back with Jack Charmichael. They talked to Jan the bartender and left, no one said a single word to Tommy Dollarhide. Jan said nothing about it and no one else did either. Tommy carried $280 home with him.

The next night there was a different manager. He walked up to Tommy and said, "I'm not a fighter, I'm a lover, so don't hit me."

"Don't be a prick and I won't," Tommy answered.

"You broke Paul's jaw."

"Good," Tommy answered. He went home with over three hundred dollars in his pocket, plus an envelope from Jack Charmichael Jan gave to him when they closed. He opened it after he was parked in his garage; it had five hundred dollars in it and a note that read:

Keep up the good work. I don't like my girls getting held up.

 Jack

On the eleventh, Linn Morrison called Jack Charmichael again at the hotel bar. On the twelfth she called him at his office. On the thirteenth she called again at his office, and his secretary told him as she handed him the message, "Here! Don't be stupid, Jack! Jake will shoot you dead."

"I ain't done nothing," he answered, and put the note on his desk.

On the sixteenth, Monday, he got a perfumed letter in a small blue envelope from the girl. It read:

Jack. I want a robin-egg blue Porsche.
Linn

Jack Charmichael sat looking at the note and read it several times, smelled it, then laid it on his desk and said softly to himself, *"You greedy little bitch! I eat women like you for lunch, a Porsche? People in hell want ice water too."*

"I heard you, Jack," his secretary said through the intercom, "You're asking for it if you mess around with her."

"Turn that fucking thing off and mind your own damn business, will ya?" he screamed, and flicked off the switch.

Wilma Smith was smiling a knowing smile at him as he left the office and walked past her desk.

"Do I need to start looking for a new job?" she asked.

"Why?" he answered.

"Well, if you get shot dead," she smiled.

"I ain't done nothing!" he answered.

"Yet!" she said, as he closed the door behind him.

Thursday the 19th of April, Mary Forbes came back to John Tru-Day's office, bringing back the finished books of the first man Charmichael had sent to him. They were in three, black, hard-back folders. She laid them on his desk with his pay envelope and another envelope, and went straight to the bar, made herself a drink, then turned and looked at him, smiled, and said, "I guess you ain't as bad as all that. You're just sort of short."

"Is that supposed to be a compliment, Mary?" he asked.

"Ya. I guess it is, if you want it to be," she answered, and then said, "You're supposed to charge 'dim wit' there at least two thousand for doing his books. Jack said if you don't charge him that much he'll think something is wrong."

"Is something wrong?" he asked.

"I don't know," she answered, "I don't do that stuff."

"I know. You do the payoffs, and you're sloppy at it," he said.

"I am not!" she returned.

"You threw away your payoff sheets in my trash can," he told her.

"I did not. Those were something else."

"What?"

"I don't remember."

"You're full of it! If someone, the wrong one, finds those things lying around, you're in for it, big time."

"No one knows what they are!" she answered.

"That's stupid!" he answered. "It took me about two minutes to figure out what they were. The first letters are the guys' names, the second is the box number, and the last is the amount you give them. I got rid of them for you."

"So? They still wouldn't know it's the Pioneer Vault Company, even if they did find them."

"Christ, you're stupid! You just told me where the money is, Mary!"

She looked at him for several seconds not knowing what to say, and then said "So what are you going to do, go down there and rob everybody?"

"I might," he answered, then smiled.

"Really?" She looked excited.

"No, stupid." he answered.

"Too bad. Are you going to tell Jack on me?"

"No! Hell no! Just be careful from now on."

"Thanks, John," she said, then she laughed and said, "So really, are you going to go to the Vault and rob everyone?"

"Jesus! You are dumb. That kind of talk will get you killed around here, Mary."

"So you're one of them too!" she said, and made herself another drink, then turned and looked at him.

"One of what?"

"Jack's flunkies."

"Screw you, fat ass," he returned.

"The last guy who had your job disappeared."

"Ya! And they found him floating in a fifty-five gallon drum out there in the water," John finished.

"You know about it?" she acted surprised.

"Ya I know about it, who doesn't?"

"Lots of people, I guess," she answered.

"Don't be throwing away your payoff sheets. Just give them to me and I'll make sure no one finds them."

"I'm supposed to burn them, but I don't like fire."

"Just give them to me and I'll get rid of them for you."

"How?" she asked.

"I'll burn them. Think! Will ya?" he halfway yelled at her.

"Now you sound like Jack!" she returned, shaking.

"You scared?"

"Yes! Wouldn't you be?"

"There ain't no 'wouldn't' about it. I am," he answered.

"You should be."

"I am. He's got two guys following me."

"I am too," she answered, then said, "No, he doesn't. The clubs call him as soon as you walk out the door. He knows where you are every minute you're gone."

"I don't care. There's two guys following me in different cars, but they're the same guys."

She looked at him and smiled, then said, "That doesn't surprise me but don't worry about it."

"Well I'm still scared," John answered.

"You should be."

"I am."

"Me too," she said.

"Ok! Stop! We're both scared."

"You want me to make you a drink, John?"

"Ya! Thank you, Mary."

"I think I'm starting to like you a little," she said.

"Good, no more insults," he answered, and followed her to the bar. She made two drinks and handed him one. They stood a few feet apart and drank the drinks and she made two more. He carried his back to his desk, and she sat in one of the chairs, and then crossed her legs.

"I wish I was as smart as you are," she said.

"And?" he answered.

"And what?" she returned.

"Never mind," he said.

"No, what?" she continued.

"So what would you do if you were as smart as me?"

She looked at him, laughed, and said, "I'd leave! What do you think I'd do?"

He looked at her then said, "If I was as smart as you think I am, I'd already be gone, wouldn't I?"

"So you're saying you're dumb like me?"

"No!" he laughed, "I'm just too damn scared to leave yet."

"Me too," she said, and then asked, "one more drink?"

"Ya, maybe two. Who re-stocks the liquor when it gets low?"

"Tell me what you want and I'll bring it to you," she answered.

"A good secretary," he answered.

"I meant booze."

"All kinds, and a good secretary," he answered.

"Alright," she smiled and brought him his drink. Then said, "Don't get mad at me for saying this. Promise not to?"

"If it's got anything to do with the size of my dick, I don't want to hear it."

"I just want to see it," she answered.

"Get out!" he told her, and stood up.

"I'm just curious," she said.

"Get out!"

"Oh, don't be so mad. I won't ask you again."

"It's none of your damn business, Mary."

"It's just everyone keeps asking me about it."

"Everyone? Everyone who?"

"Forget it," she said. "I have to go anyway." She finished her drink, and then stood up.

"I kinda like you now. Do you care?"

"Just leave my body parts out of the conversation and we'll get along fine," he answered.

She started to walk away, but he told her, "Mary, come here." She walked to him. He took her hand and placed it inside his pants and let her feel his dick.

"Satisfied?" he asked.

"God! It's bigger than Jack's," she laughed.

"Ya! Well keep it to yourself, will ya?"

"God! I don't believe it!" she exclaimed. "Why is it so big when you're so small?"

"Big man, small dick. Small man, all dick. One size fits all," he answered, and then said, "Get out!"

"I'm leaving!" she chuckled, then said, "Goodbye, Mr. Tru-Day."

"Goodbye, Ms. Mary Forbes," he answered, and she left his office.

John Tru-Day opened the two envelopes and found one had twelve hundred dollars in it, the second, a bill for the guy the books had come from, for two thousand, made out to Tru-Day Bookkeeping Service. He put them both into the safe and locked it.

He had two more drinks and went home. He left for Portland at four thirty in the morning, April the 20th.

Saturday afternoon, on the 21st, Jack Charmichael came out of the Madison Hotel and went to his car. Under the wiper blade was a small blue envelope. He knew it was from Linn Morrison. It was a picture of her sitting naked on a stool with her arms folded across her breasts and legs open, but with tiny pink panties on. It was plain she had taken the picture herself. The note read:

Let's trade Jack, unless you're afraid?

"How fucking stupid do you think I am?" he muttered, but he put the picture in his wallet.

John Tru-Day had returned home with a little over $513,000 from the five clubs in Portland. Saturday night he came back from the six clubs in Tacoma with over $408,000. He was getting smarter and thinking more and more about the Pioneer Vault Company and all that money in there. He was also getting angrier, because the two men were following him again. He saw them several times during the next days, in three different cars.

He finished the collections at nine-thirty on Tuesday the thirty-first. He had in his safe almost two million dollars.

He called Jack Charmichael and told him he was done, and he had been followed again.

"Quit worrying about it," Charmichael told him, "I got it handled."

Fifteen minutes later the truck came and took the money. He went home.

He took off Wednesday the first, and went back to his office on the second.

At ten-thirty in the morning Mary Forbes came in and had with her a tall, nice looking girl, about twenty-two or three years old, carrying a huge box of different kinds of booze. He sat at his desk and watched Mary re-stock the bar with the girl helping her, and then she made three drinks and brought one to him.

"This is Jacky! She's your new secretary. She works at one of the clubs on the north end, but she's going to school to be a bookkeeper. So she'll be helping you, if you want her to," Mary told him smiling, then told the girl, "See, he's sort of cute, ain't he?"

"Screw you, Mary," he answered.

202

"Screw you, John," she answered then turned to the girl.

"We're friends now. We used to hate each other but we don't now. Right, John?"

"So how much do I have to pay you?" he asked the girl.

"You're going to pay me too?" she beamed, "I thought I was going to learn from you."

"Oh ya! I forgot about that part of the deal," he told her, looking at Mary Forbes, and then said, "You're all right for a fat girl."

"Well you're alright too, for a short shit," Mary answered, and the girl laughed and then said, "So how much am I getting paid?"

"Two hundred a week. OK, John?" Mary answered.

"Ya, sure," John returned and the girl sort of squealed and slapped her hands together.

"Oh goodie," she said.

John thought she was as dumb as Mary, but maybe he could teach her to at least answer the phone for him.

"You got a car?" he asked the girl.

"Of course," she answered, "and a driver's license, and a house, and a son, and a boyfriend. I just want to learn to do bookkeeping. I go to school three nights a week."

"You're hired," John said, thinking maybe she wasn't so dumb after all. He walked around the desk and shook her hand, then told Mary Forbes, "Thanks, Mary."

"Can we go buy her a small desk?" Mary asked.

"Sure," he answered, "We'll put it over there by the door."

"Super!" The girl sort of laughed then said, "My own desk."

Mary Forbes took the girl and left, then returned in less than an hour followed by a truck. The men brought a small walnut desk, chair, and typing table into the office and placed it where John told them to set it, a few feet back from the door, but directly in front of it facing his own desk, then he moved his three-line phone onto it so she could answer the phone for him.

Mary Forbes sat on the couch and drank gin and tonic as they arranged her desk and put a typing table next to it. She was all set.

He had a secretary. He sat behind his desk and looked directly under the typing table, and directly up under the girl's short skirt, at her light blue panties and thought, "Oh well, you can't have everything, at least she didn't have big fat legs."

"This is great!" she said.

"You like her, John?" Mary asked, making herself and him a fourth drink. The girl refused after two.

"Ya, I like her," he answered.

"He likes me!" The girl laughed proudly.

"Maybe she is as dumb as Mary," he thought, "but if she don't drink and Charmichael don't scare her off, maybe she'll be alright."

John Tru-Day sat on the couch with Mary Forbes and got half drunk, as the girl, Jacky, took all the folders from his desk and the counter behind it, and filed them into the file cabinets, then made herself another drink, and sat in the chair behind her desk, her panties showing plainly to both Mary and John. They looked at each other and laughed at their first private joke together, then got drunker and drunker until John was afraid to drive home.

He left, and took a taxi home, leaving the two women at the office. He was passed out on the sofa when Muriel Sue got home at five-thirty.

He took the city bus to work and arrived at nine-thirty. The girl Jacky was sitting in her car waiting for him, "I brought coffee and some donuts, if you like donuts."

"That's a plus," he thought.

He spent the best day he had spent in his office, working on income taxes for people, and got five more customers off the street. Jacky greeted them and helped him every way she could. He was glad he had her. He had a key made for her and went home at three. She stayed until five-thirty every night. He was happy, except for a few things. One being Muriel Sue was upset from his drinking too much. He decided he had to slow down a little.

Tommy Dollarhide was happy. He had over three thousand dollars saved in his toolbox, a house full of furniture, and a pretty girlfriend, plus a huge freezer in the garage he was slowly filling up with food. He had just about everything he had ever wanted. He sat in his big chair and leaned back sipping a root beer as he rubbed his nice clean feet inside his nice clean socks, and listened to the songs on the record player while Patty cooked corned beef and cabbage for him in the big black iron pot he had bought for her.

Patty McShane was happy, she had Tommy Dollarhide.

Muriel Sue was sort of happy, but scared about John's work and his drinking so much. She saw Patty McShane out on the front porch washing Tommy's clothes in a big black pot and went and asked her why she was doing it.

"How else would I?" she asked.

"Use the washer and dryer," Muriel Sue returned, and Patty just looked at her like she didn't know what she was talking about. "The washing machine on the back porch, Patty!"

Again a blank look.

"Didn't Tommy show them to you?"

"No."

"Good grief! Men!" Muriel Sue shook her head and said, "Come on, girl, it's time to join the real world."

She showed Patty the washer and dryer, and showed her how to use them.

"I feel so dumb," Patty told her.

"Men are the dumb ones," Muriel Sue answered, and went back to her own house.

Doug Hicks didn't know if he was happy or not. He didn't even know he was in jail charged with murder.

Keith J. Shocko was happy just sitting in the motel room, drinking beer and watching the television, while Barbara earned enough money to leave Seattle.

Barbara Fieldsman pretended she was happy as she put away money and figured out how and when she was going to get even with Keith Shocko.

Jake Morrison was happy, he was getting ready to go fishing for the weekend.

Linn Morrison was happy. She was with two girlfriends, plotting how to get Jack Charmichael to buy the car for her, and a lot of new clothes she planned on wearing at college.

Jack Charmichael was happy, because Linn Morrison was calling him and teasing him, and he was trying to figure out a way to give her something that wasn't a car, and without her dad finding out about it. He was developing a plan while several girls who sort of looked like her in several of his clubs were watching out for him, because the more he thought about Linn Morrison, the more he took his frustrations out on the girls in the clubs.

He thought about just snatching her and then sticking her in one of his houses for his personal use, but gave the idea up as soon as he had thought of it, because of what his secretary had said, and because he remembered the big gun cabinet in back of Jake's desk, in his den.

He decided the best way was to spoil her, then cut her off until she gave in. That way, she couldn't talk about it.

Mikie, the actor, was happy. He was doing a TV commercial in southern California. His girlfriend, Sonia Re'olo, was happy, because she was Mikie's girlfriend.

Carol was happy, but her butt was a little sore from the spanking her new boyfriend had give to her the night before with a ping pong paddle.

And it was a nice day in Seattle, with the sun shining. It was four-twenty pm, May 3rd, 1963. Tomorrow was Saturday, and John Tru-Day was going hunting for hidden money, in downtown Seattle.

Three

John Tru-Day got up at seven in the morning and ate, then told Muriel Sue he was going into town to look for some bookkeeping things he needed, and some other things he didn't really need but wanted.

"So where are you going to look for these things, John?" she asked.

"Pawn shops," he answered. "In pawn shops."

"And may I ask what they are, John?"

"You may ask, but I'm not telling you because I love you," he answered and walked out of the house, got into the Olds, and drove to downtown Seattle. Muriel just smiled because her birthday was coming up in a month and she thought he was going shopping to buy, or at least find her something, when in fact he had no idea when her birthday was.

He found a parking spot and then walked north two blocks, and ended up on the corner of Second Avenue and Pine Street. There in front of him was a men's clothing store on the street level, and a sign that had an arrow pointing to a wide staircase.

Pioneer Vault Co.
Monthly or weekly rates

The staircase was closed off by a rod-iron gate with a sign:

Hours:
Monday through Fri. 9:00am - 6:30 pm

Sat. 10 till 4 Office ⟹

An arrow pointed to a small office with a barred window. It was 9:22 am. He walked back out of the building and stood looking around, then walked around the corner and stood there, looking. What he saw was what he had seen the night he left the Navy, a manhole with steam coming out of it two feet from the curb. He remembered sitting on the curb and feeling the heat, but today it was almost 60 degrees and it still had steam coming out of it. He walked down the street and got a cup of coffee, then walked back around the block and finally back to the front, then back into the building. It was 10:01. The gate was open and the office cage was open. There was a man, sitting and reading a book, inside.

He walked down the stairs and there in front of him was the vault room, completely open to the public. There were four long rows of boxes from the floor to the ceiling, one on each outside wall, and two in the center, none on the far end of the room on the street side. He walked along the rows, looking at the numbers, recognizing some of them, knowing that inside them were several thousands of dollars, and he wondered why anyone would trust their money to be left in a place as easy to get into as this one was. Then he saw the second door slide up inside the top of the front doorway, an iron barred door that slid down, completely sealing off the entrance from the stairs. It would be easy to get down the stairs, but not through the iron door.

He looked at the boxes, and the ceiling, and the pipes running along the wall, then down and out of the building through the south end of the vault. He decided they were probably water pipes, and then he got close, and felt the heat from them. He realized they were steam pipes, exhaust pipes for the condensed water from the boiler room that went into the manhole at the curb. That's where the steam was coming from.

He walked back up the stairs and out of the building, then stood looking around, and then walked back around to the manhole and wondered how deep it was. He couldn't just lift the lid, so he had to figure a way to measure it. He went across the street and got into his car, then sat there trying to think of something.

Across the street and down a few doors was a sporting goods store. He bought a roll of fishing line and some small weights. He sat in his car and unwound several feet of fishing line, and pressed a small weight on it, then rolled it up in his hand and walked back to the manhole. When no one was close to him, he dropped the line with the weight on it down through the hole used to lift the lid off. When it hit bottom he pinched it with his fingers and then pulled it back out. When he got to his car he tied a knot where the lid had been. He could measure it when he got back home and know how deep the manhole was.

Now all he had to do was find something from a pawn shop to carry home with him. He had the fishing line so he bought a fishing pole and a 35 mm Kodak camera and several rolls of film.

He gave the camera to Muriel Sue, and proudly showed her the fishing poles, telling her him and Tommy Dollarhide were going fishing when the fishing season opened in June.

Muriel Sue carried the camera to the closet in the hall way, and then opened the door. She put the camera on the shelf, next to the three she already had, and showed him the five fishing poles and two large boxes of tackle that had belonged to her and her former husband.

"So why didn't we take them when we went to the coast?" he asked.

"Because you never told me where we were going until we were already there, John," she answered.

"Oh! Well I tried," he said and got himself a beer, then saw Muriel Sue looking at him. He put the beer back and took out a can of pop, then went out to the back yard.

He sat in the lawn chair and thought about the vault, then he remembered something. He had to go back to the vault company and check it out better, but not today. He would do it when he was in town doing his collections. He spent the rest of the weekend helping Tommy do the yard and not drinking beer. He drank water and soda pop, Muriel Sue was happy. He even felt a little better.

Jack Charmichael went home and stayed there for almost three hours Saturday afternoon, then left and went to the Madison Hotel and stayed there for the weekend, drinking in the bar and thinking about Linn Morrison. She was starting to get to him. He looked at the picture several times and then put it back into his wallet.

Linn Morrison was thinking about Jack Charmichael too. She went to the VW dealer and looked at the robin-egg blue Porsche twice. She sat in it, and walked around it, and sat in it again, trying it out for size as a salesman stood watching her.

"You going to buy it or just wear it out sitting in it?" he asked smiling.

She looked right into his eyes and said, "I'm going to trade my virginity for it," then she walked out of the store.

Monday, the sixth of May, John Tru-Day went back to work. Jacky was already there sitting at her desk.

"Good morning Mr. Tru-Day," she smiled, "the coffee is made. I hope it's not too strong. I stopped and got some cream and sugar."

John Tru-Day got a cup of coffee and sat at his desk. He looked at the girl sitting behind hers. She had on a light colored sweater, slacks, and white shoes.

"I'm really glad you're here," he told her.

"I'm really glad I'm here too," she answered.

He drank his coffee and went to work. Jacky was right beside him helping and learning everything he could teach her. She went out and got lunch and brought it back. She even paid for it. But as soon as she walked out the door he got out the piece of fishing line and stretched it out on the floor and measured it, seven feet ten inches, just about the same as the floor of the vault. He put it in his desk drawer and waited for Jacky to return. He went home feeling good. He hadn't had a drink for four days.

Tommy Dollarhide spent the whole month of May working, and he went back to Boeing three times to get his application put back on the top of the pile.

John Tru-Day spent the month doing income taxes and left for Portland on the twentieth at four in the morning.

He came out of the first club and saw the white Chevrolet parked a few spaces away. He stood looking at them and then walked to a phone booth and pretended to make a call as he kept looking at the two men in the car. The car left and he didn't see it again during the rest of the collection trip. He finished at three in the afternoon on the thirtieth and called Jack Charmichael, then told him he was done and was still being followed.

Jack Charmichael told him to quit worrying again and then called the policeman friend of his and told him, "Those guys are still following my man around. I'd have someone kick their ass but I don't want any trouble. Just scare the fuck out of them, will ya?" He finished with a "please."

The policeman answered by telling him, "I'll put someone on it full time when he leaves again and have them follow him too. I'll tell you what kind of a car and you can tell him so he doesn't worry."

The thirty-first was Friday. John took the three-day weekend and let Jacky off also. He didn't tell Muriel Sue he was off on Friday and went to downtown Seattle and back to the Pioneer Vault Company. He went in and rented a box so he could have an excuse to be in the vault section. He put some papers in the box and relocked it after he examined the lock. It was nothing, the boxes could be opened with a small pry bar. Mostly, he wanted to look at the wall where the pipes went out.

He looked, and saw that the pipes were just stuck through the wall and then putty was pushed in around the hole and painted over. He stuck a pencil into the putty and saw the

214

wall was only thin metal, maybe 1/16-inch thick. The vault wasn't built to keep anyone out who wanted to get in, but he also realized the pipes went into the manhole on the outside of the wall.

He left the vault by counting his steps from the wall to the door, then counted the nine steps up out of the basement (about eight feet) then went out of the building and onto the sidewalk to where he figured the door was, then counted his steps along the sidewalk to the manhole. He came to the conclusion that the manhole was not more than two feet from the outside wall of the vault, but he knew nothing about manholes. He had to go check them out.

He looked in the phone book and found a company that made manholes out of concrete. He drove there and walked around the yard looking until a man came out and asked him what he wanted.

"Something to collect water," he said.

"Well these are for sewers."

He was told the storm drains are over there. After looking, he realized the storm drains were not as heavy as the manholes, the walls were thinner and they were shaped different.

"So what's the difference?" he asked.

"Sewer is in the center of the street and storm drains are usually by the curb so the water can drain into them."

John thanked him and went home, then realized he had forgotten one thing. He now knew how deep the storm drain was, but what did they refill the hole it was set in, with more concrete or dirt?

As he drove home he almost talked himself out of thinking about it anymore. "How could a guy get through the concrete? How could a guy get through the steel wall of the vault? How long would it take to get into the vault? How would he ever get the money out? Who could he get to help him?" His first thought about it was simply go there, get the money and go away on a long boat trip somewhere, but that was as deep as he had thought about it.

Now, it was starting to get a little complicated. He knew where the money was, but how to get it out?

Then there was Muriel Sue. That was the big question.

He got home at two in the afternoon and had two beers before Muriel Sue got home.

"How many have you had, John?" she asked.

"One and this one," he answered then asked, "want to go out to eat?"

"If you don't drink," she answered.

"That's under control," he answered, "I was just having a sort of--I don't know what it was."

John Tru-Day went back to his office at nine-thirty Monday morning, on the third of June. On the fifth, Mary Forbes came in and handed him his pay envelope. He put it in his desk drawer. She went to the bar and made herself a drink, then sat on the couch and talked to Jacky for several minutes, then asked John Tru-Day to come outside with her. He followed her out and she told him.

"I need you to help me. I took some money from Jack and I'm afraid he's going to find out I took it."

"How much?" John asked her.

"Sixteen thousand," she answered, "but I haven't spent any of it yet."

"So put it back," he said.

"It's been almost two months," she answered.

"Put it in an envelope and tell him it was on the floor of your car and you forget you had it."

"It was in my glove box and I did forget I had it. You're so smart, John. How do you know things like that?"

"Just tell him what happened," he returned.

"You think he'll believe me?"

"He'll believe you, Mary."

"Can I just give it to you and you give it to him and tell him I was too scared to tell him I lost it?"

"Hell, no! He don't trust me worth a shit. He has me followed every time I go do the collections."

She laughed, "No, he doesn't!"

"Hell, yes, he does. There's two guys following me every time I go."

She laughed again, "That's Eric and Bill."

"Who's Eric and Bill?" he asked, surprised she even knew about it.

"My sort of boyfriend and Jacky's boyfriend. They think Jack has a secret place where he keeps his money and they're trying to find it."

"Well, that's great!" he said, "Tell them to stop!" Then thought for a second and raised his voice, "So why the hell didn't you tell me the last time I told you I was being followed?"

"You didn't tell Jack about it, did you?"

"Sure I did! I didn't know who they were."

She laughed, "That's funny."

"No, it ain't funny. It scared the hell out of me! I thought I was going to get robbed, or killed, or something."

"He'll have someone beat the crap out of them again," she laughed again.

"What's so funny about that?" he asked her.

"They're both jerks," she answered

"You just said he was your boyfriend."

"He is, but he's still a jerk. He don't work or nothing."

218

"So what does he do?"

"Tries to find out where Jack keeps all his money."

"That's it?"

"Ya, he's a jerk," she laughed.

"So Jack has some place else where he keeps all his own money?"

"Ya! In a bank in Mexico," she laughed again, then said, "Jack is going to have someone beat the crap out of them," then she ask again, "Can I give you the money and you tell him I was too scared to give it to him?"

"No, just tell him it fell on the floor of your car and you just found it because you cleaned your car."

"I hope he doesn't beat the crap out of me," she answered then said, "Oh, he won't."

John Tru-Day turned and walked back into his office, followed by Mary Forbes. She had two more drinks, and talked to Jacky telling her about him being followed by their boyfriends, both women laughed.

He sat behind his desk listening to them and sort of wishing he was back in the Navy, or at least somewhere else. He was starting to realize, Jack Charmichael was surrounded by a lot of dumb people, and dumb people couldn't be trusted. He had to be very careful about what he said and who he said it to from now on. But mostly, he had to find a way to get away from Jack Charmichael without endangering himself or Muriel Sue.

Mary Forbes left John Tru-Day's office and drove to Jack Charmichael's office. She walked past Wilma Smith and into his office without knocking and handed him the envelope with the check from Doug Hicks in it.

"Here, I guess it fell under my car seat," she laughed, "I just found it this morning. I was cleaning my car."

Jack Charmichael looked into the envelope and asked her, "What's this from?"

"That check from Doug, remember?"

He looked at her for a few seconds then said, "Oh ya! The cock sucker! He's in jail. Keep it! Make your payoffs tomorrow and take yourself a vacation. Go see your mother."

"Really, Jack?" she beamed.

"Ya, really!" he answered, and tossed the envelope back to her. "Go see your mother, take two weeks. If I need you, I'll call you." He didn't want any other women around while he was with seventeen year-old Linn Morrison, who might say something to Jake, and he didn't want anything that might connect him with the Tropics two days after the girl got killed.

"Thanks, Jack," she said.

"Oh ya! Use part of that money to rent me a nice cabin by the lake up there. Rent it for two weeks and then call me and tell me where it is and don't use my name."

"You coming up there?" she asked.

"Would I have you rent me a place if I wasn't?"

"I guess not," she answered.

"Just be here at ten in the morning and get the bag."

"I will," she answered, and then walked out past Wilma Smith saying, "I got two weeks off."

"Ya, you're off alright," Wilma muttered, then walked to Charmichael's door and stuck her head in.

"If you're thinking what I think you're thinking, Jack, you take that girl up there and keep her. Jake is going to find out about it."

Jack Charmichael looked at Wilma Smith for several seconds, thought about Linn Morrison and her dad and his guns then answered, "Not too smart, huh?"

"Not smart at all," she returned, and closed the door.

Mary Forbes went back to John Tru-Day's office and spent most of the day just hanging around and drinking, and bothering both him and Jacky. She was asleep on the couch when he went home at three in the afternoon.

She went back to Charmichael's office at nine-thirty in the morning and got the payoff bag. Wilma told her to forget renting the cabin. She then went to the Pioneer Vault Company and made the payoffs, opening each box with her master key and putting in the envelopes with the money in it. It took her a little over an hour and forty minutes, and she left for Vancouver, B. C., to visit her mother.

Jack Charmichael went to the Madison Hotel at eleven-thirty, Friday the seventh, to have lunch with Linn Morrison, their first real meeting in person.

Linn Morrison was wearing a light blue low-cut sweater, and no bra. She had a pony tail in her blonde hair. She was sitting in a booth waiting for him when he walked into the restaurant. He sat across from her.

"You trying to get me shot?" he asked her.

"No!" she smiled.

"I ain't buying you no car," he said, then motioned for the waiter to come over.

Linn Morrison slipped off her right shoe and put her foot in between Jack Charmichael knees on his seat. He looked down, and then felt her foot.

"I bet you do," she smiled again.

"You think so, huh?"

"I'm not one of your whores," she smiled wider.

"I know, you're my construction boss's kid."

"I'm not a kid either, Jack," she answered, moving her foot over so it was touching his leg, "I'm a greedy little bitch and I want a car, a nice car."

"Without morals?" he finished.

"Morals don't buy things," she answered, then moved her foot and waited as the waiter stood by the table.

"What can I get you?" he asked.

"Nothing, just a Coke," she answered.

"Bring me a drink and her a Coke," he ordered, and the waiter left. She put her foot back on the seat between his legs.

"You think I'm just going to go out and buy you a new car because you're flirting with me?"

She leaned forward and said softly, "Because I'll be eighteen in three weeks and I'm still a virgin, and I'm greedy." Then she put her shoe back on and stood up.

"Where are you going?" he asked.

"Can I have some money, Jack?" she asked.

"What the fuck you talking about?" he raised his voice.

"Give me three hundred. I need to go shopping," then she said, "please, Jack."

"Fuck you," he answered, getting mad.

"In three weeks, Jack," she smiled and held her hand out for the money.

"You are a little bitch, ain't you?" he said and took his money clip out of his pocket and handed her three hundred dollars.

"Don't worry, I'm worth it," she smiled and walked out of the Madison, leaving him sitting in the booth wondering why he had gave her the money.

"She leave?" the waiter asked.

"Shut the fuck up!" he said, took his drink, and walked into the bar.

Linn Morrison met her girlfriend down the street, then went and had her hair done, then went to the most expensive clothing store in town and tried on a white low-cut evening gown. She stood next to a wall and had her girlfriend take several pictures of her, put the dress back and left to have the pictures developed, then went shopping with her friend.

Tuesday the 11th, he got three pictures of Linn Morrison in a blue envelope. Two of them were her wearing the evening gown. The third was her sitting in the robin-egg blue Porsche, wearing white shorts and sandals. Her shirt was open down to the third button, almost showing her right nipple. The door of the car was open and showing most of her bare legs. She was smiling with one hand on the wheel.

This one, Jack!

was written on the bottom of the photo. He sat, leaning back in his chair and looked at the three pictures, and was becoming more and more attracted to her, telling himself he was being a fool. Wilma Smith came in and looked over his shoulder at the picture of Linn in the car then said, "It was bound to happen sometime," she patted him on his shoulder and said, "It was nice working for you, Jack."

"I ain't done nothing!" he answered.

"Yet!" she answered, and walked back out of his office.

"I ain't done nothing to her," he called.

224

"Yet!" she called back.

On Friday, the fourteenth of June, Tommy Dollarhide got a letter from Boeing, telling him to report to the medical center on the eighteenth at nine-thirty in the morning for a physical. If he passed, he was to start work on Monday, the first of July.

On Saturday, the fifteenth of June, Mary Forbes went to a night club in Vancouver with her mother and met a man named Art Sweeney. He was from a small island in the Pacific Ocean, south of Guam and north of Australia. They talked and he told her he wanted to buy a boat and start a sightseeing and fishing excursion business on the island where he lived. He had come to Vancouver to earn money so he could buy a boat, and then take it back to the island.

Mary Forbes spent every day and every night with him for the rest of the time she was in Vancouver. Art Sweeney asked Mary Forbes to marry him and come back to the island with him. She told him he could come back to Seattle with her and she would help him save the money, or maybe find someone to loan them the money to get started with and they could get married on the island. She was in love.

Mary Forbes came back to Seattle and told her boyfriend, Eric, he had to move out of her apartment.

He argued about it until she said, "You want me to ask Jack to move you out?"

Eric packed his things and moved out and into the spare room at Jacky and Bill's house.

On Friday, the 21st of July, Art Sweeney came to Seattle and moved into Mary Forbes' apartment with her.

On the 26th, Jack Charmichael called and told Mary Forbes to come to his office. He told her he had some men from back east coming to visit for the weekend and for her to get three more girls and spend the weekend in the apartment at the Carlton Hotel with the men.

Mary Forbes answered by saying, "I met someone, Jack. I'm not going to do that anymore. We're getting married, I can get you some girls from the clubs, OK?"

Jack Charmichael answered Mary Forbes by saying, "Mary, come here. Lean over here," meaning for her to lean forward over his desk. She did as he told her.

Jack Charmichael reached across his desk and slapped Mary Forbes so hard on the side of her face it knocked her down. She lay on the floor on her back, crying, looking up at him.

"Now! Just shut the fuck up, and do as you're told," he screamed, "I don't give a fuck if you're getting married or not. It ain't got nothing to do with your job! Just get three girls and have them at the hotel by seven Friday night. If you don't want to be there, get four. Christ! Grow up! Will ya? I'm getting sick of you being so fucking stupid about things."

Mary Forbes got up off the floor and walked out of his office, rubbing the left side of her face as Wilma Smith looked at her, then called into Jack Charmichael office, "You're losing it, Jack. I think that girl is getting to you."

"God damn it! I ain't done nothing with her," he screamed back.

"Yet!" Wilma answered.

Mary Forbes went to three clubs and got four girls who agreed to spend the weekend at the hotel, then went home and told Art Sweeney, "I've been thinking about it. I have money saved and if you want to go, we'll go. We can leave after the twelfth of August when I can get my money from my stocks."

"Do you have that much money?" he asked.

"How much do you need?" she asked him back.

"Maybe seventy-five thousand dollars in American money," he told her.

"I have more than that," she answered.

Mary Forbes stayed as far away from Jack Charmichael as she could the rest of the month.

Tommy Dollarhide went and took his exam and passed it with flying colors. He was supposed to report to Boeing at seven in the morning the first day of August. He was happy.

John Tru-Day left on his collection trip on the twentieth and before he even got to Portland knew he was being followed. When he got to the first club, he watched the car park a few spaces away and then the man got out of his car and walked up to him. John could plainly see the gun inside the man's coat as he came closer. He was scared. "I'm here to watch out for you. If you see the guys who were following you, point them out to me. My name's Joe," he said, and walked back to his car.

John Tru-Day was relieved but didn't say he knew who had been following him. He counted and put into his safe in his office $2,245,785 during the next ten days, with the man in the car never more than a few feet away from him. He felt halfway safe for the first time in four months. He called Jack Charmichael and told him he was done. It was Monday afternoon, the first of August.

Tommy Dollarhide was in his first of twenty days of training classes at the Boeing plant, twelve miles from John's office. He finished, and then went to work at the Tropics. He gave two weeks' notice that he was quitting.

"That's a first," Jan said "No one ever gave notice here before."

Mary Forbes and Art Sweeney had gone back to Vancouver to get Mary a passport so they could leave from there. They had decided to buy a boat closer to the island.

On the fifth of August, Mary Forbes went to John Tru-Day's office and handed him his pay envelope. She stood there smiling and told him, "I met a guy."

"A guy? Or The Guy?" John asked.

"The Guy," she answered.

"Then get on a plane with him and move to a different country. Go find yourself an island somewhere and never come back," John told her.

228

Mary Forbes stood there looking shocked at him, and then she smiled and said, "How do you always know what I'm doing? OK, John, I will. See ya some time."

"Not if you're smart," he answered.

"I'm smarter than Jack thinks I am," she answered, and left.

Barbara Fieldsman had saved over two thousand dollars and was ready to leave Seattle. She told Keith J. Shocko she had found a club open after hours in downtown Seattle and wanted to take him there. They left the motel at ten-fifteen on the night of August the 4th. She had Keith park the Buick on the street and then walked him down into an alley. She had her left arm around his waist and her right hand in her purse feeling for the handle of the hunting knife. He had his right arm around her shoulder and his left hand in his pants pocket. She walked him into the alley, and behind a huge dumpster in front of a fire door, then stopped and turned to face him still with her left arm around him.

"You'll love this place, Keith!" she said and gripped the hunting knife in her purse.

"So where is it?" he asked, looking around for a door handle.

"Right here! Mother fucker!" she said, and shoved the knife up into his chest as far as she could shove it, making sure it went directly into his heart as she pulled him forward with her left hand. She managed to bury the full nine inches in his heart cavity.

His eyes got wide and he tried to say 'Barbara' but only managed to say "Bar--" and she let him fall. He was dead before he landed on his face in the trash next to the dumpster, his left hand still in his pocket.

Barbara Fieldsman took the keys out of his pocket and walked back out of the alley and got into the Buick, went back to the motel, loaded her few things, and drove away. She was driving south less than thirty minutes after she had gotten rid of Keith J. Shocko.

By the time the police found his body the next afternoon, she was in northern California, driving south, heading for Phoenix, Arizona.

Keith J. Shocko was gone.

Barbara Fieldsman was gone.

Monday, August seventh, Mary Forbes got a second brilliant idea. She called Eric at Jacky's house and told him she had changed her mind and he could move back into the apartment on the tenth. She said she was going on vacation and wanted him to watch the place for her.

"Why not now?" he asked.

"Because Jack has some guy staying here with me until then, if you were here he wouldn't like it," she answered.

"What time should I come back?"

"Anytime. I won't be here. I'm going to go stay with my mother for three weeks; she has to go into the hospital."

At ten in the morning, on the eighth of August, Mary Forbes went to Jack Charmichael's office and picked up the payoff bag. She had already loaded everything she wanted to take with her into her car and had Art Sweeney wait as she went into the vault to make the monthly payoffs.

Mary Forbes went down into the vault room and opened the first box, then began to play a game she had learned from Jack Charmichael. *One for you, one for me, two for you. One, two, for me. Three for you. One, two, three for me.* By the time she finished, one hour and forty-five minutes later, she had put into certain boxes four hundred and fifty-eight thousand dollars. She had taken out of other boxes and the payoff bag and put into her own bag three hundred forty-seven thousand dollars in hundreds, and fifty thousand in fifties and twenties.

Mary Forbes stopped at her apartment and left the payoff bag there with three envelopes still in it and the twenties. She hid it in Eric's closet, knowing Jack Charmichael would search her apartment trying to find out where she had gone. She then stopped and mailed a letter to Jack Charmichael telling him what she had done. With what she had taken from the vault, her own savings, and her own cash, and the leftover money from Doug Hick's check, Mary Forbes and Art Sweeney crossed over into Canada with more than eight hundred seventy-six thousand dollars, all in cash money in the trunk of her car, which was registered to Jack Charmichael. She left it at the Vancouver airport, just before she and Art and the canvas bag with wooden handles got on a plane for Mexico City.

At eleven fifteen, on the morning of the tenth, as Eric was moving back into Mary Forbes' apartment, Jack Charmichael got two letters, one in a blue envelope, one in a white one. He opened the blue one first and read the note:

Meet me at the hotel if you want to. I'll be there Saturday at noon.

love ya, Linn

He laid it on his desk and opened the second one. It read:

I robbed you, Jack! And I'm going to live in Paris.

Now you shut the fuck up!

Then in big letters she wrote,

MARY! HA HA! HA! HA! YOU ASSHOLE!

Jack Charmichael didn't believe what he had just read and called to Wilma, "You know where Mary is?"

"No, I haven't heard from her since she took the bag."

"Come here and read this."

Wilma read the note and chuckled, "I didn't think she was that smart."

"She ain't smart, she's fucking stupid. Just wait until I get my hands on her fat ass," he said. Then he said, "This is a joke. She ain't got enough guts to even think about stealing from me."

"I think she stole from everyone else to make them think it was you," Wilma returned, "She probably just shorted everyone."

"How much?" he asked, wondering who she had shorted.

"You better start calling," Wilma told him, "before they find out they got shorted."

"Son of a bitch!" he screamed, "If it ain't one thing, it's something else."

"You shouldn't have slapped her," Wilma told him.

"I slapped her before, and she never robbed me! Why now?" he answered, and Wilma sort of laughed at him.

He spent four hours calling people and trying to explain what had happened. He had a few people he knew start looking for Mary Forbes in France, even though he didn't believe she was there.

He sent a man to her mother's house in Vancouver, B. C. Mary was not there. He had a man watching her apartment but she didn't show there either. At four in the afternoon, he left his office and drove to the Tropics club and had three drinks, then looked at the girls dancing and had the manager tell Sonia Re'olo to go into the office.

"No way," she answered, "I know what happens to girls who go in there."

The manager took her by her hair and dragged her into the office, followed by Jack Charmichael who stood there for a few minutes and listened to her screaming in Spanish, and told the manager to let her go, and he left the club.

He was back in his office for only an hour when he got a call from the day bartender.

"You know that Sonia Re'olo girl? The one who goes with that guy Mikie?"

"Ya! No! I don't know! What about her?" Charmichael asked.

"As soon as you left, your new manager and some other guy raped her in the office."

"You're kidding me?" he screamed into the phone.

"No, and she kicked him in the balls. I mean she really kicked him. Then she beat the shit out of him with the baseball bat they keep in the office. She hit the other guy in the face with it and he's gone. She smashed his nose all over his face and knocked some of his teeth out, but that Jerry guy, he's on the floor by the office. He's really hurt, Jack. I think she broke his arm and maybe his ankles, and she called the cops. She's here cussing in Spanish at the top of her lungs and smashing all kinds of things with the bat here, listen--"

He held the phone out so Jack Charmichael could listen to the woman smashing his club. "Should I call someone?" he held the phone out again so Jack Charmichael could hear the girl cussing.

"Who the fuck you going to call?" he screamed and hung up.

Jack Charmichael got up and went to the Madison Hotel and started drinking.

The police came and hauled the manager of the Tropics off to the hospital, then to jail.

Mikie the actor came and took Sonia Re'olo home. All the day girls in the Tropics left, except one.

Tommy Dollarhide came to work at six, heard what had happened to Sonia, asked Jan to get his things out of the safe, and quit.

Jan the bartender followed Tommy outside and then after talking to him for a few minutes, decided to quit herself.

There was only one girl in the place and Jan told her to leave, then locked the door and went home, leaving the Tropics closed.

It was 7:12 pm on Tuesday, the fourteenth of August, and not a good day for Jack Charmichael, but things would get worse.

At nine-fifteen, the cops came into the bar at the Madison and were going to arrest him for the attempted rape of Sonia, but didn't have enough good evidence and had hoped he might slip up and say something that would make him guilty. He just told them to go to hell. He was there only five minutes, and they could check with his bartender and anyone else they wanted to.

At 10:08 on the morning of the fourteenth of August, twenty minutes before Jack Charmichael read the note from Linn Morrison that said: *"Meet me at noon in the café at Fifth and Pike,"* Mary Forbes walked into the International Bank of Mexico and handed the clerk a check signed by herself and Jack Charmichael and a deposit slip to a bank in London, England.

"We'd like to transfer our account to this bank account, please."

The clerk looked at the check, talked to the bank manager, who then made a phone call, hung up, looked at a picture, nodded his head, yes, and the clerk came back.

"All of it?" he asked.

"Yes, please." Mary answered.

"There will be a charge of four hundred dollars American."

"That's fine," Mary answered.

And the bank clerk moved three million, eight hundred thousand, four hundred and eight dollars of Jack Charmichael's money into the secret account in London, England, that she had opened three years before because Jack Charmichael had told her to do it in case he ever needed a place to hide his money from the IRS, thinking Mary Forbes was too dumb to ever use it.

Mary Forbes then took Art Sweeney back to the airport and got on a plane and flew to New York City. She rented a hotel room and they stayed there for four days, getting into one taxi and out of it, then into a different one and out of it, until she found a driver who knew where to get new driver's licenses, birth certificates, and passports made. Art Sweeney sat in the hotel bar for a day and sipped drinks, not sure what Mary was up to, while she had two new ID cards, driver's licenses, and passports made.

Then, at ten the next morning, Anna Loretta Charmichael, with her husband, Art Charmichael, flew off to London, England, and stayed for two days.

Anna Loretta Charmichael went into the International Bank of London and transferred the money to a secured Swedish bank account located in Australia.

The next morning, they got on another plane and flew off to Australia, then the next day they bought a forty-seven foot Bay Cruiser, supplied it with food, water and extra fuel, and left for the island, three hundred seventy miles to the southwest.

Mary Forbes was gone.

On the fifteenth of August, Monday morning, Jack Charmichael tried to withdraw money from his account in Mexico to repay part of what Mary Forbes had stolen.

He was told the account did not exist.

"What the fuck happened to it?" he yelled.

"If it was a sealed account, we can't tell you. We don't have any records of it ever being here. They're all burned within ten minutes of the account being closed. You would know that if you had an account with us," he was told.

It took him several minutes to get over the shock, and then he remembered he had Mary open up the account in London under some name he didn't remember. His money was gone. Even if he found Mary, he couldn't get the money back without her giving it to him.

He sat at his desk looking bewildered at Wilma until she finally asked him what was wrong.

"Mary cleaned me out. She took it all," he stammered.

"I didn't think she was that smart," Wilma chuckled.

"It ain't funny, Wilma," he choked, "we got to find her."

Wilma looked at the note and said, "She's in Paris, France."

"No, she ain't, she just wrote that!"

"Jack, if she's smart enough to take all your money and then tell you where she is, she's smart enough to know you'll make her a deal and give her some of the money if you let her go. She's in Paris, France. Hire someone to find her."

"You think so?" he looked at her.

"Or, you could go to her apartment and see if she's still there, or maybe she left a clue to where she was going."

Charmichael picked up his phone and then set it back down. "I better do this in person. For God's sake don't talk about it," he said, and left the office.

Jack Charmichael went to a phone booth and called several people and told them to meet him in his apartment in the Madison Hotel that night. Then, he went to the bar and drank until the meeting. He talked to five men, telling them Mary Forbes had robbed him and to find her. He said he didn't know where she was but she had a lot of money on her. Then he said, "If you have to, kill the bitch, but get my money back first."

Two of the men went straight to Mary Forbes' apartment, then kicked in the door and found Eric sitting on the couch eating corn curls and waiting for her to come home. They threw him on the floor and one guy stood there with his right foot on the back of Eric's neck, holding him down, and told him to stay there as they tore the apartment apart, looking at everything in it. Then they found the bag in his closet under some extra blankets with the envelopes in it. They also found Jacky's address and her boyfriend's name, plus a lot of notes about Jack Charmichael and the clubs in a different bag in the same closet.

They hauled Eric to Jacky's house and grabbed Bill, then dragged him out the door and took them both to a warehouse by the waterfront. They tied both men with chains to one of the steel uprights, and called Jack Charmichael.

Jack Charmichael came to the warehouse at eight in the morning and kicked both Eric and Bill several times while he was screaming at them to tell him where Mary Forbes had gone. He kicked them in the ribs and the back and face several times and got nothing out of them.

"They don't know nothing," he said, and walked out calling them "fucking morons."

"What do you want us to do with them?"

"Let them rot where they're at," he said, and the men left Eric and Bill beaten and tied up to the steel upright.

Two days later a homeless man turned them loose and they left Seattle in the white Chevrolet. Eric and Bill were gone.

On the eighteenth of August, Wednesday, at one in the afternoon, Jack Charmichael and two men came to John Tru-Day's office and questioned him and Jacky for two hours about Mary Forbes.

John said nothing except, "I can't believe she would do such a thing. She liked you so much."

He sat behind his desk, scared to death, as the men looked at every paper he had except the five under his desk mat, the payoff sheets. They left and Jacky went home to take her son to her mother's for safekeeping.

"You coming back?" he asked.

"Should I?" she asked him back.

"It might look bad if you don't," he told her.

"Alright, but I'm scared," she answered.

"Ya, me too."

Jacky went home and John Tru-Day followed her out the door with the payoff sheets in his pocket. He burned them as soon as he was home. He had two days to think about what had happened before he had to leave on his rounds Saturday morning. He wanted to leave right then and never come back.

Thursday morning, Jack Charmichael called John Tru-Day and asked him, "Do you know what happened at the Tropics last week?"

"No," John answered.

"Well it's closed for a few days, so go over there and inventory everything in there, will you, and get the money out of the safe and put it away. Count everything in there, even the glasses. Call me back."

"How do I get in?" John asked.

For a second he forgot about Mary Forbes and started to send her down to help John.

"I'll have Mary me--son of a bitch!" Charmichael screamed and hung up.

He called back and told John Tru-Day, "I'm sending a guy over there to change the lock on the door. Meet him there at noon."

"Then what?" John asked.

"Fuck!" Charmichael cussed, "I don't know, just inventory the place and get the money. I'll find someone to keep it open until I find someone else to run it."

John Try-Day left his office and drove to the Tropics club and met the locksmith, then went in and into the office. The safe was sitting there with the door halfway open, but with the money still in it. He took the money from the safe and counted it. There was $91,293. He put it in a bag with some of the change, threw some of the small change on the floor then put the bag in the trunk of the Olds. He spent four hours inventorying the place.

The wheels were turning in his head again and he figured he didn't have too much to lose, plus he needed some capital. He took the bills from the cash register and tossed a lot of the change on the floor behind the bar, the rest he dumped in the sack with the bills.

He left and went back to his office and called Jack Charmichael, "What happened there? The place is a wreck," he said.

"Ya, it is, what happened to it is," Jack replied, "the manager raped one of the girls and she called the cops on him. Did you get the money or was it all gone?"

"That's why I asked you what happened," John told him. "The safe was open. The cash register was open. There was no money in the safe or the cash register. A lot of change is on the floor. They were both open when I got there, but I took inventory. There's a lot of booze and there's a lot of blood on the office floor; some of the change was in the blood and I left it there."

"She did a fucking job on me, didn't she?" Charmichael asked, sounding sort of lost.

"Who?"

"Who?! Mary! Who the hell do you think?"

"You think she took the money?"

"Sure she did, she had a key. She took most of the payoffs and cleaned out my account in Mexico."

"No way!" John answered, not believing Mary to be that smart.

"She got me for over three million!"

"No way!" John answered again, then said, "If she got all that, why would she bother with the money in Tropics? Wouldn't it be more likely that the girls took it all?"

"Ya! Fuck! You're right! It must have been them, or one of the bartenders." Then Charmichael's voice changed and he asked, "You think you could wait until Monday or Tuesday to do the collections? I might need some help here."

"If that's what you want," John told him.

"Can I call you at home if I need you?" Charmichael asked.

"I guess so, but don't say who you are, my girlfriend is afraid of you. OK?"

"Sure, I understand that," Charmichael answered, then said, "Thanks, John, I'll talk to you later."

John Tru-Day hung up his phone, looked at Jacky and said, "Mary waxed his ass good, she got three million from him, all in cash."

"You think he had Eric and Bill killed?" she asked.

John Tru-Day's good mood vanished. "God! I hope not," he answered, then said, "Let's go home, I'm scared out of my mind."

He was scared, but for more than one reason. He had 91,293 reasons in the trunk of his car.

Tommy Dollarhide had tried several times to find out Mikie the actor's phone number so he could call and see how Sonia was doing. Friday night on his way home, he remembered the receipt from his tires in his glove box and called the tire man. He got Mikie's number and called him.

"We'll come over to your house in the morning, big guy. I'm really busy right now trying to put Charmichael out of business," Mikie hung up. Tommy looked out his window and saw John Tru-Day sitting in the backyard. He was drinking a beer. Tommy walked outside.

"So how's it going?" Tommy asked.

John Tru-Day was trembling as he took a drink of his beer.

"Man, I'm scared to death. Charmichael's girl, Mary, stole a bunch of money from him and he's looking to kill someone and it might be me."

"Why you?"

"Because I'm the smallest guy?" he asked.

"Start over," Tommy told him.

"Jack Charmichael had this girl named Mary working for him. She did his payoffs. She took the money and went south with it. Or, maybe not south but somewhere.

"The girl with the big butt?"

"Ya, big butt, no brains."

"How much?"

"I don't know. A lot probably, she said she wanted to get even with him and I guess she did. He was in my office Wednesday looking at everything there. They scared the crap out of me. Then, yesterday he had me go to the Tropics and it looks like someone got killed in there. He said the manager raped one of the girls."

"The wrong one," Tommy told him, "that's why I quit."

"You quit? You don't work there anymore?"

"No, not since last week when they raped Sonia."

"Man, I'm scared Tommy."

"So quit," Tommy told him.

"I can't. I have to go do the collections on Monday and I'm too scared to quit. I'd have to just leave and leave Muriel Sue and everything."

"So do the collections and then tell him you're too scared to keep doing them."

"I know how much he steals each month. He can't let me run around. I might tell someone."

"I think I need a beer," Tommy told him.

"I think I need more than a beer. I need to figure a way out of this mess," John answered, nearly crying.

"Jesus. You're really upset, ain't you?" Tommy asked, looking down at him.

"I'm scared out off my mind. What if he does something to Muriel Sue?"

"I'll be right back." Tommy went into his house and brought back two beers and handed one to John.

They sat and talked until Muriel Sue came home and John went inside his house, and Tommy went inside his. They came back outside and sat in the yard drinking beer and talking until dark. The women came out and went back in and came back out and went back in several times. Each time they came out they changed the conversation from Jack Charmichael to something else and then changed it back again when the women left.

Then, John Tru-Day said, "I bet there's about twenty million in the Pioneer Vault Company down there."

"And?" Tommy asked.

"And, if someone was to just take it, the guys who owned the boxes couldn't say anything because the money is all payoffs," and he looked at Tommy, who was already getting up out of his chair.

"It's just a thought," John said.

"Ya, and a dumb one," Tommy answered, and walked back to his house.

Both men went in to bed around ten in the evening. John went straight to bed and Tommy sat up thinking. He too was developing a hatred for Jack Charmichael and everything he did.

Four

Saturday Morning was August 20th. It was warm and the sky was full of white clouds, moving slowly from south to north. The breeze was warm.

Tommy got up and ate breakfast, then went out to mow the lawn. He had it half done when John Tru-Day came, stood next to him shaking and whispered in his ear, "I was going to tell you last night but I couldn't. I've got $91,000 of Charmichael's money in the trunk of my car. He thinks that Mary girl, or you or the bartenders, took it."

Tommy looked down at him and said, "So?" then he said, "Me? What do you mean me?"

"Well, at first he thought Mary took it but then he changed his mind and figured either you or the bartender took it. If he finds out I took it he'll have me killed and I can't give it back because I already told him it was gone."

Tommy shut off the mower and walked John into the garage.

"Why did you take it in the first place?" Tommy asked.

"I don't know," John was talking in a low whisper, "the safe was already open when I went into the office and the money was there and I just took it. Then Charmichael asked me if the money was gone when I got there and I said yes, so I kept it."

"Good for you," Tommy answered, and patted him on the shoulder, "keep it."

"Where?" John asked.

"Go get it and I'll show you."

John Tru-Day didn't carry the money back to the garage. He drove his car around and down the alley and backed it up to the garage door, then got out and opened the trunk and showed Tommy the money bag. Tommy took the bag and emptied the cash out into the grass catcher bag of the old push mower and hung it up on the wall, then tossed a couple handfuls of dead grass in with it. He tossed the bank bag into the trash can belonging to a house three doors down. He put some trash on top of it so whoever owned the house wouldn't see it before the garbage company took it away on Tuesday.

John stood watching him and then said, "You think they'll find it there?"

"Why would they find it? They don't even know you have it, so why would they even look for it?"

"What if they come looking for you?"

"Let um, I hope they do," he answered.

John drove his car back around the house and parked it in the driveway, then came back to the backyard and helped Tommy rake the yard. They were just finished when Mikie and Sonia Re'olo came around the corner of the house carrying a big box.

"Here, big guy! Mikie said and tossed the box to him. "It's for Patty, a house warming, get well, glad you're well, have a nice life gift."

Tommy looked at Sonia and asked, "You OK?"

Sonia spoke about twenty angry words in Spanish and then said, "I'm OK now. How are you, Tommy?"

"I think we need to have a nice barbecue," Tommy answered, "and a few beers."

"And a few more beers," Mikie added, then looked at John and said "I'm Mikie. This is my girlfriend, Sonia. You're John Tru-Day. I heard a lot about you."

"What?" John asked.

"Just be careful," Mikie told him then turned to Tommy, "I'm putting that guy out of business one way or another."

"Let's have a barbecue," Tommy said, trying to get off the subject of anything that had to do with Jack Charmichael.

"I'll buy the steaks," Mikie said.

"I'll buy the beer," John added.

"And I'll buy whatever else we need," Tommy finished, then went and called Patty McShane and introduced her to Sonia and gave her the box she and Mikie had brought for her.

The three men went to the store in Mikie's car and brought back enough food and beer to feed ten people and get fifteen drunk.

All six people spent the afternoon cooking, eating, and drinking. By the time it was getting dark all six of them were sitting at the table half-drunk and Mikie spoke first. "You know what I'd like to do, big guy?"

"What's that?" Tommy answered.

"Go right down into the Pioneer Vault Company and clean Jack Charmichael and all his friends out."

John Tru-Day nearly choked on his beer. He coughed and beer flew out of his nose and mouth.

"Do it!" Tommy answered.

"I need money and help. I don't want the money, I just want to clean him out so he's out of business for good."

"Tommy Dollarhide looked sideways at John Tru-Day wiping the beer off his face and then asked Mikie, "How much money do you need?"

"About thirty thousand for some trucks and stuff."

"What kind of trucks?" Tommy asked him, looking again at John.

"Three trucks, one pick up, one one-ton, and a van."

"Then?" Tommy asked.

"Then you paint them up like Seattle City trucks, put decals and tools on them and get some barricades and stuff, and park them around the storm drain next to the Pioneer building, like you're city workers fixing something in the storm drain, and go down into the manhole, bust your way into the vault and clean it out, then haul the money away in the van. I been checking it out for two years. A guy would just have to wait for a three-day weekend. I bet there's over ten million dollars in there, and it all belongs to Charmichael's friends and crooked politicians. If someone took it, Charmichael would be blamed for it and out of business."

John Tru-Day choked again and got up from the table, then walked across the lawn choking and gagging, trying to regain his composure.

Muriel Sue looked at Mikie, then at Sonia, and then at Tommy, and finally at Patty McShane who had no idea what Mikie was talking about.

"You're really thinking of doing that?" she asked.

"It's just a thought, but I'd like to if I could," Mikie answered.

"Let's do it!" Muriel Sue said, "Let's all do it together," she looked at Tommy and then at Patty and Sonia, then back at Tommy, "You think we could talk John into doing it?"

"Leave me out of it," Tommy said.

"I'll do it," Sonia said, "I hate that fucker guy!"

"What are you all talking about?" Patty asked.

"Nothing," Tommy told her, "forget it."

"Who's Jack Charmichael?" Patty asked him.

"A crook," Tommy told her, "Mikie wants to steal all of his money so he'll be out of business."

"What business is he in?" Patty asked.

"Prostitution," Sonia told her, "They raped me last week," then she spoke a string of Spanish cuss words only her and Patty McShane could understand, and Patty answered back in Spanish, "I know what that feels like."

"You do?" asked Sonia, looking surprised at her, and then asked her, "Yo Habla Espanola?"

"Pikito," Patty answered, then the two women talked in Spanish for several minutes as everyone else sat there not knowing what they were talking about, then Sonia Re'olo said in English, "Tommy will fix those fucking bastard guys when he takes you to get your son back."

Everyone looked at Patty, and she got up and left the table, walked away, and then came back. Patty turned and looked at Tommy then said, "I'll help if I can."

"Oh no, you won't!" Tommy answered, and then said, "This conversation is over with."

John brought it back up as soon as he was able to sit and talk without choking. He was astonished that Mikie had exactly the same idea as he did, but his was already planned out.

He looked at Muriel, not knowing what she had already told Mikie, and said, "How would you like to buy a three-mast schooner and spend the next fifteen years going around the world?"

Muriel Sue looked at Mikie, then at Sonia, and then at Patty, and then at Tommy, and back at John Tru-Day, then back at Mikie.

252

"I have almost a hundred thousand dollars left from my husband's insurance; you can use some of it if you want to."

Then all eyes were going from one face to the next for over a minute and no one spoke. Then Tommy said, "You're all nuts. Let's go, Patty, this is crazy."

He stood up, but Patty McShane didn't. He stood looking down at her and then sat back down.

"Are you all nuts?" he asked.

No one answered.

"It's crazy," he said.

No one answered.

"It's bank robbery!" he said.

"It's not bank robbery. It's just burglary," Mikie told him, "It's a private storage company. It has no insurance and no federal connections. Six months in jail if we get caught and if the judge doesn't have a bunch of money in one of the boxes, and even if we do it, it will all come out about how much money is in there and whose boxes they are. The whole outfit will be out of business and I bet they go to jail longer than you guys do."

"You guys do?" Tommy asked.

John Tru-Day looked at Mikie, then at Tommy, and then around the table several times, then back at Tommy and finally said, "It's my way out. I'm in all the way!"

"I'm not! Tommy said, "You guys go ahead. Leave me out of it."

He got up and went into his house. Patty followed him a few minutes later and didn't say anything to him. He sat in his chair and tried to watch the TV but couldn't think straight. He got up and went to bed, and Patty followed him.

Mikie and John Tru-Day sat and tried to figure out the first step to take. They decided to meet again the next afternoon and figure out what they were going to do.

Jack Charmichael made three more mistakes on Saturday while Tommy, John, and Mikie were having their barbecue. He first sent a man over to Jan the bartender's house and had him bring her to the Madison Hotel where he sat and talked her into coming back to work for him by telling her she could either come back to work at the Tropics or be put into a house somewhere, and be locked in there forever, turning tricks.

She was too scared to say no.

The second one was Jan told him Tommy Dollarhide was working at Boeing now. Jack Charmichael spent five hundred dollars bribing a lead man into getting Tommy fired, thinking he would have to come back to work at the Tropics, and he was going to make him the manager of the club.

The third was he met Linn Morrison as soon as he finished talking to Jan and Linn conned him into taking her out to dinner that night. He picked her up at a house belonging to her friend near the college, and took her to a nice restaurant.

Linn Morrison put her little tape recorder in her purse, turned it on, and had her friend follow and take pictures of them. Linn Morrison sat in Jack Charmichael's car after eating, and there in the lit parking lot of the restaurant let him kiss and fondle her as she sort of fought him off telling him he had to wait until the time was perfect and she was 18.

"I have no intentions of ever doing it in a car. I'm not one of your whores, Jack," she told him, but let him feel around a few minutes more, sliding his hand up under her dress as her friend stood a few feet away and took pictures.

As soon as she saw her friend was finished, she acted like she was mad and got out of the car telling him, "When you can respect me, we'll go out again," then she said, "I need some money," and held out her hand.

"What for?" he asked.

"A taxi, and clothes, and because you were so rude to me."

He handed her a fifty dollar bill.

She threw it back into his car and held out her hand again.

"How much?" he asked.

"A lot!" she smiled, "I'm expensive."

Jack Charmichael leaned over and held his money clip in his hand, "Alright, I'll play your little game, but you try to fuck me and I'll have you raped and stick you in a whorehouse. Don't fuck around with me, Linn." He handed her the money clip and said, "Take what you need."

She tossed the empty clip back in on the seat and said, "When I fuck you, Jack, you'll give me a lot more than this," then she smiled at him and walked away back into the restaurant.

He drove away, remembering how her skin had felt, and even thought about divorcing his wife. He was getting hooked.

On Sunday, John Tru-Day and Muriel Sue didn't talk about the night before, both thinking it was all the beer they had drunk, right up until two in the afternoon when Mikie and Sonia Re'olo came back.

Tommy Dollarhide saw them all sitting at the table in the backyard and came out. Mikie had a blueprint of the storm drain and the vault laid out on the table. He was explaining to John Tru-Day how easy it would be to break through the wall of the storm drain and into the vault. He had made a list of tools and he even had the time figured out. He figured it would take fifty-nine hours to open all 1040 boxes, if they got that far.

Tommy listened and then told them again they were both nuts, then he went back into his house, only to come back out carrying beer with him.

Muriel Sue started the barbecue and it all started again. They ate and drank beer all day and talked about robbing Jack Charmichael while Tommy tried to talk them out of it.

Monday morning, John Tru-Day left for Portland and Tommy Dollarhide went to work at Boeing. He parked his truck in the parking lot and tried to go into the building and was stopped by the guard.

"Sorry," said the guard, "your pass has been suspended. You have to go talk to your lead man."

Tommy walked to the office and found out he had been laid off because of lack of interest.

"What the hell is that?" he asked.

"Well, you just don't seem to be the right guy for the job," the lead man told him, and then said, "We can fire anyone for any reason within the first forty-five days, and I don't think you're interested in working here."

He handed Tommy a pay voucher and told him to leave it at the front desk and his check would be mailed to him at his home.

A very disappointed Tommy Dollarhide got into his truck and drove home. He told Patty what had happened and she cried. He sat on the porch and drank beer until it got dark, waiting for John to get home, but he was almost drunk and went to bed before he had a chance to see John Tru-Day.

The next morning he got a call from Jan. She told him she wanted to meet with him and asked him if he could come to the Tropics to meet her.

"I thought you quit," he said.

"It's not that easy," she returned, and sounded sort of scared. He knew Jack Charmichael had something to do with her going back to work there. He left his house at one in the afternoon and drove to the Tropics and met Jan. She told him what Jack Charmichael had told her and he told her in return he had been fired from Boeing.

"He did it! He paid someone to fire you," she said. "He told me to call you and offer you a job Saturday so he knew you were getting fired. He wants you back here to be the manager. I need to get away from Seattle, Tommy," she said.

Tommy Dollarhide sat and looked at her for a few seconds and saw how scared she was.

Jan looked at him and saw how mad he was.

"You're not going to do something stupid are you, Tommy?"

"Probably," he smiled at her.

He told her, "When you get off work, don't stop anywhere, just come to my house and I'm going to give you some money. Leave, Jan. Just leave here and don't come back."

"You sure, Tommy?" she answered, and then said, "Where should I go?"

"Don't you know anyone in a different state?"

"Back in Kentucky," she answered.

"Then go there."

"What about all my things? God! I don't know what I'm doing," she exclaimed, then sort of shook a little and cried.

"I'm telling you right now, Jan. I'll give you some money and you rent a truck, take your stuff and get away."

"Are you sure it's the right thing to do?" she asked.

"Positive," he grinned. "Rent a truck and go somewhere. Be gone in the morning."

"You're not going to burn the bar down, are you?"

"Hell, no!" Tommy halfway laughed but then answered, "I'm just going to wipe his nose for him."

Tommy Dollarhide went home and called Mikie, the actor, and told him, "I'm in, let's clean the bastard out. He got me fired."

"If anyone can do it, you can, big guy. I'll be there in a half hour."

Mikie arrived at four and Jan came at six-thirty. Tommy Dollarhide took them both out to the garage and took down the mower bag. He then counted out thirty thousand dollars and handed it to Jan.

"Here," he told her, "go have a good life."

"Where did you get this?" she asked. "Did the girls give you all this money?"

"Never mind, just consider it a going-away present from Charmichael."

Jan reached up and kissed him and said, "You're the magic man, Tommy." She left, rented a U-haul truck, and her and her boyfriend, with the help of her next-door neighbors, loaded her things, and she left Seattle at one in the morning.

Jan was gone.

Mikie stood smiling, a few feet to the side, as Tommy gave the money to Jan. He said nothing, and then Tommy took the rest of the money and put it in a paper sack and handed it to Mikie. "Here, buy the trucks and stuff."

Mikie took the money and put it in his trunk then came back. "We have to make a plan," he told Tommy.

"We have to wait until John gets home and then figure all of this out. He's doing his collection and won't be done for a week," Tommy told him, "so just sit tight and wait and see what happens when Charmichael finds out I won't go back to work for him, and Jan is gone."

They decided to meet again on the 5th of September when John was finished.

Wednesday, the 24th of August, Jack Charmichael called the Tropics and got no answer. He drove down there and found it closed. He called one of his men and told them to go to Jan's house and see what was going on with her. The guy called him an hour later and told him the apartment was empty. She had moved away during the night.

"Go find that Dollarhide guy and bring him to the Madison," Charmichael told him.

The man drove to Tommy Dollarhide's house and parked in the alley beside the garage, then went to the door and Tommy answered it.

He told Tommy to get his shoes on and come with him without even saying who he was.

"What?" Tommy answered.

"Get your shoes on, Jack wants to see you."

"Get lost," Tommy told him, and shut the door.

The guy just opened the door and stepped into the house and started to tell Tommy Dollarhide he had better come with him, except Tommy reached out and grabbed him by his throat with one hand and by his hair with his other one. He twisted his head to one side until it was laying on his shoulder and he was looking at his own butt, then picked him up off the floor and took him back outside the house and stood there with his hand around the guy's throat, pulling his head sideways by his hair, choking him and asked, "Who wants to see me?"

"Jack Charmichael," the guy choked, barely able to speak and trying to touch the ground with his toes.

"He sent you to get me?" Tommy asked, choking him harder and twisting his head around backwards by his hair.

The guy tried to shake his head yes, but could only get a grunt out. Tommy Dollarhide dragged the guy around the corner of the house, slammed him against his car four times, caving in both side doors, and hit him in the belly four times until he had almost lost consciousness.

"You tell him I ain't interested," Tommy said, then shoved him into the back seat of his car and put it in gear, letting it roll down the alley and out into the street and across the street, finally running into a light post across the street, smashing the front of the car in.

The cops were there before the guy could regain his composure, and had to try and explain what had happened. He got a ticket for reckless driving and his car was towed.

He walked down to Rainier Avenue and called Jack Charmichael and told him, "He said he ain't interested. He almost killed me and smashed my car up."

"Go get him and bring him here," Charmichael demanded.

"Fuck you! He almost broke my neck and pulled half my hair out! My fucking car is wrecked," the guy said. "You better send about five guys over there, big ones, and I don't think they could do it either. I ain't going back, and don't call me anymore." He hung up.

Jack Charmichael gave up on getting Jan and Tommy Dollarhide back to work.

The Tropics nightclub was still closed when John Tru-Day finished his collections on the third of September. He called Jack Charmichael and told him he was done and that Tropics was not included in the receipts.

"I know. I need to find someone to run it. You want the job?" he asked.

"No, I don't, thank you anyway, Jack," he answered.

"I don't blame you, I wouldn't want it either. Thanks for doing a good job down there, John," Charmichael said, and then told him for the first time, "Thanks for calling me. Bye."

John Looked at Jacky and said, "I think Mary took the starch out of him."

The truck came and picked up a little less than two million dollars and left with it. John Tru-Day had lost all interest in keeping his bookkeeping business going and told Jacky the same.

"So what do we do now?" she asked.

"We just sit here and do as little as we can until I figure out something."

"Like what?" she asked, then said, "I'm out of money."

"I'll give you some, don't get excited; just go on like everything is good and fine."

"I need some now, my rent is due."

He got up and went to the safe and handed her a thousand dollars, and asked, "Will that hold you for a couple weeks?"

"I guess so. Thanks," she said, "but I'm still scared."

"We're all scared, Jacky," he answered.

They both went home for the weekend. Tommy was sitting on his porch drinking a beer when John walked out the back door.

"You're not working?" he asked.

"The son of a bitch had me fired so I would have to go back to work at the bar."

"It's still closed," John told him, "anyway, it was this morning when I went by there."

"Good. I hope it stays closed."

John watched Tommy drink part of his beer. "I'm in," Tommy said.

"In what?" John asked.

"Robbing the son of a bitch," Tommy answered. "The bastard tried to strong-arm me into going back to work for him. He sent some punk over here to get me. The guy walked right into my house and tried to tell me to go see Charmichael."

"He knows where we live?" John asked.

"Of course he does."

John stood there looking at Tommy. "What are we going to do?"

"I gave your money to Mikie to buy the trucks and tools with."

"All of it?"

"No. I gave some to Jan so she could get out of Seattle and away from him."

"It's all gone?"

"Ya, it's all gone."

"Thank God!" John said.

"Mikie is coming over here Sunday and we're going to figure out how to do this thing."

"I'm losing weight, Tommy, and I ain't got that much to lose," John said.

"Get yourself a drink and relax. Just figure out what you and Muriel Sue are going to do after it's done."

"I got that part figured out," he said. "There's a boat down in San Francisco I want to buy."

"A big boat?" Tommy asked.

"A big boat, one hundred twenty-five feet long. It's a schooner named 'The Searcher.' The captain is a guy named Michelangelo Augustus, after the artist that carved David. You've seen it, haven't you?"

"The boat or the statue?"

"The statue," John smiled, and then said, "I get excited just thinking about it. I was on it once and it's so--you have to see it, Tommy. A guy could go anywhere in the world if he had it."

"Buy it!" Tommy smiled. "But first, get yourself a beer and come talk."

Tommy Dollarhide and John Tru-Day sat and talked with Patty McShane, listening until Muriel Sue came home, then all four of them sat and talked until well after midnight.

It was decided. They were going through with the robbery. Muriel Sue was going to put the houses up for sale, cash in the insurance policies, and they were going to buy the boat.

Mikie was going to supply the trucks and tools needed, and Tommy was going to put them all together and make them look like Seattle City trucks.

Tommy and Patty were going to go to Wyoming and buy a small ranch there and raise horses.

All four of them were mostly drunk, including Patty McShane, who had her first drinks that night. She got sick and threw up.

For all their drunk plans of grandeur, the first thing they had to do was talk to Mikie.

Sunday September 4th, it was decided they needed a little more than the money Tommy had given to Mikie and the money Muriel Sue had, if they were going to buy the boat and the trucks and everything else.

Mikie insisted he wanted none of the money and he wanted to stay in Seattle, but he would help in every way he could help by getting the trucks and tools and everything else to make it happen.

Monday was the 5th of September and John Tru-Day went back to work. He sat in his office and did little.

Tommy Dollarhide met Mikie and they went to the Pioneer Vault Company, and looked it over, then went and played a few games of pool. Mikie won each one of them.

Patty McShane stayed in bed most of the day, sick from drinking the five beers the night before.

Muriel Sue filled out the papers to cash in the insurance and listed both houses with a friend she knew.

Tuesday, the sixth, not much happened except a man came and put a "for sale" sign up in front of the houses, and as soon as John saw it, he took it down, not wanting one of Charmichael's people to drive by and see they were planning on leaving.

Tommy Dollarhide went to look for a garage he could rent to work on the trucks in. He was two days away from finding out there was more to painting a truck than just spraying the paint on it.

Wednesday, the seventh, a man came to John Tru-Day's office and asked him a lot of questions about Tommy Dollarhide and the bartender, Jan. Had he seen them and had Tommy been spending a lot of money? He called Jack Charmichael and told him, "There's some guy down here asking me a lot of questions. What should I tell him?"

Charmichael was silent for a few seconds, and then said, "let me talk to him."

John handed the phone to the guy and after he listened for a few seconds he said, "All right, I guess you're OK with Jack," then he left, but John was still scared.

An hour later, Charmichael called him back and said, "I guess you're going to have to make the deposits this month. I got no one else to do it."

"I don't know what you're talking about, Jack," he answered, "What deposits? The truck took all the money except what you gave me."

Again Charmichael was silent for a few seconds, then he said, "Never mind, I'll do it myself."

Charmichael hung up and told the guy with him, "He doesn't even know about the payoffs. He's straight as a fucking yardstick."

"Ya? Well I don't trust those short guys," the man replied, "they all got a chip on their shoulder."

"He's straight, I trust him," Charmichael answered, and then said, "He's got it made down there. He's got his own business and a pretty girlfriend, a nice car and a house. Fuck! Six months ago he was in the Navy. He doesn't know anything, forget him."

"So what about that guy Dollarhide?"

"My advice is don't fuck around with him either; from what I've heard, he'll twist your head off and feed it to the chickens. He ain't the kind that steals. I'm betting on that guy Jerry and the guy that was with him when they got my place all torn up by that Mexican chick."

"Maybe she took the money."

"She was the one that called the fucking cops. Jesus Christ, man! Why do I pay you guys? Go find out where that guy Jerry lives and check him out, and his friend. I want my money back, I need it."

The guy left Charmichael's office and gave up trying to find the money stolen from the Tropics. He got into his car and said to himself, "Ya! Well you don't pay me enough, ya prick!"

Thursday, the eighth, Tommy decided he would practice painting on his own truck, so he rented a compressor and a spray outfit, then bought some masking paper and tape. By five in the evening he stood there looking at a mess. He was covered with paint, the truck was covered with paint, most of which was running down the side of it, and the dirt from the garage walls and roof was all over it, stuck in the wet paint. He stood looking at it, and decided he was no better at painting trucks than he was at wolf hunting. He took a shower, then bought five gallons of paint thinner and spent all day Friday washing the truck off for a second time.

Jack Charmichael went to the Pioneer Vault Company, and made the payoffs and used all of his own money to make up for what Mary Forbes had taken. He was not a happy man when he walked out.

"How you been, Jack?" the clerk inside the cage asked him.

"Not worth a shit, so shut the fuck up," he answered, and walked out.

John Tru- Day came home and walked out to the garage to see what Tommy had done. When he saw the truck and then saw Tommy standing there looking at it too, all covered with blue paint, he turned around and walked back out, then took Muriel Sue out to eat. He didn't want to be around Tommy, he was not happy either.

Friday, the ninth, Mikie called Tommy and asked, "Did you find a place to do the truck?"

Tommy thought about his own truck and answered, "Whose idea was it for me to do the painting?"

"I guess we just assumed you could do it. Why? Is there a problem?"

"No, I didn't find a place yet. I'm looking."

"I found you one not too far from your house. It's even got a paint booth in it."

"I ain't guaranteeing nothing," Tommy answered.

"Why don't you practice on your own truck first and figure it out?" Mikie asked.

"I did that already," Tommy answered. "You think I just painted the garage floor blue because I like the color?" He sounded disappointed and Mikie started laughing.

"Oh, OH!" he said, "not too good?"

"I guess I'll figure it out," Tommy answered.

"Want to meet me in the morning, about ten?"

"Where at?"

"I'll come get you. See ya, big guy." Mikie hung up and Tommy opened a fourth beer.

Saturday, the tenth, Mikie came and took Tommy to a garage behind an old building that belonged to a friend of his. It was an old painting company, and looked pretty good to Tommy. It had plenty of room to put all three trucks in, and it had no windows so he felt it was alright if he could learn to paint.

At four in the afternoon Mikie called him and said, "I got it all taken care of for you, big guy. My friend is going to let you work for him in his body shop for a week and learn how to paint."

"That's great," Tommy answered.

"You don't sound very excited about learning a new trade," Mikie kidded.

"Oh but I am," Tommy answered, then said, "I am." He hung up without saying goodbye, and Mikie laughed.

"What's funny," Sonia asked.

"Tommy's frustrated," Mikie answered.

"Oh, ok," Sonia answered, and walked off.

He spent the rest of the day mowing the yard and raking the grass as John Tru-Day sat and watched him and drank a couple beers. Every so often he pointed to a place Tommy had missed and finally Tommy looked at him and he got up and went into the house.

Sunday, the eleventh, Mikie, Sonia, John, Tommy, Patty McShane, and Muriel had another barbecue in the backyard, and then Mikie took Tommy and John back to look at the garage again. He gave Tommy the door keys.

Muriel Sue, Patty McShane, and Sonia Re'olo sat and talked about what was about to happen. All Sonia would say is "I hate that fucker guy, Mikie will take care of him one way or another."

Muriel Sue was ready to do whatever she had to, to get John away from Jack Charmichael, and Patty just said, "I'm not drinking beer anymore."

Mary Forbes was on a small island in the South Pacific, walking around on the beach and acting like she was the queen of the island, and she almost was. Every child on the island either followed her around or wanted to follow her around. She was giving away money to any family who need some.

Barbara Fieldsman was lying on her back on an air mattress, in a swimming pool, in Mesa, Arizona, getting her tan back.

Jan was in Kentucky with her family.

Jack Charmichael was in the Madison Hotel bar, getting drunk and talking to Bill Tacki. He was thinking out loud about Linn Morrison and Bill Tacki just looked at him for a few seconds, thinking, then said, "I saw her," then he walked off and started cleaning glasses.

At eleven pm, after the lights were turned out, Doug Hicks tore his t-shirt into several strips and then tied it around his neck and the faucet of the sink, and sat down with his butt four inches off the floor choking himself to death.

Doug Hicks was gone.

Monday, the twelfth, John Tru-Day went back to work and tried to do taxes, but in his mind he was thinking more about the Pioneer Vault Company than he was his work. Jacky answered the phone and tried to be cool, but she was also fidgety.

Tommy Dollarhide went to work at the body shop and learned how to mask off a car so the paint wouldn't get on places it wasn't supposed to be. There was more to it then he thought. It took him almost all day before he was told he was doing it right. Mikie's friend told him if he wanted he could paint his truck in the paint room and the painter would help him do it so it would turn out nice.

"Man, that's real nice of you, thanks a lot!" Tommy answered.

"Thank Mikie," the man said, "if it wasn't for him I wouldn't have a shop to paint in."

About 2:00 pm some girl John Tru-Day didn't know came into the office. She looked sort of like Mary Forbes, and her butt was about the same size. She brought back four folders belonging to the guy whose taxes he was supposed to have done three months back.

"I'm Sherry. I'm Jack's new personal," then she smiled and said, "whatever you call it, errand girl? Well you know, Jack said to charge him fifteen hundred. He gave me a bill. It's for you," then she looked at the bar and said, "Can I make you drink?"

John looked at her and said, "You got an envelope for me too?"

"Oh Yes! I almost forgot," she laughed.

"I don't suppose you got a sister named Mary, do you?" he asked.

"I do, do you know her?"

"No," he answered, "but you remind me of someone with that name."

"You mean Mary, Mary? She robbed Jack, you know, you want a drink?"

"No, and neither do you; goodbye," John told her.

She looked at him then said, "Jeeze, you're no fun. Mary was right, you are a creep!" and walked out.

John shook his head and muttered, "I didn't think there could be two of them."

Jacky looked at him and said, "Kinda strange, isn't it?"

"What ain't?" he returned.

The envelope had his normal ten hundred dollar bills in it and a bill for the guy's taxes. He gave Jacky five hundred of the thousand and put the rest in his wallet.

"Why are you paying me so much?" she asked

"Give it back if you don't want it."

"I want it." She stuffed the money in her purse.

"We might need all we can get real soon," he said and went home.

Tuesday, the thirteenth, the painter, John, gave Tommy Dollarhide his first lesson on how to mix paint and let him paint a couple old things. They turned out pretty good.

John Tru-Day sat at his desk, turned around in his seat, looked at Jacky's underpants, watched the news on TV, smoked a big black cigar until Jacky asked him to do it outside, and he told her to "buzz off." So she went outside until he put it out. He had a few drinks then went home.

Jack Charmichael spent most of the day on the phone about construction problems with Jake Morrison and several other people who wanted money.

Linn Morrison spent the day in school and at her friend's house, making plans to get the car from Jack Charmichael.

Wednesday, the fourteenth, Jack Charmichael came to John Tru-Day's office in the early afternoon to meet with Jake Morrison next door. He waited in John's office, and sat on the couch sipping a drink and looked at Jacky for a long time, then asked her if she wanted to work at the Tropics club. He wasn't mean or pushy. He offered her a good salary and told her she would be the manager as well as the day bartender.

She asked him if she could talk it over with John and he said "yes," then said, "He's the one guy I can trust right now," then added, "Hey, no hard feelings if you don't want to. I'll understand, it's a rough place." He left after talking to Jake Morrison for a few minutes in the other office.

Jacky ask John Tru-Day if she should take the job and he said it was up to her, she knew what she was getting herself into.

"You think he'll rape me?" she asked.

"Probably," John told her, "unless you just give in to him."

"He never has yet," she said.

"Maybe he ain't interested in you that way," John answered.

They went home and Jacky decided to start managing the Tropics. She told Jack Charmichael the next morning that she wanted the job and she was supposed to start the next Monday. John was disappointed and knew she was headed for trouble, but he didn't care. He wasn't going to be around that much longer to worry about her. Then, as he was driving home he got another of his ideas. He had seen a money bundler that had been rigged to steal money while he was in the service, and thought it pretty smart, except the guy talked and got caught before he had a chance to use it. They would never have caught the guy, but he bragged about it and someone told on him. No one was going to tell on him, and he needed money to buy a ship with. What was the worst that could happen? Charmichael could kill him.

Mikie drove Sonia Re'olo to a car lot and bought a repossessed, almost new, Chevrolet 3/4-ton van truck. She drove it home.

Muriel Sue put both houses up for sale and cashed in the insurance account from her late husband. As Tommy was learning about painting trucks, and Patty McShane was cooking, Muriel Sue signed the papers and sold both houses. She started worrying as she started picking out some things and putting them into boxes.

On Thursday the 15th, Jack Charmichael got another letter in a blue envelope:

Meet me at the hotel Saturday at noon.

Linn

He was pissed, and tired of her acting so smart. He decided he was just going to take her some place and do it to her, and not just do it to her, he was going to do it to her until she was used up and then he was going to stick her in a house somewhere and keep her there. Except, he got carried away Friday night when he went to a different bar and saw a different girl who looked a lot like Linn Morrison.

He had her dance for him and bought her a few drinks and got a little too drunk himself, then took her into the office. She told him she wanted fifty dollars to have sex with him and he got mad. He smiled and handed her fifty dollars, then turned her around and pushed her down onto her knees, then shoved her face down into a chair and almost smothered her while he pulled off her costume bottoms, then shoved himself into her back door. She screamed and cried, and finally gave up and let him finish.

Jack Charmichael let her stand up, and then watched her standing in front of him crying.

"That hurt me!" she cried.

He bent over and picked up the fifty dollar bill she had dropped on the floor and put it back in his pocket and walked out of the office. He was only eight blocks from the club when he got pulled over by three cop cars. He was arrested for rape and went to jail, cussing all the way there.

The girl was taken to the hospital and had to bend over and let a nurse examine her backside while a female cop stood there watching.

"She's been penetrated, but there is no sign of forced entry," the nurse said.

"Did you try to fight him off you?" the cop asked her.

"No, how could I?" she answered.

"Did you try to scream for help?"

"No! I couldn't," she answered, "he had my face in a chair, I could hardly even breathe."

"Well, did you tell him you didn't want him to do it to you like that?"

"No," she answered.

"Did you tell him to stop?"

The girl looked at her, and then cried, "You just try to talk with some guy's dick up your butt and see how you like it."

"Did he pay you?" the cop asked.

"No! He took the money with him," she cried.

The female cop called the detectives and told them she was a hooker who just got stiffed.

"I guess she did. Right in the ass, huh?" the detective answered and hung up. He went and told Jack Charmichael, "You're lucky, fella. Really lucky, if I had my way I'd lock you up and keep you locked up. You can go."

"How about giving me a ride to my car?" Charmichael asked him.

"Don't push your luck. I can still charge you with assault."

Jack Charmichael was shaking as he left the jail. He wasn't going to do that again.

Friday, the sixteenth of September, John Tru-Day went out to the garage and took the money bundler he had bought apart, and then made a little adjustment to the machine. He put a rubber band hooked to a bent paper clip inside the rollers so every twentieth bill would not be counted but shuffled past the roller and dropped into the bottom of the machine. Most of the time, the manager of the club would stand and watch him count the money. This way, they couldn't see his stealing it. He figured even if Jack Charmichael found out about it he would already be gone. And he wasn't going to steal Charmichael's money, but the money from the clubs. He would steal Charmichael's later. Right now, he needed the money to get the boat and supplies.

Tommy had painted two cars that belonged to a used car lot, so if the job was a little bad it didn't matter too much, but they turned out pretty good.

"You want to paint your truck this weekend?" the painter asked him.

"Sure, what color?" Tommy returned.

"It's your truck, I don't care what color you paint it."

"Red?" Tommy asked.

"Any color you want," the painter told him. "Be here at seven, and we'll get it done."

Saturday, the seventeenth, Tommy went to paint his truck.

John Tru-Day slept until almost eleven in the morning while Muriel Sue packed a few more things and Patty McShane washed clothes.

Jack Charmichael was in the Madison Hotel in his room, more or less waiting to meet Linn Morrison at noon. He had just gotten out of the shower when Bill Tacki knocked on his door.

"I got some bad news for you, Jack," he said.

"What now?" Charmichael asked.

"Your wife died last night. They want you to come home right away."

"Son of a bitch, that's all I need!" was all Charmichael said, and closed the door. He got dressed and went home.

Linn Morrison came to the Madison and sat and waited for him for about an hour, then stomped out, giving Bill Tacki a dirty look as he grinned back at her.

"It's not funny," she sneered.

"His wife died last night," Tacki told her.

"So what's that got to do with me?" she asked, and walked out.

Jack Charmichael went to his house and stayed there until they took his wife's body away. His daughter was crying and he told her to shut the fuck up.

"Now are you going to make me move out of the house?" she cried.

"I hadn't thought about it, but now that you mentioned it, how old are you?"

"I'm only seventeen," she cried.

"You finish high school yet?"

"No, I had to quit," she cried, "I had to take care of Mom. You were never here."

He turned and walked out of the house, leaving her standing there, crying.

He went back to the Madison and got drunk. No one spoke to him and he spoke to no one. He went up to his apartment at six and stayed there all night.

Tommy had his truck all masked off and ready to paint. In the morning, he borrowed a truck from the paint shop and came home. He ate a steak and some mashed potatoes and green beans, and three slices of bread and butter, and drank three big glasses of milk, then ate two pieces of apple pie, then took a beer and went out into the yard and sat in a chair with John Tru-Day until it got dark, then they all went to bed.

Sunday, the eighteenth, Tommy went to the shop and painted his truck red. It turned out good. He was proud of himself. He felt he could paint the three trucks well enough so no one could tell the difference, unless they looked real close at them. He drove it home and Patty McShane said it looked really nice, so did John Tru-Day, and so did Mikie.

Jack Charmichael stayed at the Madison and didn't answer the five phone calls from his daughter. He was trying to decide what to do about her, maybe just give her the house and let her go on her own, or send her to a school. He thought the school was the best thing to do for her, if he could find one that would take her. He got drunk and almost fell when he stood up from the bar stool. He went to bed at seven-thirty.

Monday, the nineteenth, John Tru-Day went to Portland and started his monthly rounds, but this time, his money machine was playing the same game Mary Forbes had played in the Pioneer Vault. Only he just took five percent of the clubs' money.

Tommy Dollarhide went to the garage and started cleaning it so he could paint the trucks.

Mikie and Sonia Re'olo brought the van to the garage and parked it inside, then left.

Jack Charmichael spent most of the day taking care of his wife's needs and trying to decide what to do about his daughter.

Patty McShane and Muriel Sue spent most of the day talking about what was going to happen to them if Tommy and John got caught.

Jacky spent her first day at the Tropics, not knowing what to do or how to do it, because Jack Charmichael was busy doing other things.

John Tru-Day came home and put $99,641 in the safe for Charmichael and then emptied the bundler into a sack and took it home and put it in the old lawn mower basket in Tommy's garage without counting it. He knew there was $8,316, all from the clubs.

Tuesday, the twentieth, he went to Tacoma and came home, then put $101,375 in the safe, and another $9,266 in the lawn mower basket.

Jack Charmichael went to the Tropics and showed Jacky how to do the tills and gave her a guide book for bartenders. "Hell, most of them know how to make the drink they want, so just ask them how to make them. The night bartender is supposed to be here early and help you out for a few days if he shows up," and then he said, "You'll get the hang of it pretty quick," and left.

An hour later, a young man named Tony came in and spent the day helping her get started. He was the night bartender, but by the time he was supposed to go to work he was already drunk and Jacky called Jack Charmichael but got no answer. She called John Tru-Day and got no answer. She went home, leaving Tony to work behind the bar drunk.

Tommy Dollarhide started masking off the van truck and cleaning it. He finished, then drove his truck to the tire shop and had the guy take his tires off and put them inside out to hide the blue paint he had let drip on all of them. The truck looked almost new. "Nice and shiny and red."

Wednesday, the twenty-first, Mikie came to the garage and told Tommy, "If we're going to do this, we have to do it before Thanksgiving weekend, or all the money will be gone. They'll take it out and use it over the holidays."

Tommy answered by saying, "If? Is there an 'if'?"

"What you're doing looks good," Mikie told him. "I'll have Sonia bring you a spray rig in the morning. See ya, big guy." He left.

Jacky did better, and the night bartender didn't get drunk so she went home feeling a little more relaxed.

John Tru-Day came home and dropped another $11,771 in the basket.

Muriel Sue saw him go into the garage and come back out two nights in a row, and asked him what was in there.

"Trust me, you don't want to know," he answered.

"What am I going to do if you guys get caught? And what about Patty? She has nothing if Tommy goes to jail," she said.

"Wait?" he answered.

"Twenty years?" she returned.

"Even if we get caught, they won't do anything to us. I'll just say I was going to turn in the money and put Jack Charmichael in jail where he belongs."

"We don't even have an attorney. I don't even know one, do you?"

"Mikie has one or two, or knowing him, probably a dozen of them that will help us. I'm not worried," he said, and kissed her.

"I feel really insecure right now, John," she said.

"And I know the answer for that too," he returned and led her into the bedroom.

Jack Charmichael went to the funeral home and picked out a coffin for his wife. The funeral was to be Friday. He went to the Madison and got half drunk and didn't return the seven calls from his daughter.

Thursday, the twenty-second, Charmichael went home and stayed there all day because his wife's family came for the funeral. He told his daughter he was going to send her to a private Catholic school in West Virginia on Monday.

She told him she wasn't going and he answered by telling her to shut the fuck up, and she was going there or to reform school until she eighteen, and she wasn't getting one red cent of his money if she didn't go and try to graduate.

"What about my boyfriend?" she cried.

Charmichael didn't answer her, just walked away.

Mikie and Sonia Re'olo brought a spray rig in the back of a Ford pickup he had brought to the garage for Tommy to use.

John Tru-Day put another $12,300 in the lawn mower basket.

Jacky went to work and had a nice day of it. She earned over a hundred in tips. Eleven of the girls were back and all of them were giving her advice about everything.

Friday, the twenty-third, Charmichael spent the day going to his wife's funeral and then with the family. He went to the Madison Hotel bar at nine in the evening and got drunk. He stayed in his apartment and didn't go back home.

Tommy started painting the van truck, but stopped after one coat. It looked like hell. The paint was running, and he started washing it down. The garage was too cold. He had to get a heater.

Linn Morrison called Jack Charmichael at his office. Wilma knew who it was and told her, "You listen here young lady, you're heading for a lot of trouble and you best just stop right now before your dad finds out what you're up to."

Linn hung up on her.

Saturday, the twenty-fourth, Jack Charmichael packed his daughter up and sent her off to school. She was not happy.

Tony came in drunk and told Jacky he couldn't work. She was not happy.

Linn Morrison called Jack Charmichael five times and got no answer. She was not happy.

Tommy tried again and figured out he had too much pressure turned on the spray gun. He started washing down the truck a second time. He was not happy.

It dawned on Muriel she was going to have to leave her house and friends when she gave notice she was quitting her job at Boeing, and she and all her friends cried. She was not happy.

Patty McShane burned her roast and the cake she was trying to make. She was not happy.

John Tru-Day came home and put another $13,446 in the basket. He was getting happier every day and had five beers before Tommy came home.

"Who the hell decided I was supposed to paint these damn trucks?" Tommy said as he walked by John sitting on his porch.

"Not going well?" John asked him.

Tommy lifted up his foot and showed his boots, all covered with paint, to John.

"What the hell do you think?" he walked off to his house.

"If I knew how, I'd help you," John called after him.

"If I knew how I wouldn't be so damn frustrated," Tommy closed the door.

"Can we go out to eat, Tommy?" Patty asked.

"I ain't hungry," he answered, and got a beer from the fridge, on his way to take a shower.

Jack Charmichael sat in the bar at the Madison Hotel and thought about what had happened to him in the past month. He was not happy either.

Sunday the 25th of September Jacky closed the bar at 2 am and started to put the money in the safe then saw how much was already in it and got scared because she didn't have a key to lock it with. She tried to call John Tru-Day and got no answer. She tried Jack Charmichael and got no answer. She put the money in a paper sack and carried it out to her car with the intentions of taking it to John's office and putting it in the safe there. She sat the bag on the top of her car and unlocked the door, then put her things in the back seat, then put her purse in the front seat and got in the car and drove five blocks before she realized she had left the bag on the roof of the car. She stopped and it was not there.

"Oh my God!" she screamed, and went back to look for it. She found it. A car had run over it and the wind was blowing money everywhere. She got out and tried to pick as much of it up as she could while cars were driving past making more wind and scattering it everywhere. Then a cop came and she had to stop while he asked her what she was doing, and showed him her ID cards and driver's license. Then he tried to help her. When it was done, about one third of the money had blown away, across a fence and into a field.

"God, I'm in trouble now," she cried.

And when the cop found out who she worked for he agreed, "I'd say you're in trouble," he said, then told her, "I wish I could help you, but I think you're on your own with this one, lady, good luck."

"I'm dead. God, I'm dead," she cried, and drove to John Tru-Day's office, and put the money in his desk drawer, then went home.

She went back to John Tru-Day's office in the afternoon and waited for him to come back from north Seattle.

"God! You won't believe what I did, John," she cried.

"Yes, I will," he answered, and she told him the story.

"Don't worry about it. Just come here in the morning and I'll go through the receipts and give you the difference. Jack will never know it happened."

"Thank you, thank you!" she cried and left.

Except the cop who was a deputy sheriff told the sheriff and the sheriff called Jack Charmichael and told him what had happened, and before Jacky got to her house, two men grabbed her and took her to the Madison Hotel to meet Jack Charmichael.

She told him why and how it happened, and that the rest of the money was at John Tru-Day's office.

Jack Charmichael blew up and screamed and cussed at her, then told the men to take her to Tacoma and put her in a house he had down there, and she was going to work it off.

Jacky cried and screamed and cried some more, as the two men put her in a car and drove her to Tacoma and then dragged her into a two-story house, and locked her in a room.

Jack Charmichael called John Tru-Day the next morning and asked how much she had lost. John said, "Maybe a few hundred, a thousand at the most," then he did the books and replaced what was missing with seven thousand dollars from the money he had taken from the clubs in north Seattle.

Charmichael thought a night in the house would teach her to be more careful. He called the madam and told her to let the girl go in the morning, and only keep her overnight, but don't make her do any tricks, just scare the hell out of her.

The madam went to the room and took Jacky out and down into the basement into a small bedroom and told her, "You owe Jack five thousand dollars and you're going to turn tricks until you pay him back. You charge fifty a trick and the house gets twenty-five. You pay five for new sheets each trick, and fifty a day rent for the room. And I get half your tips, so don't try to hold out on me because I'll know if you do. I've been doing this for thirty years and I know every story you can make up.

"I'm getting twenty dollars each man?" Jackie cried. "How many do I have to do every day?"

"Oh, fifteen or twenty," the madam told her. "You'll have him paid off in no time, honey." Then she left the room and locked the outside door from the inside with a padlock and went up the stairs and locked the stairway from the outside. Jacky sat on the bed and cried until she saw three things: a crowbar, a can of gas by the lawn mower, and a pile of old newspapers and magazines. She took the crowbar and pried the lock off of the outside door, then took the can of gas and started at the pile of papers and ran a trail across the room, up the three stairs and outside, then down the driveway until the can was empty, then she lit the gas and ran as fast as she could, until she saw a taxi and flagged it down and had the driver take her to John Tru-Day's office in south Seattle while Jack Charmichael's most profitable whorehouse burned to the ground.

While Jacky was en route to John's office, the madam called Jack Charmichael from the phone booth across the street and screamed at him, "That girl burned my fucking house down, you stupid moron bastard! Why'd you bring her here anyway, what am I going to do now?"

"What the hell are you talking about?" he asked.

"She burned my fucking house down. She set it on fire and burned it down. Listen," she held the phone out so he could hear all the people and the fire trucks.

"Did you get the money out?" he asked.

"Fuck, no, I didn't! I was damn lucky to get the girls out. You're paying me for my house, Jack, or I'll, I'll, by God, I'll do something to get even with you!" Then she slammed down the receiver and carried the cash box with her and went to her sister's house as seven girls stood on the street watching the house burn down along with all their clothes and wondered where to go.

Jacky knew exactly where to go, straight to the safe in John Tru-Day's office, where she grabbed one big sack of money and went to her boyfriend's house and then to Florida. She was in Idaho, four hours after the madam had called Jack Charmichael, going east at seventy-five miles an hour.

Jacky was gone with $7,200 of Charmichael's and John's money.

John returned from his last day of doing the clubs, and the phone was ringing when he walked into the office.

"You seen that Jacky girl?" Charmichael screamed.

"No," John answered.

"She burned my fucking house down," he yelled.

"What house?"

"The one on Ninth Street, in Tacoma."

"What was she doing there?"

"I sent her there to teach her a lesson."

"It didn't work very well, did it?"

"You know where she went?"

John looked at the open safe and said, "No, but I know where she's been."

"Where?"

"Here, the safe is empty."

"What do you mean empty?"

"I mean it's empty. The door's open, and the safe is empty."

"She went there and took the money from the safe?"

"If she didn't, someone else did," he said.

"How'd she get a fucking key? You give her yours?"

"No! I don't know where she got one, was there a duplicate?"

"Ya, and Mary Forbes had it!" he answered, then said, "Son of a bitch! First she loses my money, then she burns down the whorehouse, and then she robs us?"

"I think mine's still in there. Anyway, the envelope is still in there, let me look," John said, and laid the phone down. When he picked up the phone again there was no one on the other end. John Tru-Day wasted no time in grabbing the other six bags of money and stuffing them in the trunk of his car, thought about it, and returned four of them, keeping enough to make the down payment and stock the schooner.

He called Jack back and told him, "She dropped four of them in the planter in the hallway, I got them back."

"So how much did she get?"

"I don't know which bags are here, you'll have to come and open them before we know."

"Alright, I'll be there in an hour. Boy! Has this been a fucked-up two months or what?" he said, and hung up.

"It's just starting," John said under his breath, "it's just starting."

Tommy Dollarhide stayed home all day Sunday and wondered why John was so late getting back.

Mikie and Sonia Re'olo spent the day looking for a third truck and other things needed to rob the vault.

Patty and Muriel spent the day first shopping, then talking, and finished up drinking mixed drinks and then wine. Patty was sick as a dog by eight at night and threw up again.

Jack Charmichael came to John Tru-Day's office and sat there for about an hour as John used Jack's only key and opened the sacks, then told him how much was in each one.

He had three drinks and said, "I'm fucked! I'm a fucked duck on a stick. I'm going to have to sell something to make up for all this. It's like all these people are just trying to fuck me. You know what I mean? Hell, I ain't the fucking boss of this program. Shit! Every time I really get a good grip on it, some cocksucker comes along and fucks it up again. I got half a mind to just go back into the construction business and forget trying to make so much fucking money, but I'm in so deep. I can't get out. You know how many people I have to pay off each month just to keep going? Every fucking official in the fucking state

293

has his fucking hand out and reaching into my fucking pocket. It just pisses me off, John. You know what I mean?"

"No, but I can imagine," John answered.

"Well, let me give you some good advice, my small friend," Charmichael got up and made himself another drink, then motioned with his glass if John wanted another one too.

"I got enough left," John told him.

"Get the fuck out and away from me as soon as you can. This is a bunch of fucking bullshit. I'm going to have to sell one of my apartment houses to pay off what Mary fat-ass and that fucking house burner took. I got to pay for Helen's house too. You got any idea how much I'm losing each month now that it's burned down?

"About sixty-six thousand dollars?" John answered.

"You're pretty fucking smart, ain't you? You figured that out all by yourself," Charmichael was weaving as he walked back to the couch. John realized he was drunk as a skunk.

"So what should we do?" John asked.

"You got the brains in this outfit. You tell me, I'm going home." Charmichael tried to set his drink on the table and missed, it fell on the rug.

"Now I suppose I have to pay for that too," he said, and walked out the door. John watched him drive away up Rainier Avenue, and wondered if he could even make it to town. He left as soon as Charmichael was out of sight. He went straight to Tommy's and told him what he had in the trunk of his car.

"You're trying to get yourself in trouble, ain't you?" Tommy said, and told him to bring the money to the garage in the morning.

"I don't want to leave it in my car overnight."

"How many clubs you got left to do?"

"I'm done tomorrow."

"Throw them in the damn bushes and I'll take them to the garage in the morning," Tommy answered and started to walk away.

"If I open the trunk, the light will come on and someone might see me," John returned.

"You handle it. Patty's sick as a dog and I'm going to bed." Tommy walked back to his house and closed the door. John left the bags in his trunk all night and took them to the garage on his way to north Seattle to finish his rounds for the month. He was done at six in the evening. He didn't bother to empty the bundler. He just put it in the trunk of the Olds and left it there.

It was Monday, the twenty-sixth of September, and the weather had warmed up, plus Tommy had brought in two heaters. He painted the van Seattle City white and it looked good. Mike would bring the magnetic decals as soon as he got them.

At four in the afternoon, Mikie brought some things he had gotten from a city worker who worked in the city garage: top lights for the two pickups and traffic signs. He dropped them off and told Tommy the van looked perfect. He would bring another truck that afternoon.

Tuesday morning, John Tru-Day and Muriel Sue left for San Francisco on a plane with the money from her insurance policies and some of the money John had taken from the clubs, a total of $113,000, all in hundred dollar bills. They arrived at seven in the evening. They stayed in a hotel near the airport overnight.

Wednesday morning, they took a cab across the Golden Gate Bridge and went to a marina, a couple miles from it. They walked down a long pier, and there it was, sitting at the end of the pier, all three masts stacking up with small colored flags on them. The gate to the gangway was closed and locked, so they couldn't go on board, but Muriel Sue wanted it as soon as she saw it. The sign on the gate gave a phone number, and John Tru-Day went back and called it. One hour later, as they sat on a bench on the pier, a man about the same size as John Tru-Day came walking down the pier.

"That's him, that's the captain," John stood up, excited, and Muriel Sue stood up as the captain stopped in front of them. He was exactly the same size as they were.

"You remember me?" John asked.

"Ya, sure I do," he said in an Italian accent, then put his hand out to Muriel Sue, "Michelangelo Augusta," he introduced himself, "Would you like to go on board?"

John Tru-Day and Muriel Sue walked around on the schooner, and Muriel Sue fell in love with it, the mahogany walls and the small kitchen. It even had a laundry room with a steam press in it. All the dishes had the ship's name stamped on them with a small scroll under the letters written in gold leaf.

"I want it, John," she said. "I want it!"

They went into every compartment and Muriel Sue asked, "How does it stay so warm in here?"

"Central heating," The captain told her, "it has an oil-burning furnace."

After they had gone through the entire ship, John told him they would buy it.

"How would you like to pay for it? Cash or check?" Michael asked John.

"Cash!" John told him. "One hundred thousand down, and the rest as soon as we're in international waters. "

"I'm afraid that won't work," the captain smiled.

"How much does it cost?" Muriel Sue asked.

"The asking price is $950,000," Michael told her.

"Then there's the marina fees and the crew fees and the supplies and a lot more than just buying the boat. It has to be made seaworthy."

"So how much are we needing to get her underway?" John asked.

"With me or without me?" the captain asked.

"With you," John answered.

"About one million three should do us for at least seven or eight months, but then we'll have to stop once a month and outfit her again. Spoils, you know the things that don't keep forever," he smiled.

He had taken with him $23,000, plus the ninety Muriel Sue had in a check. He took the brown envelope containing the twenty three thousand in cash out of his overcoat and handed it to the captain.

"I'll come back down here in two weeks and give you enough to outfit her and I'll pay it in full the day before we leave, is that fair?"

"If you don't come back, I can't return any of this, you understand that, don't you?"

"If I don't come back, I won't need it," John answered.

Michael smiled at John and said, "Oh, I understand. It will take me exactly forty-five minutes to call the owner and tell him I have the cash in my hand, and then we could leave, assuming all other fees have been paid. I can carry the cash to him in person sometime after we have ported in a different country if you want it that way."

"That's how I want it. So how much should I bring you to buy supplies and pay all the fees and charges?"

"Do you want an American crew or the crew she has now?"

"Your crew," John answered.

"Where are we going?" the captain looked at Muriel Sue and she looked at John.

"All over," she answered.

"If you want it fully stocked and crewed, I would say," he thought for a few seconds and then told him, "one hundred twenty-five thousand dollars, and she will be seaworthy and ready to leave within one hour, whenever you're ready."

"How long will it take you?" John asked.

"About twenty days, depending on what you want for food and such things."

"I'll come back down here on the 17th of October and bring you the money," John told him.

They left the boat and Muriel Sue asked as they walked back up the pier, "Shouldn't you have gotten a receipt from him or something?"

"That schooner has been sitting there for two years. He'll do anything to get out to sea with her again."

"I guess you know what you're doing, John," she answered.

"No, I don't, none of us do," he returned.

They spent the rest of the week in San Francisco and came back on Sunday night, the second of October.

Wednesday, the twenty-seventh of September, Mikie brought the first pickup to the garage and Tommy told him,

"I want to go and look at this place before I ruin any more of my clothes."

Mikie took him to the Pioneer Vault Company, and they walked down into the vault room and Tommy looked at it. Mikie opened his own box and showed Tommy what the boxes were made of, and the locks. When they had left and were out on the street Tommy said, "A piece of cake, they're cracker boxes." He checked out the wall and manhole, the street and surrounding streets, and the way to leave town after they were finished. Then they drove around until they found a crew working and looked at everything they had, the barricades, and the railing, and the tent, and the blower mounted on the back of a tool truck with a huge compressor.

"Can you get all that stuff?" Tommy asked him.

It's in the works right now. We should have it all in a couple days," Mikie assured him.

"What about the tent? We need a tent and then just hope to hell it's raining."

"I got it all covered," Mike told him again, then said, "Don't worry about it. If there's the slightest thing wrong, we just wait until it's right, then do it."

"Where are we going to get a blower and a compressor like that?" Tommy asked. "And what about a jackhammer to go through the side of the manhole, and we need a cutting torch."

"I got it covered," Mike told him. "There's a used equipment place about eighty miles south and I'll send Sonia and her brother down there to get the stuff."

Jack Charmichael got a call from Linn Morrison and she asked him to meet her. He hesitated, and then agreed. He said they could meet at a place somewhere else, but not at the Madison Hotel. She told him about a restaurant she knew where her and her friends hung out and he said he would meet her there at five in the evening. He picked her up and drove her to downtown Seattle, and they went into a small bar restaurant, and drove right past Jake Morrison, who saw his daughter in the car with Jack Charmichael sitting right next to him on the seat, and exploded. He turned his truck around and tried to follow them, but lost them by the time he got through traffic.

He was mad, to say the very least, and as soon as he got home he took one of his handguns out of the cabinet and put it in his truck, then drove back to downtown and went looking for Jack Charmichael. He kept calling his wife and asking if Linn was at home yet, as he drove from one place to another, looking for Jack Charmichael, with every intention of just walking up to him and shooting him in the head.

He looked for them until after ten in the evening when he had gotten over being so angry. He drove home to wait for Linn. As soon as she walked in through the door, he dragged her into his den and told her, "If I so much as hear about you talking to him again, so help me, Linn, I don't know what I'll do, but you just better not ever talk to him again. He'll rape you and put you in a whorehouse and we won't be able to ever find you. He'll get you hooked on drugs and dope and you'll be dead in two years. You got it?"

And of course Linn Morrison lied and said, "But it's him, he's been calling me at my friends' houses, and he waited for me at school. He was mostly talking about you and asking me questions about you."

"I know you too well, and I know Jack Charmichael," he said. "Don't call him again. I mean it."

Linn Morrison paid absolutely no attention to what he said and tried to call Jack Charmichael from her room and tell him to watch out because her dad knew about them. The problem was, Jake Morrison saw the light on his five line phone light up and put the phone on speaker, as he listened to Linn Morrison leave Jack a message.

"Jack, my dad knows about us seeing each other, be careful. I told him you were just asking about him." Then, before she could hang up, her dad came into the room and ripped her phone out of the wall and threw it across the room.

"You think I'm kidding?" he screamed, "I mean it. I'll beat the living shit out of you. I will, Linn. I mean it. Don't talk to him again."

Then, the next morning he walked past Wilma and into Jack Charmichael's office and stuck the gun in Jack Charmichael's face and cocked the hammer, then told him: "You mess with my daughter, mister, and I'll blow your God damn head off."

Jack Charmichael looked down and into the 3/8-inch opening of the barrel of the .44 Magnum and couldn't talk because he was too scared to say anything or even move. He thought he had lived his last minute on earth when he saw the gun hammer being pulled back. He could see the head of the bullet, halfway down the barrel. He sat there and didn't move until Jake Morrison walked out of his office.

"Satisfied?" Wilma called into his office.

For the first time since she knew him, he had nothing to say. She looked in and he was sitting at his desk. His face was a very pale grey, and she could see him shaking all the way from the door, fifteen feet away.

Twenty minutes later, Wilma stuck her head in his office and said, "She's on the phone, you want to talk to her?"

Jack Charmichael picked up the phone and screamed into the receiver, "You fucking almost got me killed, you little bitch! If you ever call me again, I'll have someone haul your ass off and stick you in a whorehouse and leave you there fucking for a dollar a trick. You hear me? I mean it! Don't call me again!" He slammed down the phone.

For all practical purposes, Linn Morrison was gone, and so were her hopes of trading her virginity (which she had already lost when she was fifteen, to a boy she didn't even know) for a robin-egg blue Porsche.

At four in the afternoon, Mikie came back to the garage and brought with him four sets of coveralls and hard hats, plus a box full of Seattle City decals and numbers for Tommy to stick on the trucks after he had them all painted and outfitted. He said Sonia and her brother were down in a different town, buying a blower and a few other tools. He said they were getting an electric jackhammer. It was lighter and more quiet. He said Sonia's brother was a construction worker and knew a lot about tools.

Thursday, the twenty-eighth of September, not much happened, except Tommy painted the second truck and Sonia, her brother, and Mikie brought a third truck loaded with tools and a tent. They unloaded it, and Sonia's brother stayed to help Tommy install the generator and the blower on the truck he had finished painting. Then he put the decals on it, and the lights on top.

"The only thing missing is the license plates," he said, "but if you park with the back of the truck to the tent, you won't need them. No cop is going to look twice at a city truck going down the street." They finished at two in the morning.

Friday the twenty-ninth, Tommy and Sonia's brother painted the third truck and went home, leaving it to dry overnight.

Jack Charmichael's new errand girl was in trouble. She had tried to manage the Tropics bar and had everything all messed up. None of the girls liked her and Charmichael told her to go back to wherever she had come from. He closed the bar again and told Wilma to put an ad in the paper for a manager and bartenders.

Mike came to Tommy's house and told him it was going to happen the weekend just before Thanksgiving, the weekend of November 12, 13, 14, if Charmichael made his payoffs on the tenth or eleventh like he always did. If not, they would do it the next weekend, the 19th.

"Kinda soon, ain't it?" Tommy asked.

"If we wait any longer, most of the money will be gone. They'll take it out for the holidays."

Tommy looked at him sort of funny and said, "Shit!"

"What?"

"I got to get ahold of my sister and have her come out here."

"What for?" Mike asked.

"I ain't leaving my furniture and truck," he told him. "I got to send her some money so she can bring a U-haul truck and a tow bar."

"Western Union," Mike said.

"There ain't no Western Union in Miles City. She'll have to go to Billings and start from there, but first I got to get a message to her, and have her call me."

"Call her."

"She don't have a phone, and the closest one is in town. Now, who do I call?" he asked.

"I don't know," Mikie answered then said, "I'll see ya, big guy." He left.

The only person Tommy knew well enough to have them go tell his sister to call him was the clerk at the ranchers association, and he was H. C.'s brother-in-law, so he didn't know if he would do it or not, and it was the only phone number he knew.

He called the number and the clerk, Raymond, answered, "Rancher's Ass."

"This is Tommy Dollarhide."

"Hey! You a mind reader? We were just talking about you, you want to talk to Two Trees?"

"Is he there?"

"Standing right in front of me, here."

"Hey Tommy, how you doing?"

"Listen. Go tell my sister to call me. You got a pencil?"

"Raymond does if he lets me use it."

"Write down my phone number, and as soon as you hang up, go tell my sister to call me collect. You got the pencil?"

"Ya but I don't have any paper. Raymond, can I use a piece of your paper? Go ahead, Tommy."

"7-5-4-6-7-8-1, in Seattle. Tell her to call me right now! Not tomorrow, or this afternoon, right now, as soon as you can walk over there and she can get to the phone."

"She's over at the store right now, shall I go over there and tell her?"

"Ya. Don't make jokes, this is important. Go tell her to call me collect right now."

"See ya, Tommy." Two Trees hung up.

It took his sister over an hour to call him back. As soon as he said he would accept the charges she told him, "Tommy, Yackaty-Yack Carol was on the phone. You know how long she talks to her mom. I had to tell her to shut up and get off the phone. How you doing, Tommy?"

"Listen," he said.

"OK, Tommy," she answered.

"I want you to get Two Trees and Joe Jackson and go to Billings.

"What for, Tommy?"

"Listen!"

"OK, Tommy."

"Get Two Trees and Joe Jackson and go to Billings, then go to Western Union and I'm sending you some money. Get on a Greyhound bus, and come to Seattle."

"When?"

"Right now, if you can."

"How are we going to get to Billings?"

"Have George Morgan drive you. Tell him you'll give him fifty dollars if he does."

"Tommy, I ain't got fifty dollars."

"I'm sending you money. Have him call me. Go find him right now."

"He's over at the tavern drinking beer."

"Where's Joe Jackson?"

"Where he always is, standing right by Two Trees."

"Go to the tavern and don't say anything, just have George Morgan call me if he don't believe you, and bring your good clothes because you ain't going back there."

"What clothes are those, Tommy? I don't got no good clothes" she asked.

"Never mind, just go tell George to drive you to Billings and go to the Western Union, and make sure you got your ID and Two Trees has his driver's license on him. Call me as soon as you get the money and don't drink, and don't let those two drink, not one beer until you're here, and don't lose the phone number, call me in three hours."

"OK, Tommy. I'll try to do what you said," he heard her tell the two men, "We got to go to Seattle and help Tommy do something," then the phone went dead.

He drove to the Western Union on Rainier Avenue, and sent two hundred dollars to Billings, then came home and waited.

It took a little over four hours, and his sister called back.

"George only wanted twenty dollars, Tommy."

"OK, you got the money?"

"Yes, two hundred dollars."

"Ok, go get on the Greyhound and call me when you get here."

"All three of us?"

"Yes, all three of you. Get the next bus out of there today and you'll be here tomorrow afternoon, and call me from the bus station, and no drinking until you get here."

"OK, Tommy," she said then asked, "Can we spend some of the money on eating?"

"Just don't drink!" he said.

Thirty minutes later, she called again, "OK, Tommy, we're at the bus station."

"I said call me when you get here, not when you get there."

"You said to call from the bus station, so I did."

"OK, I'm glad you did. When does the bus leave?"

"We'll get there tomorrow at five twenty," she said, then asked, "Is that OK with you?"

"That's fine with me. I'll be at the bus station when you get here."

"Bye, Tommy. I hope I don't get sick riding on the bus. I did one time, remember?"

"Just get on the bus and get here, OK? Did Two Trees bring his driver's license?"

"Yes, so did Joe Jackson, but he can't drive a truck with a clutch because of his knee, you know, just a car."

"Fine, just don't drink."

"OK, Tommy, bye."

Saturday, September thirtieth, Tommy took Patty McShane with him and went to the garage. They took the masking paper off the one-ton truck, and cleaned up the garage so Muriel Sue could store the things she hadn't gave to Tommy and Patty in it. Mikie was going to send them to her wherever she and John Tru-Day ended up settling.

At three-thirty they drove to downtown Seattle in Muriel Sue's car and went to the bus station and waited for Two Trees, Joe Jackson, and Tommy's sister. They got off the bus and looked like they had just come from the reservation, all ragged and worn out. People were looking at them and Tommy's sister told him, "I don't think I like city people too much. We ain't going to have to stay here, are we? Because I don't like it that much, Tommy. It smells like something bad."

"Two weeks, maybe three," he answered. Then took the two men to a motel on Rainier Avenue and got them a room. He brought his sister home with him, then went back and picked up Joe Jackson and Two Trees and took them across town, and had Two Trees rent a U-haul truck for November 1st.

Sunday, October first, John Tru-Day and Muriel Sue came back home in the afternoon and John got ready to go back to work.

"I'm about out of money," Tommy told him.

"Go look in the mower basket," John answered, then went and got the bundler out of the trunk of his car and took it with him out to the garage. He showed Tommy the money in the basket and then emptied the bundler out on the

310

workbench. Together, they counted $96,368. Tommy took eight thousand and intended on using it to buy a trailer to put his truck and freezer on, and pay for Two Trees to move to Wyoming and wait for him there. John intended to use the rest and what Muriel Sue had from the insurance and the houses to outfit the schooner. He told Tommy, "It looks like we're just about set to do it. Now all we have to do is cover our departure and make sure it looks like Charmichael did it. I want everyone to think he was behind all of it," John said.

"And how are you going to do that?"

"I got the wheels turning," John answered. "I spent a lot of time thinking during the past few days."

"Ya, I did too, and I found out I don't like painting trucks or being a mechanic," Tommy answered.

"But you're done now, just about, ain't you?"

"In more ways than one," Tommy answered.

"You're not pulling out on us, are you?"

"No, I'm just worried about Patty."

"I'm worried about Muriel Sue too. I mean, she sold her houses and cashed in her insurance, and quit her job."

"That's what I mean, if this thing goes wrong, John--" Tommy walked away, leaving John Tru-Day standing in the garage with $88,368, cash, stacked in little piles in front of him.

He shrugged his shoulders and said out loud, "What can go wrong? It's all falling into place like a set of Tinker Toys." He put the money away and went back to his house.

Monday, October second, Tommy went to see Two Trees and Joe Jackson at the motel. Two Trees was sitting in a chair, and Joe Jackson was lying on one of the two beds.

"I got to tell you guys something, and I don't want my sister to know anything about it. And I'm serious, not a word, give me your word on it." Both men gave their word and Tommy told them, "We're going to rob a crook, Two Trees, you're going to take a truck and my sister and my things to Wyoming and wait for me and Joe there."

"Where in Wyoming?"

"Jasper," Tommy told him.

Neither man spoke, they just looked at Tommy.

"Joe, you're going to help me and my friend, if you want to. If you don't it's OK, you can go with Two Trees.

"What are we doing?" Joe asked.

Tommy explained the whole plan, saying Joe Jackson would be up at the street level, pulling up the sacks of money, if there was as much as John thought there would be, while he and John were down in the vault opening the boxes. And after he was done, Joe asked, "They feed you good in jail, don't they?"

"Probably better than you been getting," Tommy answered.

"But no beer," Joe smiled and then said, "Hell, I need to stop for a while anyway. I been drinking too much lately."

"Lately?" Two Trees kidded.

"For a few years, lately," Joe returned.

They talked for a while, and then Tommy took them to the garage and showed them the trucks and equipment. Then he gave Two Trees five of the eight thousand dollars for traveling money and Two Trees took it and said, "Hell! I never seen this much money in my whole life before."

"No drinking, only when you're at my house. Got it?"

"We got it," both of them answered, and all three shook hands on the agreement.

They left the garage and went to Tommy's house. Patty and Tommy's sister Olla had food cooking on the stove, steaks and mashed potatoes and veggies, with Patty's apple pie still cooking in the oven.

"You sure got a nice house here, Tommy," Two Trees said then said, "You sure you want to leave it and go to Wyoming?"

"What did we agree on in the room?" Tommy asked.

"Oh, sorry, Tommy, I slipped up."

"Well, you do it in the wrong place and if the wrong guy hears you, we're all cooked meat. Don't forget it again," Tommy warned him.

They spent the rest of the afternoon eating twice and drinking a few beers until John Tru-Day came home, walked out into the backyard and stopped dead in his tracks when he saw the two Indians.

"Friends of yours?" he asked.

"Best friends," Tommy answered.

"You didn't tell them about the vault, did you?"

"No, but you just did," Tommy answered.

"What vault? What is it?" Joe Jackson asked him.

"It's where this guy keeps his money."

"Oh, OK," Joe answered as though it didn't really matter to him.

Tommy explained to John Tru-Day that Joe was going to be up with the trucks and Two Trees was going to take his truck and furniture to Wyoming, because Joe couldn't drive and Two Trees could come back and post the bail money if they got sort of caught.

"I don't think there's a sort of getting caught, is there?" John asked him, laughing.

"How much do you think is in there, Tommy?" Two Trees asked looking at John then Tommy, "twenty thousand?"

"Million," John answered.

"Twenty million dollars? How much is that?"

"In money or volume?" John asked him back.

"I mean, is it a gunny-sack full?"

John thought for a moment then told him, "About twelve gunny sacks full, if most of it is twenties and fifties, but I'm thinking most of it will be in hundreds," and then he said, "about eight or nine gunny sacks full."

"What in hell are you going to do with it?" Two Trees asked.

"We don't know, just take it away from him. After that, who cares?" John answered, and then asked, "Any beer around here?"

"In the cooler by the porch," Tommy answered, and they spent the rest of the evening talking, and eating, and drinking a few more beers.

Tuesday, October third, Jack Charmichael was in the bar at the Madison trying to figure a way to recover his losses without selling off his property. He was talking to Bill Tacki and getting no help at all. Each time he asked him something, Bill Tacki answered him the same way, "I don't know anything about your business dealings. I been a bartender all of my life," and then he would walk off and clean glasses.

John Tru-Day was still figuring, but he was figuring a way to make it look like Jack Charmichael was the one who robbed the vault company to regain his losses. A plan was forming, but he needed Jack Charmichael's name on a piece of paper, then he remembered the note he had in his sea bag and the other one he got when he was at the Hotel. He left his office and went home at eleven in the morning, leaving a note on the door saying he was across town doing taxes and would be back in the morning.

Tommy, Two Trees, and Joe Jackson were in the garage, finishing the three trucks.

Muriel and Patty were just sort of hanging out together at the house and waiting to go to San Francisco.

Wednesday, October fourth, John Tru-Day spent almost all day taking the two notes Jack Charmichael had written to him, and tried putting together a small note on the bottom of the last list of payoffs, except he was about ten words short of what he need to say, he was trying for: "Do these first, they belong to me, you can have the others."

He didn't have nearly enough of the right words. So he decided to just write it himself and then sign Charmichael's name on it, but wrinkle it up and smear it and wad it up, so it would be impossible to really tell who wrote it. He was practicing signing Charmichael's name when Jake Morrison walked into his office and tossed a set of keys on his desk.

"What's going on?" John asked him.

"I caught the son of a bitch with my seventeen-year-old daughter," Jake answered, then said, "oh, it was as much her doing as it was his, but I'm just sick of the bastard and the way he does things."

"You're quitting?"

"Ya, I'm quitting and he's fucking lucky I didn't kill him. God knows I wanted to so bad I could just--Well never mind that. Here are the keys to the truck and the office over there. If he asks you, tell him I said for him to go fuck a goose, the son of a bitch." Jake Morrison walked out of the office.

John got up and went across the hall and into the construction office. Right there in front of him was everything he needed to blame Jack Charmichael, papers with his name on them and all kinds of tools belonging to him. He looked for receipts and found a drawer half full of them, but the one he liked best of all was one for a generator that was sitting right in front of him on the floor. All he had to do was leave it in the truck and the receipt in the glove box, and then he saw a blueprint on the desk and right on the bottom of it was a note from Jack Charmichael. He was referring to several jobs in the works, but the note said:

Do these first. Then call me when you're done.

It was signed by Jack Charmichael using his full name. John cut the note off of the blueprint and then pasted it on the bottom of the third page of the payoff sheet, then cleaned the edges with whiteout and copied it. It looked to him like it was perfect, just a copy of a note Jack Charmichael had written to someone on the bottom of the third sheet."

He was proud of himself, and then as he looked further through the desk drawers he found three checks signed by Charmichael in the checkbook for the construction account.

He called the bank. There was a little over eleven thousand in the account. He knew what he wanted to do and closed the office, then went home taking the three signed checks with him. He told Tommy he needed to see Mikie in the morning and for Tommy to come to his office and get one of the pickups parked in the construction yard, plus the generator and a few more things to leave laying around.

"What's on your mind?" Tommy asked him.

"Nothing but good things," John answered, then said, "I need a couple beers, got any?"

"In the cooler," Tommy answered.

Five

Thursday, October fifth, Tommy Dollarhide called Mikie and told him John needed to talk to him. Mikie said he'd be over first thing in the afternoon.

Joe Jackson, Tommy, and Two Trees went to John's office and got the generator and the pickup. When John asked him to paint it, Tommy just looked at him, and then walked out.

Jack Charmichael came up with an idea of his own. He'd sell his apartment house on the south side to make up for the losses and pay everyone what he owed them. When he finally decided it was the only way out for him, he walked across the room and kicked over a $2200 statue, then stormed out of his apartment and went down to the bar in the Madison and sat there looking at Bill Tacki. Finally he said, "What the fuck makes you like you are?"

Bill Tacki smiled and leaned over the bar, "Clean living, Jack, clean living," then he went to polish his glasses.

Mike met with John Tru-Day at a tavern close to John's office, and John handed him the three checks and asked him, "You think you can find three men who want to leave town?"

"Maybe, why?"

"I was thinking if you found three men and gave them each say, $1500, and told them to cash them on the fifteenth, then to leave and not come back for a few months."

Mikie looked at the checks and saw who had signed them. "I'm liking you more and more every time we get together, John."

"I am a pretty smart and likeable guy, ain't I," John smiled and sipped his beer while Mikie put the checks in his pocket and started thinking.

"Three homeless men from the park downtown, that should be easy," then John told him, "You're going to have to put them on a bus heading back east, or they might just cash them and stay here."

"It's no problem," Mike answered, and then said, "see ya around." He walked out and John went back to his office.

Friday, October sixth, Tommy, Joe Jackson, and Two Trees painted the pickup, and Two Trees volunteered to spray it for Tommy. He did a better job than Tommy could ever have done. There was not a single run in the paint, and it turned out shiny and smooth.

"You done that before, haven't you?" Tommy told him, smiling.

"About two hundred times when I worked in the body shop in Billings, remember?"

"I was in the Marines then."

"Oh ya, glad you're out now," Two Trees returned. He didn't have any paint on his shoes, or his face, or hands.

Saturday, October seventh, Muriel Sue got her money from the houses. They had to be empty by the first of November. She and Patty McShane were going to go to San Francisco on the 20th and give the money to Michelangelo Augusta, so he could outfit the schooner, and then stay there until the men arrived, if they did arrive. Patty didn't want to leave Tommy, but he told her she had to and that was that. They spent the weekend doing little of anything.

Monday, October ninth, Two Trees found a box van truck in the paper while he was looking for a trailer to haul Tommy's truck with. They went and bought it and a trailer for $3500. Two Trees mounted the first generator Sonia Re'olo had bought on the trailer. He told Tommy, "This way we can keep the freezer running and not lose the frozen food you have in it."

All the trucks were finished and stocked with all the things they needed to set up over the manhole.

Muriel Sue was taking her time separating things and packing things in her house.

Patty was spending her time worrying about Tommy getting caught.

Tommy's sister was spending her time wondering what the hell was going on with everyone, and she kept asking Tommy, Two Trees, and Joe Jackson, "Will you tell me just what the hell you all are up to?"

Every time she asked she got the same answer, "Not yet."

Jack Charmichael was spending his time in the bar at the Madison explaining to a lot of different people why they had not gotten their money last month.

"I got you covered, so don't worry and don't call me every fucking day asking about it," he told them.

"What's wrong with all these fucking people?" he asked Bill Tacki.

"If you don't know, I can't tell you, Jack." Bill Tacki went to the other end of the bar and polished his glasses.

Charmichael sat there looking at him then said loud enough for Tacki to hear him, "Rightist bastard."

Bill Tacki walked back and stopped in front of Jack Charmichael, still holding a glass with the bar towel in it. He twisted the glass polishing it and asked, "Do I insult you, Jack?" Then he looked through the glass at the light to see if it was clear, then at Jack Charmichael as if to say, "Shame on you."

"Fuck you, Tacki," Charmichael answered, and left the bar, leaving his drink half empty.

Tuesday, October tenth, Wednesday, October eleventh, and Thursday, October twelfth, Tommy used Muriel Sue's car and took his sister, Joe Jackson, and Two Trees to the coast, because they had never seen the ocean. They all went deep sea fishing and Patty McShane was the only one who didn't get seasick and throw up.

Friday, the thirteenth of October, no one did anything except sit at the house, drink beer, and eat. John Tru-Day didn't even go to work.

But Jack Charmichael did. He went and reopened the Tropics, his newspaper ad was answered by about twenty people. He hired four of them, two female bartenders, and two men to be bouncers, and then he went to try and find Jake Morrison to find out why nothing had been done at the construction site for several days.

"Hell, he quit a week ago, didn't you know about it?" the security guard told him.

Saturday and Sunday, the fourteenth and fifteenth, Jack Charmichael hung out at the Tropics bar and drank, and watched the new manager and the girls, making sure they didn't rob him blind.

Tommy, Two Trees, and Joe Jackson worked on the box van truck and began loading some things in it. They had the freezer mounted on the front of the trailer.

John Tru-Day sat in the house and drank a few beers until Muriel Sue told him he was drinking too much, so he went to the garage and drank more beer with Tommy and the other guys.

The sixteenth, seventeenth, eighteenth, and nineteenth, John Tru-Day sat in his chair in his office and spun around and around behind his desk, waiting for Friday to get here. He had all the money ready for Muriel Sue to take to San Francisco, and remained drunk almost all week, sipping at drinks from the bar to pass the time faster. He and Muriel sue had collected $88,800 from the bundler, $86.000 from the houses, and $92,000 from Muriel Sue's insurance. She was going to hand over $200,000 to Michelangelo to get the schooner ready. She had a small U-Haul trailer completely full of things she collected over the years, and had loaded from the house.

Patty was not wanting to go and leave Tommy Dollarhide.

Muriel Sue was more than ready to start a new life aboard the schooner.

323

Linn Morrison moved out of her parents' house and into a friend's apartment, and then tried to call Jack Charmichael again. He had no intentions of ever answering her calls.

Tommy's sister sat on the couch, watching the TV and asking, "What the hell are you guys doing?"

Friday, October twentieth, Muriel Sue and Patty McShane left for San Francisco, and John Tru-Day left for Portland, following Muriel Sue to make sure everything was alright. They arrived in Portland and had breakfast, then Muriel Sue and Patty went on their own, driving south, pulling the small trailer behind her car, as John went across town, and again began to steal money from the club managers and stash it in his car trunk.

Tommy, Two Trees, and Joe Jackson were loading furniture from his and Muriel Sue's houses. Muriel Sue had told him to take whatever he wanted and just leave the remaining things in the house for Goodwill to come and get. Nothing was left by the time his sister had decided what to leave. The truck was loaded, and Tommy's pickup was on the trailer. At seven in the evening and in a light snowstorm, Two Trees and Tommy's sister left for Jasper, Wyoming, to wait for Tommy and Patty McShane.

John Tru-Day came home at nine and saw the house was completely empty. He walked through it and then stood looking at Tommy Dollarhide.

"We're giving up a lot, ain't we?" he said. It was more of a question than a statement.

"Ya," was all Tommy answered. They were both a little worried.

Tommy went to the motel with Joe Jackson, and John Tru-Day slept on his couch in his office.

Saturday, October twenty-first, Mikie found three men from the local mission that he thought he could trust half way, or enough to at least get them out of town after having them cash Jack Charmichael's checks. He took them to the bank and had them fill out the checks, writing their own names on the pay line, and then signing the backs of them and cashing them. He drove them to the bus station and sent them off to three different towns across the country. He met with John Tru-Day on Sunday night after he finished his trip to Tacoma and explained what he had done.

On Monday he drove to the vault and saw a sign on the front of the entrance:

We will be closed from Nov. 15 through Dec. 1

"How perfect can it get?" he laughed after he read the sign, but then realized if the vault was going to be closed, most of the people would take their money out as soon as Charmichael put it in on the eleventh. They were going to have to move the job forward.

"We can't," John told him, "It just won't work. We can't go in there during the week. It has to be on the twelfth, that's all there is to it."

The problem solved itself on Wednesday, after about ten of Charmichael's payees called his office and asked him what the hell he was trying to pull on them. "We want our money after Thanksgiving, so don't try closing the vault on us," they told him.

325

Jack Charmichael went down to the vault and told the man operating it to keep it open.

"I'm going on vacation," he answered.

"You close the fucking vault, and you'll go on vacation all right! A permanent one," Charmichael warned him, "You go after Thanksgiving."

He took the sign down.

For the next nine days, Tommy and Joe Jackson sat around, went to the garage and fooled around, played a lot of pool at a local tavern, and John Tru-Day did his clubs and stole $87,000, put it in a small box and gave it to Mikie, so that in case they got caught he could bail them all out of jail. He called Jack Charmichael and told him he was done, but the count was a little off because the machine had kept plugging up. "I don't think you're short. I think you got about ten percent of their money."

"Fuck um," Charmichael answered. "I'm in so much hot water now, I need all the extra money I can get my hands on."

"I know, a couple guys asked me if you were thinking of running?"

"What? Which ones?"

"I don't know, they've been calling me on the phone and the phone in the other office over there is ringing all the time. You heard from Jake Morrison?"

"I'll send the truck down there," he hung up without saying goodbye.

John was done on the twenty-ninth. The truck came and took the money and he was done with Jack Charmichael. He went to the airport and bought a ticket in his own name to Hawaii, then to Puerto Rico. He drove downtown and gave it to Mikie, who was going to give it to some homeless guy the day after the vault was finished, someone who wanted to go to Hawaii.

Mikie and Sonia Re'olo sat in a restaurant across from the Pioneer Vault Company all day Thursday the 11th, and watched for Charmichael to go into the vault to make the payoffs.

They saw him at 10:30 Friday morning, right when they were supposed to.

Mikie smiled at Sonia and she said, "I hate that fucker guy."

Everything was ready for tomorrow night, the trucks were ready, the money was in the vault, and it was raining hard. Everything except Tommy Dollarhide was ready to move.

Friday night, November 13th, 1963, 6:15 pm, four light blue trucks left a garage six blocks off of Rainier Avenue in south Seattle, and followed each other to the corner of First Avenue and Pine Street. Sonia Re'olo drove past the manhole, then backed up to it and parked, then left Joe Jackson to help the others park.

Mikie parked the tool truck in front of the alley, blocking it off, and south of the manhole, so the trucks were backed up against each other, blocking the outside lane of the street, and got out. He and Sonia Re'olo walked away across the street to the restaurant to watch. They took their place in a booth in the restaurant directly across the street from the vault, and ordered coffee for Sonia and a beer for Mikie. They sat there and watched while Tommy backed the other tool truck up to the manhole and John drove the van down to the corner, turned around, and came back, then backed up on the west side of the manhole. All three men set out the barricades, blocking off the sidewalk and the street. They put the tent up over the manhole, turned on the generator, turned on the lights, and then lowered the lights down in the manhole. Tommy Dollarhide lowered the jackhammer down, then climbed down after it, as two Seattle police officers stood under a store overhang and watched for several minutes, then walked past them and up Second Avenue.

"Nice night for ducks," one of them said.

"Double overtime for us," John Tru-Day answered.

"Glad it's them and not me," one of the cops said, then said, "but I'd take the overtime if I could get it. I've been looking at a boat."

"Looking or leering?" the other one answered.

"Still a hell of a way to spend a weekend, ain't it, down in the fucking sewer?" both of them laughed and turned the corner onto Third.

"Storm drain, you dumb fuck," John muttered under his breath, and tossed Tommy's gloves down to him, then started the blower.

It took Tommy Dollarhide exactly forty-two minutes to knock a four-foot hole in the side of the storm drain manhole. He found sand outside it and as soon as he removed the concrete, the sand began to run out and into the storm drain, and was carried down the pipe by the water running through it. By the time he had finished making the hole and removing the broken concrete, the sand had run down and cleared the way to the outside wall of the basement.

It was built out of cement blocks, and the jack hammer tore them apart like paper blocks. Ten minutes, and he had a three-foot opening to the steel side of the vault.

John lowered the cutting torches down to him and he cut a round hole two feet in diameter through the 3/8-inches of steel. Five minutes later, he was standing inside the vault.

Fifty-nine minutes after he climbed down inside the manhole, he was inside. John followed him, and Joe Jackson stood at the top.

John took out the list of payoffs and started making check marks with a felt tip pen as Tommy started blowing off the outside locks with the cutting torch. After ten or so, he stopped and just used the crow bar and pried them open.

They completed one row, and began opening the boxes. Every one had cash in it, some more than others, and some of them were stuffed full completely. It took only a few minutes to fill the tool sack with money. John carried it to the opening, hooked it on the line, and yanked on it. Joe Jackson pulled the sack up and emptied it in the van on the floor, then dropped the sack back to John Tru-Day.

Tommy compared opening the boxes to back when he was removing the rims off of the tires in Spokane. He was opening one every few seconds, and filling the sacks faster than John and Joe could haul the money out of the vault.

They were in the vault at fifteen after eight and at midnight, they had opened about thirty-five an hour, about a hundred and five boxes, hauling thirty-six full sacks of hundreds, fifties, and twenties up out of the vault along with watches, rings, and about sixty small gold bars. Joe had a pile started on the floor of the van, and a pile of empty boxes and fives, ones, and change was forming on the floor of the vault. They were stepping over the empty boxes, and Tommy stopped and stacked them neatly against the wall.

"No need to be slobs, right?" he said, joking.

By eight in the morning, they had opened two hundred fifty-five boxes and the floor of the van was covered with money two feet deep. Joe had to get in and push it all forward, making a pile right behind the seats.

They worked all day Saturday and Saturday night, stopping only once, when Mike had Sonia Re'olo walk by and drop some sandwiches down to them. They stopped and ate, and then went back to work.

At seven am Sunday morning, they had opened all of the numbers on the list, plus a hundred seventy-five other ones, all of the larger boxes. A total of four hundred fourteen boxes were emptied and stacked in the aisles. The van had a stack of loose bills in it almost to the ceiling, from the front and almost to the back door.

John Tru-Day stuck the sheet with the payoff numbers and Charmichael's note on it on the wall by the hole and they left the vault.

Tommy and John climbed up out of the manhole at ten-thirteen am Sunday morning, and Tommy had to go back down and help John up the ladder because he was so tired.

They got into the van and drove south, down First Avenue, and then on to highway 99 south, stopping at the airport to let John out.

John Tru-Day got on a plane at 11:55 Sunday morning, with a reserved ticket Sonia Re'olo had bought for him, and flew to San Francisco. He arrived at one forty and Muriel Sue met him at the airport.

"Piece of cake," he said, as he got into the car and he fell asleep as soon as they were back on the road.

Tommy Dollarhide drove south all day Sunday, as Joe Jackson slept. They crossed the California border at nine-thirty. They were in Redding, California, at eleven and slept in the van at a rest area until nine in the morning on Monday. They went to a packing company and bought twenty-five cardboard boxes, some tape to close them with, and some labels, and then went across the street and had hamburgers. Tommy was ready to drop, he was so tired. He drove to an isolated spot off the highway and down along the river. The men stacked the loose money into twenty-one 14" X 24" X 24" boxes, taped them shut, and put labels on them that said, "t-shirts".

Tommy slept three more hours while Joe Jackson stood and watched, then they drove on to San Francisco, across the Golden Gate Bridge, and to the marina. Patty McShane ran down off the schooner and hung around his neck, kissing him and crying because she was so relieved he was not in jail.

"Nothing to it," he told her.

Joe Jackson sat on the bench and started shaking because he had been so scared all the time, and now he let it all go.

The men carried sixteen of the twenty-one full boxes onto the schooner and down into a storage room, except one that John took into his and Muriel's stateroom.

All of them sat as John emptied the box on the bed and separated the bills, and then counted the money. He finished, and turned and smiled at Tommy, "Are all the boxes about the same?" he asked.

"Close," Tommy answered.

"So how much you think is here?"

"On the boat or the bed?"

"The bed."

"Nine hundred thousand?" Tommy guessed.

"One million one hundred seventy-six thousand. We got almost exactly what I said, about twenty-two million dollars, not counting the bearer bonds, that's another three million, plus the gold bars."

"No way," Tommy answered.

Monday morning, the fourteenth of November, two police officers first looked at the three trucks parked blocking the alley and the street with no one around them, then stood over the manhole and looked down into it.

"Is that money down there?" one of them said, seeing several bills stuck in the concrete.

"Sure as hell is," the second one answered.

The police officers climbed down into the manhole, then into the vault. They saw all the empty boxes, and the floor covered with one and five dollar bills.

"Whoa! Shit, is someone in trouble! Look at this."

And because Batman was the most popular show on TV at the time, the second one said, "Holy Vault Robbery, Batman! I think this place has been violated."

Then one looked at the other and they both began to fill every pocket they had, plus the inside of their shirts, with five dollar bills, and then climbed back out of the manhole, emptied their clothes into the trunk of the patrol car, and called their sergeant, to tell him the Pioneer Vault Company had been robbed over the weekend.

By eight in the morning, no less than fifteen cars were parked around the corner, and the lead detective took one look at the list stuck on the wall and said, "Go get Jack Charmichael," and then he walked around and looked at his box to see if it was one of the ones that had been opened. It was; his fourteen thousand dollars and two rings were gone. He wadded the sheets up and stuck them in his pants pocket, then asked, "Who's got that list of numbers that was on the wall there?"

No one answered.

"It just didn't blow away! Who's got it?" he screamed.

No one answered.

Jack Charmichael was brought to the Pioneer Vault and the detective took him into a room, and then closed the door and showed him the payoff sheets with his note signed on the bottom of it, and told him, "You're paying me back, and you're paying me a lot more from now on."

"I didn't write that," Charmichael answered, stuttering.

"That's your handwriting, ain't it?"

"Looks like it, but I didn't write that." Then he said, "Fuck!! Mary, I never thought you were that fucking smart."

"What?" the detective asked.

"That fucking fat ass Mary Forbes did it. She set this whole thing up. She cleaned out my account in Mexico too."

"You're paying me big time, Jack. I had fourteen thousand in here and you're paying me back before Christmas or you're going to the fucking pen, Jack." He grinned that detective grin, and walked out of the room only to have another officer tell him, "One of the trucks is registered to Charmichael Construction."

The detective turned around and said, "You're under arrest, Jack."

"I didn't do it! You cocksucker, you know I didn't do it," Charmichael screamed.

"He was in on it! He did it! He and Mary Forbes set it up. She's the only one that could have done it and he had the list in his pocket. Look, he's got the list in his fucking pocket and he's trying to pin it on me. I gave him that truck three months ago to haul some trash from his house," and then he charged the detective and tried to hit him.

The detective stood there, looking astonished that Jack Charmichael could think so fast. He looked like a rat in a trap and handed over the papers without saying a word. He was trying to decide which was the worst offense, robbing the vault, or taking the payoffs and bribes. He walked out of the vault and didn't say another word.

Mikie and Sonia Re'olo sat in the restaurant and watched Jack Charmichael being put into a police car in handcuffs.

"He'll get out of it, but he's out of business," Mikie smiled and told Sonia, "Let's go; he's finished."

They got up and as they walked out the door Sonia said, "I hate that fucker guy."

Charmichael was taken downtown and booked into jail, and then turned loose on bail four hours later, but he knew he had lost it all; he was out of business for good and in a lot of trouble with a lot of people. He would have to sell everything he owned to break even.

October 15th, 1963, 12:06 pm, John Tru-Day stood at the rail and watched the van drive away from the schooner and out of sight, with Tommy Dollarhide, Joe Jackson, and Patty McShane in it. Muriel Sue asked him, "Will they be alright, John?"

"They have their lives and we have ours now, Muriel Sue." Then he turned and looked up at Michelangelo Augustas and called to him, "Ready to cast off, captain."

Michelangelo called the orders and the crew pulled in the gangway and cast off the lines. The schooner began to slowly back up away from the dock.

Tommy Dollarhide drove Joe Jackson to the train depot and gave him a sack full of money and told him to go to Jasper and wait for him and Patty McShane. Joe Jackson got on the train and settled down in the club car and ordered a beer.

Tommy Dollarhide drove out of San Francisco and turned south.

"I thought we were going to Wyoming?" Patty asked, looking at the map.

"We'll get there in a couple days," Tommy answered. He drove straight east through Reno and then turned south to Alamo, Nevada, and even though Patty McShane was afraid, he simply walked into the house, and when Doug McShane opened it, he knocked Doug out cold with one punch and took the baby, and then they left for Wyoming.

Patty McShane was completely happy.

Tommy Dollarhide leaned back in the seat, tossed his package of smokes out the window, and stuck a match stick in his mouth.

He was driving northeast at fifty-five miles an hour.

Total assets: a lot! He was happy.

The schooner backed away from the dock and then slowly moved forward, the bow turning into the bay and then past the other boats, and finally into deep water. It passed under the Golden Gate Bridge and out into open water.

"Prepare to hoist sails."

John watched the men scramble up the rigging and wait.

Michelangelo called from the helm, "Rig main sails," and the three huge sails fell and were tied off, then snapped open and filled with wind, and the schooner surged forward.

"Hoist all sails and set the jibs," Michelangelo ordered, and the other eight sails were dropped and filled with wind. The schooner leaned over to the port side slightly, and surged forward again.

Michelangelo cut off the engine and they were under wind power. The ship slid through the water, making little splashing sounds as the water slapped against the sides.

"Directions, Mr. Tru-Day?" the captain called down to John.

"South, captain," John called back.

He stood at the rail with his arm around Muriel Sue and said, "This is going to be the adventure of a lifetime, Muriel Sue."

"It already has been, John," she answered, and walked off down into the kitchen to help Mrs. Augustas with food.

John walked up the five steps to the helm and stood beside the captain with his hands folded behind his back and looked up at the white sails pulling the schooner forward at twelve knots.

"You ever been to the Galapagos Islands?" he asked.

"No, is that where you want to go?"

"Sure, let's start there," John answered.

"Would you like to take the wheel, Mr. Tru-Day?" the captain asked, looking proudly at him.

John Tru-Day thought for a few seconds and answered, "No, thank you, captain. I think I already took enough to last any man a lifetime."

About the cover

The Vault is a fictional story about a real happening.

On Valentine's Day weekend, in 1953, persons unknown broke through the wall of the Pioneer Vault Company on First Avenue in downtown Seattle, and opened over four hundred boxes, all belonging to certain officials and business owners around the Seattle area.

They were in the vault for over two days, cutting open the boxes with a cutting torch and crow bar which they left in the vault, and even stopped to go for lunch, leaving sandwich wrappers and coffee cups on the floor when they left.

The floor was also covered with one dollar bills and change the robbers didn't bother to take. Even though most of the victims said they got nothing, only five thousand dollars at the very most, I believe they took over fifteen million dollars, and up to twenty million, all silver certificates and gold certificates, and all of it was money no one wanted to admit they had in the boxes.

This crime is still unsolved and probably never will be solved now.

My story is fiction and the characters are fictitious, but it was fun to write and it's fun to read.

J. D. McDougal